EAST OF WARSAW

BASED ON A TRUE STORY

EAST OF WARSAW

A Family's Journey from Terror and Destruction into the
Light of Hope, Freedom and Life's Rewards

E.J. Harris

TATE PUBLISHING
AND ENTERPRISES, LLC

Published by Tate Publishing & Enterprises, LLC
127 E. Trade Center Terrace | Mustang, Oklahoma 73064 USA
1.888.361.9473 | www.tatepublishing.com

Tate Publishing is committed to excellence in the publishing industry. The company reflects the philosophy established by the founders, based on Psalm 68:11,
"The Lord gave the word and great was the company of those who published it."

Book design copyright © 2015 by Tate Publishing, LLC. All rights reserved.
Cover design by Joana Quilantang
Interior design by Mary Jean Archival

Published in the United States of America

ISBN: 978-1-63418-918-7
1. Fiction / Sagas
2. Fiction / Romance / Historical / 20th Century
15.03.17

A man can be destroyed but not defeated; if he is standing, he can fight.

—Ernest Hemingway

I dedicate this book to the memory
of Joseph, Eva, and Pepi.
May their miraculous story and life
inspire others, as it has inspired me.

I also write this in memory of the
six million souls who perished during the
Holocaust without a voice, yet will never be forgotten.

—E. J. Harris

FOREWORD

August 23, 1939

After WWI, Germany lacked the resources to rebuild. Russia had always been fascinated with German war toys.

Friedrich Muller had the distinguished title of Procurer General. It was his job to obtain the natural resources that Hitler required for the Third Reich. A secret trade and cooperation pact would provide each country with what it needed and it would clear up a nagging problem—Poland. There was no easy way to transport millions of tons of raw materials to Germany and war technology to the Soviets. Poland was right in the way. After the invasion, the new pact would divide Poland into two "spheres of influence." Instantly, the Soviet Union and Germany would share a common border if all went well. After the signing, Muller was quickly recalled to Berlin.

1

September 1, 1939

It was so comfortable. So quiet. Muffled voices faded, echoing. A sense of peace and eternity, just within reach. All I had to do was let go and let the darkness take me...

BREATHE, my lungs screamed.

BREATHE!

I tried but something pressed me down. My lungs cried for air. An immense weight smothered me. As my mind cleared, the pain set in. I've been buried alive. But no, I am alive, not dead. I tried moving my fingers. They could wiggle slightly, but not my hands—they were pinned. My head throbbed. But I can't move! My heart sped up as I panicked, and soon I grew lightheaded. Calm down, I told myself. Relax. Breathe. The thick, suffocating air could be sipped very slowly. As I relaxed, I felt better. The pain returned. My ears rang. I've got to gather my strength.

As I rested, my mind wandered. How did I get here?

Muller.

I remembered a shiny nameplate on a crisp uniform. Muller. My heart sped up. Got to remain calm, to breathe evenly. I tried overinflating my lungs to provide a little extra room. It worked. I got my first full breath of air. It was like every part of my body was slowly reattaching itself. I felt the coldness around me. The air smelled stale, metallic. Like dried blood. I tried moving my jaw and pain shot across my head. Red sparks of light danced across my field of vision.

Pop! That was the last sound I remember.

"Janek," I groaned, but nothing came out; only a cracked gasp of exasperation. The pain intensified. My head pounded. Each heartbeat pulsated in my ears. Janek had fallen. His eyes were distant, unfocused. He had fallen away from me, slowly rolling, falling.

I turned my attention to my legs—one was immobilized, the other numb. I looked down the long expanse of my body to the distant horizon of my stomach, and noticed light filtering in from above and bouncing off my jacket. Cool air rushed in from an opening and blew gently on my face. My vision was fuzzy so I simply lay there, enjoying the little air that leaked through from above.

I slept. I don't know for how long. My head still hurt but I felt better. My mind was now fully clear.

In 1938, things were pretty normal for a kid in Poland. I was fresh from school, had a beautiful girlfriend, and was following in my father's footsteps at the tannery. Life was good. I ran the big horizontal boiler. We used it to remove the hair from "fresh" skins.

"It's not a problem for me but Eva's father won't let her go," I told David. "Shabbat." The Sabbath-Saturday. I took another heavy hide and dipped it carefully into the steaming, iron cast cauldron.

"I forgot about Rabbi Rozenfeld," David responded. "But…couldn't she sneak out for a few hours?"

"He watches her like a hawk."

"The talkies are the biggest thing to hit Poland in years."

"I'll ask her, but I already know the answer."

David shook his head. "It's not going to be much of a double date if she doesn't come."

"Three's a crowd anyway. You guys have fun. I'm sure Rachel will keep you entertained."

David scowled and was about to respond when we were interrupted by the foreman.

"Joseph!" he yelled.

I looked at David and smiled.

"You'll just have to try and have fun without me."

I ran over to the boss, leaving David speechless. He nodded toward a messenger at a near doorway, and my stomach dropped. It wasn't that I wasn't ready for it. I just didn't want it to happen right now. I walked over and stood in front of him. He looked tired.

"Joseph Mitsen?"

"Yes?"

He handed me a plain brown envelope. I turned it over and looked at the stamped seal of the Polish government on the back, then glanced out the door to see a messenger ride off on his bicycle. I took the envelope in both hands and walked back to the boiler. A rush of steam wafted over me with the smell of wet fur. David opened the boiler and watched me as he stirred the skins with a blanched pole. He saw the look on my face as he closed the door and started rotating the big drum again.

"What is it?"

"My papers."

"How do you know? You haven't even opened it. Give it to me." David yanked the envelope from my hands and tore it open. "Probably some sort of tax notice," he said.

He unfolded the packaging and his face dropped.

"You're right," David whispered. "You've got to report to the Military Bureau in Warsaw next week."

———

I ran straight to Eva's house after my shift ended at the tannery. We sat on the front porch together while her mother kept a watchful eye from behind the front-room drapes.

"I thought we were going to get married," she said, her voice thick with disappointment.

"We can. Your father can perform the ceremony… before I leave."

"That's not fair."

"What do you mean?"

"I wanted a beautiful wedding with flowers and guests. One week."

"I only have five days."

"Five days isn't enough time to send out invitations!" Eva let out a long sigh. "I don't even have a gown. It's just not right. I want this to be special."

"It will be special," I said, looking her in the eyes. "It's just special to you and me."

"But I don't want to rush it. I want this to be one of my happiest memories…not to get married one moment and then have my husband run off to the army the next."

"Then we'll wait until I get out. It's only two years. Plus I'll come back on holidays and visit. You can write me." I dropped my eyes to the dusty wooden porch floor.

"I don't want you to go," said Eva. "I want you to stay here. What am I going to do when you're gone? You're my best friend."

She grabbed my hands, and I immediately heard a cough from behind the curtains. Eva looked up and quickly let go.

"We'll get through this," I said.

———— ✺ ————

My father sat in the tannery truck in front of the house, as I brought my carpet bag with the bare essentials— prayer book, prayer shawl, underwear, shirts, galoshes, a loaf of bread, and a hunk of cheese for the trip. Eva met me on the steps, adjusted my shirt, and gingerly brushed away invisible dust. I could tell she was trying to be strong. Her lip quivered; her eyes held back tears.

"I'll pray for you everyday," she said.

"Thank you, I'll need it," I breathed. "I promise I'll write often."

My father pumped the accelerator loudly. Clearly he was ready to get this over with.

"I'd better get going," I said, trying hard not to notice the sadness in her face.

Eva looked over my shoulder to her house. Her mom was watching from the bedroom. In Orthodox Judaism, a woman is not allowed to touch another man other than her husband, or even be alone with another. I could see her upbringing in the hesitation of her thoughts. She bounced on the balls of her feet and chewed on her lip. Her eyes flicked back to the house at the silhouetted outline in the window, sheepish. She looked up at me and readjusted my collar a second time. She brushed my shoulders again and her face contorted into strain. She knit her brows and bit her cheek.

"Eva?"

Tears now streamed down her cheeks. She stomped her feet and then in an explosion of arms, emotions, and tears she grabbed me in a hug. I had to hold onto the railing to keep from falling over. She cried loudly, letting all her emotions burst outward. I guess I was more surprised than anything. I put my arms around her and smiled. That's when I heard her front door open (our houses were next to each other).

"Eva!" her mother yelled.

Eva didn't let go of me. She tilted her head up and looked deeply into my eyes.

"I love you. Promise you'll come back to me."

"I will."

Eva let go and wiped the tears from her cheeks.

I kissed my mother good-bye and walked to the truck. I stopped and turned around to look at Eva.

"I love you too!" I said. I didn't care if her mother heard.

Truth was, I genuinely loved her. Ever since we were little she was always there. We grew up together—I knew what she liked, and she had always been my friend. Now that she had grown up into a beautiful woman, it seemed natural to tell her that I loved her. It was the first time we had openly expressed our affection. We had crossed a line neither of us could retrace, taking those perilous steps from childhood friends to lovers—not in the physical sense; rather, our souls had become entwined. For the first time in my life, I had a real fear that I might not see her again. Maybe it was the jitters of going into the service, but I wanted to run back, grab her, and take her far away from parents, from the government, and from civilization. I wanted it to be her and me and no one else. I waved from the truck, and she waved back weakly. Her mom stood beside her, annoyed at first. But she eventually warmed to the situation and calmly waved too. I turned and cried as I walked around the truck. I didn't look back.

———✦———

I loaded my bags onto the bus in Warsaw, and waved good-bye to my father. The bus then drove us new recruits to a camp on the western border with Germany. We were part of a mounted battalion, with cavalry, infantry, artillery, and all the support personnel that goes with it. The barracks were heated with pot-bellied stoves at either end of the large room. It was the new guy's job to bring in coal when it was low. Fortunately, in three months' time, winter had arrived, and more recruits showed up. Another three months and I'd have enough seniority to get a bottom bunk.

The conditions of the camp were deplorable, to say the least. There was no running water anywhere in the camp, and the latrine was outside amidst thick drifts of snow. During the day there was no electricity, and at night the officers ran a generator for a string of light bulbs in our unit. We got used to it, however, and eventually things settled to a mind-numbing pace. We went through the same drills every day, learning armed combat, weaponry, and discipline.

I remembered hearing angry shouts one night before lights out. A big guy was fending off a little guy with a knife. The little guy was Polish and the big guy was a Jew. Apparently they were bunkmates and the big guy had basically claimed the upper bunk. Tempers tend to flare when three thousand men are stuffed together in tight quarters, so they will find different ways to entertain themselves. Personally I was horrified that the other men were *encouraging* these two to fight. The big guy grabbed his boot and stuffed his hand in it. Every time the little guy would slice with the knife, the big guy blocked it with the boot. After a few more swings, whistles blew and the MPs rushed into the barracks to break it up. Both the men got latrine duty for a month. Surprisingly they ended up being good friends by the time graduation rolled around.

I wrote to Eva every night and told her about my day and how I longed to be with her. I never hesitated to tell her I loved her. Nor did she.

After basic training, they assigned me as the main mechanic for the generators. It was my job to start them up and make sure they ran in the evenings. In training I was part of an antitank artillery team. My bunkmate, Janek, was the spotter and I was the gunner. We became good friends. We were from the same area. His home was in Lublin, just a few kilometers from mine. We spent countless hours talking about what we wanted to do when we got out of the military. Of course we also talked about our sweethearts. Janek had a girl in Lublin. He loved her but wasn't sure if she reciprocated his affection.

"She hasn't written in a week," he whispered. It was lights out, and we were in our bunks, trying hard not to wake the other recruits.

"Maybe the mail's just slow," I said.

"She's ignoring me. All she talks about is this new family that moved in down the street. She's always going to their house for dinner with their daughter. But there's an older brother. I think she's got eyes for him."

"Has she said she doesn't love you anymore?"

"No."

"Then you're just worrying. You need to worry about what's going on here."

Another voice echoed in the darkness of the dorm. "You need to shut up and go to sleep!"

"Mind your own business!" Janek said.

Another voice yelled out, "Shut up, will you?"

Then a chorus of grumbling murmurs chimed in agreement.

"I'll talk to you in the morning," I said.

"Good night."

I was shaken awake from my bunk by the first explosion. I looked around the barracks and the men were scrambling about, dizzy from sleep and the concussion wave that had blasted shards of glass into the room. It was still half an hour before sunrise but the sky was already lit up like noon. I hastily jostled into my pants when another blast shook the camp. I could hear the horses scream and men taking their stations. The commander was yelling instructions on a portable loudspeaker.

"We are under attack! Secure your positions!"

Attack? But they would have to cross the border first! Besides, they would be seen by the patrols long before they got near, I thought to myself. By the time I got my boots on and grabbed my gear, I could hear the air crackle with cannon fire. Over the yelling men, I heard a new sound—one I had never heard before. It sounded like swarms of angry bees.

There was only one thought in my mind—I had to get the generators going, then join my squad at the Bofors 37mm antitank gun. As I ran out of the unit toward the power shed, I looked up. The morning sky was littered with hundreds of ominous silhouettes of bombers. The shed was chilly and it took longer than expected to get the propane heaters going on the big diesel engines that powered the generators. The engine puttered to life and soon drowned out the chaos of the camp. I ran back outside and could already see arc lights scanning the border. There they were. A wall of dust in the distance confirmed the approaching tanks.

My team scrambled to prepare our gun. We ignored the wave of aircraft overhead and uncovered the ammo. We loaded the first round while Janek called out coordinates as he sighted the enemy.

Thunder and lightning accompanied the bombs that dropped in a deluge. I watched in horror as the first volley crashed in the middle of the open field. Row by row the bombs exploded, and this fiery chain grew closer and closer to us. The earth rippled in waves under the thundering bombardment.

I woke out of my initial shock and fired a sighting round.

"Fifteen down and five right!" Janek yelled. He wiped the sweat from his eyes and refocused his binoculars. I spun the wheels while the firing team reloaded.

"Ready!" the primer called out.

"Fire!" Janek yelled.

The cannon leaped violently as the round whistled away. Janek waited, staying focused on his target. In the distance, a tank exploded in a black cloud.

"Yeah!" Janek yelled triumphantly. "Let's do it again!"

As my squad hustled to ready another round, the world around us exploded. The housing units were blown outward. The roof flipped away in spinning sheets, and the pulverized walls spewed shrapnel in all directions. We had to take cover. As we ran, whistling mortar rounds discovered our gun placement, instantly obliterating the two men who were operating it. The shock wave knocked me forward. When I got to my feet again, I could see German infantry crouching behind a battle line of approaching tanks. We were outnumbered. I was shocked at what I saw next. It wasn't the enemy but one of our staff cars rolling toward the approaching line. A soldier sat in the front seat, frantically waving a white flag out the window. We were surrendering. How? Why? I couldn't believe it.

"Throw down your weapons!" a voice clipped with a German accent hollered over a loudspeaker. "Your generals have surrendered! Put down your weapons!"

We didn't wait to find out if he was telling the truth or not. I thought it was a lie; a ploy to ferret us out. But then I noticed our car rolling to a stop as German soldiers surrounded it.

"Like hell I'm surrendering!" a soldier hunkered down next to me yelled. He suddenly took aim on a German and fired, and the shot hit him in the shoulder in a bloody explosion. The Germans immediately opened fire on the staff car and then us.

A line of trees led into a dense forest behind the camp. Our group retreated into the shadows. We backed away from the clearing as the first of the half-tracks reached the mine field. The explosions were a welcome sound.

"Those were ours!" someone yelled.

A cheer went up but the *pop pop pop* of the shots behind us propelled us forward. As we neared the dark tree line to the forest beyond, a German unit emerged from its cover, their weapons drawn. We were surrounded.

"Hände hoh! Hände hoh!" a German soldier yelled, the tip of his rifle motioning upward. We dropped our weapons and raised our hands high.

They threw a few shovels at us and made us dig a trench. The ground was frozen, making the work difficult, and by the afternoon, we had only dug down a few feet. We weren't allowed to talk. We exchanged a few worried glances but kept digging. A German staff car eventually pulled up, and a sergeant saluted a thin man in a black duster and cowboy boots in the backseat. The odd man stepped calmly out of the car, flipped a quick hand salute, and spoke with the officer. The man wore a black bowler hat and gloves, and brandished marshal pips on his collar.

Even though he wasn't much older than me, he seemed gaunt for his age. The marshal motioned to our work and then looked us over. He said something to the sergeant with a dismissive gesture toward us, prompting the officer to snap to attention and salute. He then started yelling orders to his troops. The guards made us drop our shovels and broke us up into groups of five. They forced us to tie each other's hands behind our backs, and then led us to the edge of the shallow pit.

A guard came up behind the first group of five, put a pistol to the back of each man's head, and fired. My friends and fellow comrades fell forward and out of view. These executions continued for fifteen minutes, but it seemed like hours. Then our group was brought forward. I could see the backs of my friends lying below, their heads now gaping holes with smoke still pouring out. My stomach burned. I swallowed dryly, then looked at Janek. His eyes pleaded but I couldn't help him.

The soldiers approached us and raised their Luger pistols. Janek reached his fingers toward me through his binds. It was an insignificant gesture but I knew it meant good-bye. Janek jerked as the first gunshot went off, killing the man next to him. The body fell solidly on top of the others in a loud thump. The guards moved behind Janek, and I squeezed my eyes shut, expecting the same blast and accompanying thump of the body below. I waited, but there was no shot. I peeked an eye open and saw the marshal from the staff car approach us. The guard pointed at Janek's boot, and the marshal bent down to study it. He reached into Janek's boot cuff and removed an ornate dagger. The officer stood up and examined his prize. The dagger had rows of precious stones wrapped with gold filigree. The leather sheath had a silver tip with exquisite engraving. The officer slowly removed the knife from its sheath.

"What is this?" he asked Janek in a quiet voice.

Janek darted his eyes to the ground.

"Answer me!" the officer yelled at the trite Pole.

"It's a family heirloom," Janek whispered.

"It's very nice. It must have taken years of working in the fields to earn enough to purchase this."

"It was my great grandfather's. He was from royal blood."

"We have royalty with us," the officer looked around in mock surprise. "We must show him proper respect." And he laughed. It was a strange laugh—high pitched like escaping steam, a vibrato of hissing that ended in several constipated hacks. The officer leaned next to Janek's ear.

"I think you are lying. I think you were planning on attacking us with this. You have wasted my time. This entire venture is a waste of time. I should be sleeping in my bed but instead I'm here with you. Do you want your knife back?"

Janek slowly nodded his head, so the man drove the gilded knife straight into Janek's back. Janek breathed in short rapid breaths with his mouth open. He choked out a spittle of blood.

"There, quiet…you've got it back. Now we can see your royal blood."

The officer yanked the knife out and let Janek go. Janek turned toward me, his mouth opening and closing involuntarily. He slowly spun, falling backward into the pit. His body jerked through the last throes of death until he lay perfectly still. His eyes stared blankly at me, and I didn't leave them, despite the tears stinging my eyes, and the rage that was filling my heart. I felt the warm breath of the officer on my neck. It smelled sour, like rancid garlic.

"How does that make you feel?" he asked. "You would like to take revenge for your friend?"

The officer grabbed my cheeks in a gloved hand and spun my head around. He paused for a moment, startled.

"But you… you have blue eyes. You are not like the others, eh? But I see your anger. You would like to kill me."

He snorted, turned me around, and cut my bonds.

"There. Go ahead. I'll give you the first shot. Attack me."

I looked to my left, right at the two guards with their weapons drawn. I rubbed my wrists as I looked the officer in the eyes. A bronze nameplate said "Muller." The man smiled with crowded teeth.

"A real man doesn't stab another in the back, but faces his enemy in a fair fight. You aren't a man but a spoiled child," I said, trying hard not to reveal the unsteadiness in my voice.

Muller slapped me hard with the back of his hand. My cheek stung but I gritted my teeth and showed no emotion. Muller calmed and leaned into my face. He wiped the blade of the knife on my coat then held its tip under my chin.

"It's a shame that you and I are enemies. Your kind of bravery is rare. I've seen men piss themselves for less."

"I'm not afraid of you."

"That…that is exactly the problem. Kill him."

A guard stepped forward and I tried to block the gunshot as he pulled a pistol and fired it point blank range into my face. The world went black.

2

I opened my eyes once more, and was determined to try again. As I swung my leg back and forth, more light appeared through the widening cracks above me. After much effort, my numb leg was free. I had to rest every few minutes but now I could see snow. It was wonderful. I bent my knee and caught my toe against something solid. I pushed and the thing cracked and slid a few inches. I pushed again and it moved even more. For the first time, both my legs were free. Because I was wearing an inner coat for warmth and an outer oil cloth, they slid against each other. Lifting and scooting a bit at a time, I squirmed free, feet first from my hole. My coat scrunched up and I felt the biting cold on my belly.

When I rolled over, I was blinded by the brilliance of recent snowfall. I sat up, surrounded in a field of pure white. An approaching grumbling noise grew in intensity until I thought a freight train was rolling over my head. The noise filled my ears and my head, and made so dizzy, I blacked out. When I came to, my stomach recoiled and I threw up. I felt better. As I looked around, I saw the hole

I had crawled out of. I pulled my coat from it and put it on for warmth. Buried in the snow beneath me, I noticed an outstretched, gloved hand reaching out, grasping for a hope that had not come. I patted the snow around me, and realized I was sitting atop the bodies of my comrades, now buried in a thick layer of ice and snow. My comrades had kept me sheltered from the harsh cold until I could recover. I looked up and saw the sun hanging low in the sky. I had no idea how long I had been buried or what day it was. My lips were cracked and my tongue stuck to the roof of my mouth. In survival situations, you're not supposed to eat snow directly as you lower your core temperature and hasten hypothermia. But I couldn't wait. I scooped up a handful of snow. It melted in my mouth and I had a precious sip of water.

By now the prickly feeling in my leg was abating. My toes on that leg hurt. They had been exposed to the snow during my entombment, and I prayed I didn't have frostbite. I then touched the side of my head, right on the spot that was throbbing dully. I felt something break in my hand like a dry cookie, and pulled away a scab nearly the size of my hand. It was shaped just like my head. Then I felt the warmth of blood from my wound. I quickly dug through the snow. I tore some clothing out of the pile, after wrapping several layers over my head, the bleeding finally stopped. I then stumbled around the bodies, searching for more clothing. I eventually found a fur-lined cap which held my bandage in place, a sweater, two mismatched gloves, an extra pair of socks, and a nice pair of thick leather boots. I hated taking the clothes but I knew my friends would do the same. I found two nice outer coats and by the time I had layered myself comfortably, the warmth returned to my core. I crawled out of the pit and immediately found the tracks of a vehicle compacted in the snow. I knew if I stayed here I would eventually be captured. And I dared not go back to the camp, they would be sure to look there. I had to get home. I knew if I went east, I would eventually get to Warsaw. I stood up and felt woozy. I found a tree branch and made an impromptu walking stick. A curious pile of snow near the road covered layers of canvas corners sticking out from it. I went over to it, shook off the snow, and discovered our packs! I put together a field kit and some rations. The taste of crackers and melted snow on my tongue sent shivers down my body. I must not have eaten for quite some time, because my stomach was rumbling for more. Once I had regained some energy, my mind wandered back to the events that had led me into that hole. How quickly my world had turned upside down. I needed to get home. I needed to warn my family. I had to get to my love. To Eva.

———◦◦◦———

Eva was at her "office." She called it an office because that's where she typed up her weekly hometown newsletter, *The Rejowiec Reporter*. In reality, her office was a hallway waiting room in the back of a downtown office building. She had cheered it up with potted plants, a wood desk she had refinished herself, and a filing cabinet. On her desk sat an old typewriter with a missing *E* key. She didn't mind the little hiccup in her operation; in fact, she had gotten quite good at penning in the missing letter throughout all her documents when she finished her typing. She was working on a new issue, collecting snippets of stories and related gossip.

She walked to the telephone in the main hall to make a phone call, and noticed the tax assessor's son, Joel, leaning against the door frame nearby, chewing on a toothpick.

"Anything new?" he asked.

"The usual: a cow fell in an old well, Main Street is getting new lights, three new babies, two deaths, and a music concert next week," Eva responded.

"We're finally getting new street lights?"

"The mayor put them in the budget two years ago and they just came in. I was just going to call my other stops."

"Oh, don't let me stop you," Joel said, taking the toothpick out of his mouth. "Never want anyone to say I got in the way of progress."

Eva smiled and picked up the phone. Joel flipped his toothpick in the trash can. He ran his hand through his black hair and leaned back against the wall. Joel was twenty-six and had completed his mandatory service last spring. He was in peak physical condition, and there was speculation as to how he had managed to come out of it without a scratch, but it was written off due to his athletic ability. It wasn't that Eva hadn't been attracted to his physique. But she didn't have a history with him. She didn't know him and that was the most important thing for her.

"You goin'?" Joel asked as Eva searched the rotary for a phone number.

"Where?" she asked.

"To the music concert," he said and then smiled. He squinted, then raised his eyebrows several times—a flirting move he had learned at the army's R&R spots. It never failed.

"What's wrong with your eyes?" Eva asked.

Joel, startled, quickly stepped back and rubbed his eyes. "Oh, must be Dad's smoke. Always makes 'em water."

"I wasn't planning to."

"Hmm?"

"I wasn't planning to go to the concert."

Joel drew in a long breath. "Oh, well…if you change your mind, let me know." Joel had lost his script. He had practiced his delivery; his choreography to the finest detail. He even practiced the comebacks and rejections. But the squint *never failed*. He quickly returned to his room. Eva stared on, puzzled at this odd behavior, then shook her head. She found her number and lifted the receiver.

"Operator," a monotone voice sounded through the speaker.

"Stettin 44, 14, 0," Eva said.

After a few moments, the operator broke in. "I'm sorry but there is no ring at Stettin 44, 14, 0. Would you like to try another number?"

"Yes, please." Eva quickly flipped to another page in the rotary. "Please try Posen 61, 22, 4."

The operator went silent for a moment, then returned.

"I'm sorry but there is no ring at Posen 61, 22, 4." The operator was obviously getting annoyed. Eva was puzzled; her eyes darted back and forth, searching for an explanation.

"Miss?"

"Uh, yes. Sorry."

"Would you like to try another number?"

"Yes. Krakow 81, 21, 5."

The operator asked her to hold, and soon Eva could hear a phone ringing on the line.

"Krakow 81, 21, 5," the operator said.

"Thank you," responded Eva.

"Hello?" a feminine voice chirped.

"Rachel?"

"Eva! Thank goodness it's you." Rachel's voice moved away from the phone, and Eva realized her contact in Krakow was talking with someone else in the room with her. "No, just the records. Leave everything else." The voice then returned to the phone's speaker. "Eva, we're packing up. The Germans have crossed the border. You've got to leave. They're—" the line went dead.

"Hello?" Eva's eyes widened.

She clicked the receiver.

"Operator?"

"Number please?"

"Krakow 81, 21, 5," Eva said nervously.

"There is no ring at Krakow 81, 21, 5. Would you like—" Eva hung the receiver onto its cradle.

She ran to Joel's office. Several people sat at wooden desks writing in ledgers.

"The Germans have crossed the border! We've got to leave!" Eva yelled. She disappeared down the hall.

The accountants and assistants looked at each other and then at Joel. Joel pursed his bottom lip, raised his eyebrows, and lifted a shoulder, confused. The accountants turned back to their work. Joel turned back to the mirror and practiced squinting.

—◦◦◦—

Joseph marched through the thick snow for several miles. He stopped often to rest and drink the water from his friend's packs. It would have been a beautiful day if he hadn't had the memory of being shot and left for dead among the frozen corpses of his friends fresh in his mind. Joseph rounded a curve in the road and came upon a grizzly scene. A man was hunched over a dead horse, cutting at its underbelly. Joseph limped by, hoping the man was too occupied to notice. The man was cutting strips of flesh and laying them across the horse's ribs. The man grunted and turned around as Joseph passed him on the opposite side of the road.

"Hmm? You scared me. I thought you were one of the Germans."

Joseph kept walking without responding.

"Hey, soldier!" the man called, now directing his full attention at Joseph. "Didn't you hear me? Hey! Come here. I want to talk to you."

Joseph didn't slow down. The man stood up and started to walk toward him. Joseph knew he couldn't outrun him so he stopped and turned in surrender.

"Come here." The man motioned with his knife. "I want to give you something." Joseph stood his ground, suspicious. "You look like you've been through hell. What's your name?"

"Joseph."

"Joseph, eh? You Jewish or something?"

"Or something."

The man laughed and took a bite from a strip of horse flesh.

"You hungry? You ever eat horse?"

"Yes."

"Well, come on and join me. Shame to let it rot. It's a German horse. Tastes like sauerkraut and schnapps." He gave a hearty laugh. Joseph wasn't amused. The man frowned and said, "So you don't think I'm very funny, eh?" Joseph stared at him, his expression blank. The man walked over to him. "Looks like you got hit on the head," the man said as he tapped his own head with the tip of his long knife. "I bet that's gotta hurt."

"What do you want?" Joseph asked.

The man looked surprised.

"Well, since you mentioned it, I like that pair of your boots on your feet and that nice warm jacket. Why don't we make this easy, huh?"

Joseph looked at the man who was now licking his lips and tapping the knife in his hand. Joseph bent down and unlaced one of his boots. He took it off and put it on his hand.

"What are you doing?" the man asked.

Joseph looked at him and dropped his pack and walking stick.

The man laughed. "You think you can take me? Look at you. You can barely walk. One blow from me and you'll fall over dead. Save yourself and give me them boots." Joseph circled him in a ready stance, still mute. "Fine, then. I'll take them myself."

The man flipped the knife from one hand to the next, all the while keeping his two dark eyes focused on Joseph. He smiled wide and suddenly lunged forward. Joseph jumped back with a surprising agility, and the man grunted with the effort.

"You're a quick kitten, huh? You think Boris can't catch a cat?" He lunged again. This time Joseph deflected the blow with the boot. "Ah, very clever you are. You see, I used to be in the army too. So I know all your tricks." The man jabbed again and Joseph deflected the blow with a sweep of his left arm. This enraged Boris, and he cursed Joseph at the top of his lungs. He then charged Joseph with a downward stab. Joseph held the sole of the boot up and the knife point pierced the boot heel and held firm. The man tried to jerk the knife away but Joseph countered with a solid punch to the man's diaphragm. The man doubled over, the wind knocked right out of him. Joseph pulled the knife out of the boot and swung the heel as hard as he could against the side of the man's jaw. The man's head snapped back and he fell hard against the ground. He was out. Joseph scanned the man's face to make sure he wouldn't get up, then put the knife in his belt, slipped his foot in the boot and tied it up. He then picked up his pack and stick, and headed on his way. He looked back and the man lay spread eagle on his back, his chest calmly rising and falling.

———

Rejowiec was a small but busy town, and Eva had to look both ways before crossing the two-lane Main

Street. Work crews were digging footings for the new light poles, and a handful of cars jostled for position behind horse-drawn carts. She stepped carefully around flattened cow pies.

The mayor's office was on the southern edge of the Rynek, the town square. In the middle of the square was a bronze statue of Henry Rejowiec, who had brought Spanish Jews to Poland after fleeing the Inquisition in 1492.

Gustav Zikowski was a rotund man with a pert goatee and an impressive handlebar mustache. He had been mayor for eight years and was encouraged by the progress his little town had made during his administration.

Eva burst through the door while the mayor was supervising the hanging of a new portrait he had recently commissioned. "Mayor Zikowski!" she yelled.

The assistant hanging the picture was startled by this sudden outburst and lost his grip. The large picture slid down the wall at an angle and bounced on the floor.

"No, stupid! Pick it up! Pick it up!" the mayor yelled. Eva ran to his side.

"The Germans have crossed the border. I tried several of my stops but there was no answer. The lines are dead. One answered but then it went dead. They're coming. We need to get ready!"

"Eva, what are you talking about?"

"The newsletter! I was working on the newsletter."

The mayor chuckled, his great belly bouncing. "You had me thinking they were rolling down Main Street."

"They will be. We've got to leave."

"What do you mean?"

"I called Rachel in Krakow. She said they had crossed the border, then the line went dead. They cut the lines. They're coming. We've got to leave. You've got to sound the warning. We've got to mobilize now."

Mayor Zikowski looked at Eva. She looked like a lost puppy with her frazzled hair and helpless expression.

"My dear, dear Eva, I think you've got yourself all worked up over a simple matter. The Germans are always teasing the Polish forces at the border. How many times have they "crossed" over only to scurry right back over some disputed territory or another? It's been like this for years and will continue to be like this for years to come. It's their way of testing our strength, to let us know that they're still mad at us. Our troops are stationed along the border. They'll handle the situation." The mayor looked up as if inspired. "Ah! Now I know the root of your fears. It's your boyfriend, isn't it? What's his name?"

"Joseph."

"You are worried about him, aren't you? I'm sure he'll be fine."

"But—"

"Look, if it will make you happy." The mayor held up his hand. He turned to his assistant who was fixing a wire on the back of the painting. "Charlie, call the station. Ask if they've heard any reports." The assistant leaned the painting against the wall and it fell over again. The mayor quickly caught it as Charlie turned back too late. "Leave it before you destroy it. Go call." The assistant quickly walked out of the room. "Worthless whelp." He looked to Eva as he carefully leaned the painting back against the wall and supported it with a chair. "You wouldn't be interested in working as my assistant, would you?"

A moment later Charlie returned. "No reports, sir. He asked if you would like to issue an alert."

"No. That will be all." He turned back to Eva. "There. See? No reports. Nothing to worry about."

Eva stared in disbelief, speechless. She turned and walked toward the door, her hopes vanishing.

"Are you coming to the music concert?" the mayor called behind her. She didn't acknowledge his question; instead she simply slammed the door behind her.

Eva returned to the office. Joel reclined at his desk and quickly dropped his feet to the floor upon seeing Eva. He ran his fingers through his hair.

"Eva, you're back! I thought you had left." Joel started squinting again. "Have you considered—"

"Stop that!" Eva said. She grabbed his arm. "Can you give me a ride home?"

"Sure!" Joel smiled.

She pulled him out the door.

When they arrived at her house, Eva promised Joel she would think about going to the concert with him. She thanked him for the ride, and then walked up to her front porch and opened the door. When she closed it behind her she called out, "Papa?"

Most of the homes in Eva's community were single story, yet her neighborhood was more affluent and had many two-floor homes, like hers. Being the daughter of the local rabbi had its advantages.

She found him praying in his study. When she looked at him, he acknowledged her with his eyes but didn't speak. She waited in the hall until he was finished praying.

Once he had finished, he closed his eyes and drew in a deep breath. He then acknowledged his daughter.

"Eva?" Rabbi Rozenfeld said, noticing the concern on her face. Eva entered and kissed his cheek.

"Papa, there's a problem. I was calling my contacts in other cities but most of the lines were down. I spoke to a girlfriend in Krakow. She said the Germans had crossed the border. It sounded like they were getting ready to evacuate. She told us we needed to leave."

"Did you speak with Mayor Zikowski?"

"Yes. He called the station but they said there was no alarm. He told me not to worry."

"There you have it, then." The rabbi stood and took Eva's hands in his own. "I know you're worried about Joseph, but I've told you we will find you someone better."

"I don't want someone better."

"Eva, you can't expect Joseph to make a good husband. He's too...ambitious. You need someone who'll get a good job and support a family."

"Joseph is a good man. He'll make a great father. His ambition is why I love him. The others are just—well, they're boring. Joseph is alive. He has desire, a destiny. He's someone special."

"Special? He has no plans to go to college! He's worked at the tannery for years and from what I've heard he is perpetually late for work—if he shows up at all."

"Father, you know that's not true."

"He doesn't even show up for prayers. You remember when we needed him to complete our Minyan so we could pray? I came home and he was fixing his motorbike. He's irresponsible. What kind of man is that? He follows his own religion."

"That was only one time."

"Hmph."

Eva tried another tactic. "Who brought you food when you were sick? Who took care of the animals when you traveled?"

"I paid him well for those services."

"But he would have done them for free. He told you that."

"He was just trying to get on my good side. To get close to you. I'd rather him consider his roots. His faith. He's out of control."

"You're missing the point." Eva sighed in frustration.

"I know what's going on. Who are you to lecture me?"

"But, Papa—"

"I will not speak about this further. Stay away from him!"

"But, Papa, I love him."

"Love? Love! You think you understand love? I have loved your mother for decades. I have sacrificed my dreams for our family. I have given up everything for my kids. That's love. That's commitment. Do you think he'll do that? That boy doesn't have a committed bone in his body. You say 'love,' but it is more like lust. I tell you now—if you go with that boy, he will use you and dump you on the curb for the first pretty girl he sees after you're all used up. I hope for your sake you don't have children when that happens."

Eva felt the tear well up in her eyes.

"But, Papa—"

"No more!" Rabbi Rozenfeld exclaimed. "I don't want to talk about it. You should respect your father."

Eva ran from the room. She went up the stairs and threw herself atop the bed and wept.

Downstairs, Rabbi Rozenfeld shook his head in frustration. A slight figure entered quietly behind him. Soft hands massaged his neck.

"You know she is just like you."

The rabbi patted his wife's hands.

"I know. That's what I'm most afraid of, I guess." His wife bent over him and encircled his neck with her arms. She placed her chin on his shoulder and looked at a photograph of Eva with Joseph.

"They were a good looking couple."

"Yes, they were."

"As I remember, you had your mind set on a beautiful young girl from around the corner. You fell madly in love with her and your father thought that her family wasn't good enough. Do you remember that?"

"Yes."

"What did you do?"

"I disobeyed my father and married her anyway." The rabbi turned in his chair and gently kissed his wife.

<hr>

Eva felt a bit relieved after releasing her emotions. The stress of the day had taken its toll. She wiped her eyes and looked out the window to the house next door. How many times had she seen that handsome face looking back at her? In her mind, she saw Joseph as a little boy. At first playing hide-and-seek behind a curtain, then as a teenager who didn't know how to bridge the gap from best friend to girlfriend, but was clearly fascinated by the physical changes in her body. She caught him staring at her as she got ready for bed one night. He was so embarrassed the next day at school—it was very sweet. In fact, she was having the same thoughts. She always liked him, just being around him. She knew his smell, like leather and sweat. It was his signature. She felt safe around him, protected. He wasn't like the other boys. She could tell him her deepest secrets and he would always understand. She came to accept him as more than a friend—as part of her life. He was her muse, her inspiration. He could read her like a book. And, he knew when she was unhappy. With a look, he could trigger an emotional outpouring that left her empty. She had always known she would marry him. From the first time she saw those beautiful blue eyes, her heart had taken him in and she had made him a part of her being. Without a doubt, she knew *HaShem* (G-d) had chosen him as her *bashert*, her partner, her soul mate. That's why it was so hard when he had to report for conscription. She prayed that no wars would break out and he would do his duty and return home to her safe and unharmed. Then he would prove to her father that he was worthy to be called his son-in-law. Her father would see then. He would give his blessing without any reservations.

Maybe she was getting worked up over nothing. Maybe her father was right—she was just being overprotective. *Like a good wife*, she thought. She smiled to herself and took out a picture of Joseph and Janek after their graduation from basic training. They both looked so handsome in their crisp uniforms and fitted wool jackets. She laughed. Joseph always did things his own way. Her father was right—the boy followed his own rules. They had told him to wear his cap level across the eyes, but in the picture, he had it tilted, one eye almost completely obscured by the hat—just enough to show his personality but not enough to be disciplined.

"Pepi!" she exclaimed.

Pepi would know what to do. If Joseph was Eva's soul mate, then Pepi was her conscience. Joseph's older sister was a strong woman, she could give as good as she got. Where Joseph protected Eva from school bullies, Pepi protected her from salacious girls who made jokes about being the "rabbi's daughter."

Yes, Pepi would know what to do.

3

Joseph made his way along a desolate stretch of road. Occasionally he would hear a gunshot echo in the distance, and would have to duck for cover. The going was slow. His head pounded with each step he took.

Once when he was resting, he heard the approach of distant machines. He slid down a mild embankment and lay prone behind clumps of dead grass. Soon a parade of German might passed by—armored personnel carriers with large-caliber machine guns, half-tracks, a few Panzer tanks, and truck after truck of soldiers. Joseph laid low until they were out of sight. He cautiously followed the bend of the road where he could quickly slip behind trees if more vehicles approached.

He reached a forested hilltop and descended carefully, but stopped short when he smelled a burning cigarette. If the wind had been blowing the other direction, he'd have walked right upon the German soldier. Joseph crossed the road and crawled up to the edge to get a better look. The man was sitting on a stump behind some bushes, alone, enjoying his cigarette. Where'd he come from? Joseph crept a little further down the road, and suddenly his heart nearly burst from his chest. Sitting on the road twenty yards ahead was the soldier's motorcycle! He turned quickly when he heard the German soldier grunt and cuss. *I've always wanted to drive a German bike*, Joseph thought.

Joseph crossed the road quietly past the motorcycle and well out of view of the soldier. He then backtracked to the bike. His heart sped and the adrenaline tweaked his senses. This was crazy. He could barely see the cloud of blue smoke rise above the bush where the German squatted. Joseph inspected the bike from across the road—it was in excellent condition, clearly hadn't seen any combat yet. He studied its operation and judged that it was ready to ride. Joseph slipped across the easement and ducked down behind the seat. He peered over it to see if the soldier could see him. Luckily he was too busy smoking and messing with a pile of leaves he had pulled from a tree. Joseph turned his attention to the controls, then found the kick starter lever. He eased himself onto the seat and carefully put his weight on the bike. After lifting the kick stand, he twisted the throttle twice and kicked the starter. The engine puttered and died.

The German let out a yelp and quickly stood. "Halt, Schweinhund!" the German yelled.

Joseph kicked the bike again and turned the throttle. It sputtered and backfired.

"Get off my motorcycle!"

Joseph shot a glance at the soldier, who was now reaching for his holster.

"Come on, come on, come on!" Joseph screamed.

He kicked the crank again and gave it full gas. The engine roared to life. He slammed the gear and spun the back tire as the bike took off.

Pop! Pop! Pop! He didn't stop to find out if the soldier's aim was accurate.

He sped down the dirt road for a while and thankfully didn't see any other vehicles. Most of the people he met were farmers, and after the German parade had gone through, Joseph didn't expect to see any locals milling about.

The wind chilled his knuckles and froze his cheeks, but luckily the German had kindly left his glasses so Joseph's eyes were protected. The countryside was beautiful, and Joseph found a semblance of calm in his heart. Rolling meadows were covered in blankets of fresh snow, and were sprinkled with forested thickets. He also passed a herd of deer on his way, expecting them to sprint away. But they eyed him cautiously and lazily went back to digging for shoots. The steady drone of the engine felt good and massaged away the stress mile by mile.

The faint smell of smoke drifted past Joseph, tapping his mind to attention. As he ascended to the top of a hill, he could see black fountains of billowing smoke rising over the trees ahead. A moment later, he passed a smoldering farmhouse. The charred remains of the timber frame clung to a section of unburned roof. Cows wandered wildly, snipping leaves off the trees, and bumping into each other in a craze. Further down the road, another house was burnt, and another. All burnt. The farther he traveled, the more flames he noticed. The Germans had started at one end and worked their way into the community. Joseph coasted to a stop at a row of homes. The first few dwellings were burning, but the others had not been lit. *Too busy to mess with them, or maybe they found what they were looking for.*

Joseph dropped the kickstand and turned off the engine. He then walked to the first unburned home and found a family of three, dead in the melting snow. They had been shot, execution style, in the back of the head. In the distance, a dog barked, echoing across the small valley. It was a strained noise, lost and confused.

Joseph went to the open door of the house and listened. There was no sound. The front room was littered with the results of a detailed search. The entire house had been ransacked. Even the kitchen cabinets were bare.

Joseph went to the next house. Apparently a struggle had taken place as two dead Germans lay in the front room. The man of the house was hanging from a beam, with his family dead at his feet. From the looks of it, they had watched him die before they were killed.

As Joseph rode his bike slowly through the village, he decided to stop at the very last house on the road. A man lay in the basement where he had tried to hide, but the hole in his head indicated that the Germans had found him. Joseph went to the kitchen to find food, but again discovered that the cupboards were empty. He decided it was a fruitless effort. He'd have to try further down the road.

As he was walking back to his motorcycle, Joseph heard a faint cry in the distance. He froze in his tracks. He heard it again. It was coming from the woodshed at the side of the house. Joseph pulled his knife out and listened at the door. A high-pitched voice, clearly grunting in pain. A cold sweat ran under the layers of Joseph's clothing. For the first time in days he felt hot. He hesitated for a moment, then kicked the door open. He scanned the interior with his fists up and found no one there.

Light beams cut through the dust swirls. *Must have been an animal,* Joseph thought. He started to leave when he noticed something different about one of the wood beams on the floor. It wasn't covered with dirt and straw like the rest of the floor. Joseph knelt down and slid his fingers under the edge of the board. He flipped it back with a thud and heard a gasp. Looking carefully into the darkness, he could barely discern a large black hole descending deep into the ground. As his eyes adjusted, he saw two eyes glistening up at him. A young boy clung to the iron rungs on the curved wall of an old well. Below him, water shimmered.

"It's okay," Joseph said. "I won't hurt you."

The boy looked at him with frightened eyes.

"Do you live here?"

The boy slowly nodded.

"Come on, I'll help you up." The boy shook his head no.

"It's all right. I'm not German," Joseph reassured him. "I'm Polish, just like you."

"You're a soldier," the boy whimpered.

"I'm on your side. You can't stay down there."

"My daddy told me to stay here and hide until he came and got me. He made me promise."

"How old are you?"

"Ten."

"Really? You're big for ten and very strong to hold onto that rail for so long. What's your name?"

The boy hesitated. "Itzak."

"Well, Itzak. I'm sorry to tell you this, but your father is not coming to get you."

"Yes, he will. He promised."

"Itzak, sometimes things happen and we can't keep the promises we make."

"You're lying. He'll come! You'll see."

Itzak began to cry, and Joseph sat on the floor of the shed, exhausted.

"How long have you been down there?"

"I don't know."

"Your hands must be getting tired. Come on up and I'll make you something to eat."

"I'm not hungry."

"We need to go back in the house. It's dangerous out here. Did you hear the soldiers come through earlier?"

Itzak nodded.

"They may come back. We can't be out here. They will see us." Joseph thought for a moment. "If you come up, I will take you to see your father."

Itzak's eyes brightened.

"You promise?"

"I promise."

Itzak slowly climbed the rungs, and Joseph helped him to his feet. Itzak held his hand as they made it back to the house. When they reached the front steps, Joseph retrieved the motorcycle and hid it behind a woodpile with a tarp.

Joseph then opened the basement door and walked down several creaky steps with Itzak close behind. Itzak peeked from around Joseph's jacket and saw his father lying still on the floor next to an old mattress. Itzak made no sound—he just looked, trying to understand. Joseph put his hand on Itzak's shoulder, and let the boy back up the stairs. Joseph closed the door behind them and the two sat at the kitchen table, silent as the dead. After several minutes of silence, Itzak looked at Joseph and said, "He was trying to protect me. He didn't want the Germans to find me. That's why he put me in the well."

"You're right. You wouldn't be alive if he hadn't."

Itzak looked at his hands, now stained darkly with rust. Joseph hoisted his pack into the chair next to him and pulled out some crackers and a tin of sardines.

"It's not much, but it's something."

Itzak looked at the crackers and the tin of sardines. He then studied Joseph with incredulity and rolled his eyes. He hopped down from his chair and walked to a segment of wall partition that looked like all the rest. He slipped his fingers into a small hole and pulled. The partition pulled back, revealing a fully-stocked pantry.

Joseph started a small fire in a large bucket on the back porch. He figured the smoke rising from outside the house wouldn't be noticed as most homes were either burning or smoldering, but smoke coming from the kitchen chimney of an intact house was sure to arouse suspicion. The two roasted potatoes and canned wieners over the bucket. The meal wasn't too bad, considering it was the first Joseph had had in, two, three days? He had lost count. The adrenaline had kept him going but now he felt the exhaustion catching up from his effort. When they had finished eating, Joseph leaned back and stared at the woods behind the house. The lone dog continued its hoarse bark, consistent, eternal. The world went dark, but this time, in an envelope of comfort.

He awoke with a shove from Itzak. It was getting cold and it was already dark, so Itzak led Joseph inside, where he had lit a single candle in a lantern. Itzak had laid blankets and clothes on the front room couch as well. Hot water sat in a basin on a table with lye soap, a rag, and a fresh towel.

"Those are my dad's clothes," Itzak said. "They might be a little big but he doesn't mind if you use them." Joseph thanked him, and watched as the boy disappeared into his bedroom. Joseph wondered if he had ever been so responsible.

Joseph closed the heavy drapes over the windows and made sure to keep the candle reflector's back to the window. He found a mirror in the tiny bathroom and took off his snow cap to view his wound. The bandage had stuck to the dried blood, so he decided to leave it for later. He disrobed, taking one layer of clothing off after the other. His uniform and shirt were stiff from Joseph's perspiration. Once he had peeled this layer of clothing off, he stood before the mirror and examined his bare body. He hardly recognized himself—his face was covered in dried blood and thick layers of dirt, rimmed only by the riding goggles from the motorcycle. *No wonder he wouldn't come out of the hole. I look pretty scary*, Joseph thought, showing white teeth against an ashen face. He unwrapped the blood encrusted shirt from his head and examined the wound. Little by little he washed the blood away, and the water in the basin turned a dark brown. He was careful not to reopen the wound. It wasn't as large as he thought—a centimeter wide starting from above his left ear, and running slightly upward along the side of his head. A graze. He was sure it had dug a groove in his skull. The entire length of the wound was sore and throbbing. He cut away the matted hair as best he could with a small pair of scissors from his kit, then cleaned the rest of the wound with soapy water. *I need to get this sewn up, but not now. Soon.*

He took cotton gauze from his field kit and packed it in the wound and wrapped a long bandage around his head. He tied it off and checked his work. Not bad—it would do for now. He dumped the basin in the kitchen and refilled it with fresh, cold water from the pump. He then washed his whole body using a sponge from the kitchen. Once he was clean, he put on an oversized wool shirt that was very warm, a pair of pants, and a pair of thick socks. He organized his pack, stuffing extra food and clothes in it for the journey ahead. What was he going to do with the boy? He decided to check on Itzak, opening the boy's door a crack so as not to disturb him. Itzak was sleeping soundly in his bed, peaceful despite the terrible events of the day. Joseph went back to the front room, sat on the couch, and stared at the candle. He suddenly felt so small, so insignificant—he was completely out of control of the world around him. Questions came but he was too tired to think. He laid back and quickly fell asleep.

Joseph awoke, startled. He had heard a voice crying out in the darkness. He stood and heard it again. It was a soft voice, and it was talking to someone. It came from the basement.

Joseph grabbed his knife and quietly felt his way to the basement door, which was slightly ajar. He stepped carefully down the side of each step to make as little noise as possible.

Below, Joseph could see a faint light flickering, dancing across the tiny room's walls. When he reached the threshold, he stopped and stared in awe of what was before him.

Itzak was standing over his father's body, which was now lying on the mattress, tucked under a sheet as if ready for bed. The dead man's eyes were closed and he was wearing a fresh white shirt. Itzak was wearing his dad's prayer shawl, and was reading from a copy of the Sidur (prayer book). The boy was praying, Joseph realized. Creeping back to the stairs to observe, Joseph watched as Itzak pulled back the shawl so it draped around his neck.

"It's okay, Daddy. Joseph is taking care of me. HaShem has sent him to rescue me. Rest in peace. Tell Mommy I love her. I love you too, Tata."

Joseph quietly ascended the stairs, closed the door to the basement, and went back to bed.

The smell of meat cooking roused Joseph from a deep sleep. Light streamed through the window, heralding in a new day. The house was warm...too warm. Joseph quickly turned to the fireplace and noticed a fire burning brightly in the hearth.

"No!" he yelled.

Joseph jumped up from the couch and nearly fell. He found the basin of water and dumped it on the fire, sending steam into the room. Joseph quickly made his way to the kitchen and found the dining table set for two. Fresh rolls, potatoes, and tea adorned the center of the table, and Itzak was placing slices of cooked meat on each plate.

"I found a dead sheep," he said.

"Itzak, you can't—they'll see the smoke."

Joseph quickly doused the fire in a square cast iron stove.

"I was just trying to make breakfast."

"I know, but if a German patrol sees us…"

Joseph went back to the front room and closed the curtains. He looked out and saw nothing. Then he heard a truck. Leaning close to the edge of the window he could see a German work crew. They must have come to collect the two dead German soldiers and finish burning the houses, Joseph surmised.

"We have to leave."

"I don't want to."

"I heard you tell your dad that HaShem sent me to protect you. So you have to trust me."

Itzak looked up at Joseph, his eyes wide. He then slowly nodded his head.

"Good, grab a change of clothes," Joseph commanded. "Wrap up the potatoes and meat and put them in my pack. And bring the pack outside when you're done. Go, quickly!"

Joseph hastily dressed and tucked his knife in his boot. He went out the back door and uncovered the tarp from the motorcycle. He rolled it behind the house and began to crank it, but it sputtered and died, sputtered and died. With each crank, the sputtering lasted a little longer, so Joseph rocked the bike between his legs, sloshing the gas in the tank. He tried again. Several houses down, he saw a curious German soldier stick his head around the edge of the neighbor's house. He yelled to Joseph.

"Hey! What are you doing? Quit playing around and come help us. You can ride later. Did you hear me?"

The bike roared to life.

"Itzak!" Joseph yelled.

Itzak appeared with his pack at the back door. Joseph unfolded the cycle's rear foot pegs and shouted, "Let's go!" Once Itzak appeared, Joseph grabbed the pack and secured it to the back of the frame.

The soldier blew a whistle and yelled to the others. Itzak jumped on the back of the bike and Joseph cranked the throttle. The bike slipped across the front yard as the tires eventually gained purchase on the gravel road.

A tree next to the road exploded as a round from the 50 mm hit. Joseph and Itzak instinctively ducked on the speeding bike. Another round zinged over their heads and kicked up dirt in front of the accelerating bike. Joseph swerved just in time, and throttled the bike to full speed. The rounds grew quieter and quieter as the two quickly put distance between themselves and their aggressors.

4

Itzak and Joseph rode directly toward Warsaw as fast as the motorcycle would allow them. At forty kilometers from their destination, traffic on the main road increased with refugees fleeing the German advance. Most were walking in the middle of the road, carrying their possessions with them, while ox-drawn carts piled high with passengers and belongings rolled along with them. It was clear that the city had already been attacked. Wheelbarrows served as litters for the wounded, and one man was pulling the lifeless body of his wife in a small, makeshift wagon.

Joseph weaved the motor bike through the throng of pedestrians, ignoring the cries for help from those on foot. Their universal expressions, however, were distant and downcast. They had already lost so much hope. They had nowhere to go, and carried everything they owned. The shock and desperation was palpable. Mud covered everything.

Suddenly Joseph felt the motorcycle's rear tire slip from one rut to another. As the bike swerved wildly, Itzak clung tightly to keep from falling off. Joseph regained control, and pulled up behind an old cattle truck loaded with women, children, and the elderly. A young girl smiled and waved from between two wood slats. Joseph smiled. She looked upward as something caught her attention. A shadow passed over them. She turned to her mother and pointed to the sky. Joseph tried to see but couldn't tilt his head far enough. The engine from whatever it was soon drowned the noise from the street out. More heads turned skyward, as the realization registered on their panicking faces. Several pedestrians started yelling and pounding the sides of the truck bed. Arms stuck out both sides and frantically waved, trying to get the driver's attention.

Joseph was able to glimpse a single engine airplane. It was too small and fast to be a Polish P.7 Fighter. It was German! More specifically, it was the deadly Messerschmitt.

The Messerschmitt turned in a long sloping bank and lined up perpendicular to the road. It dove and came in fast. Joseph gassed the motorbike and pulled alongside the truck. He yelled at the driver and pointed at the sky, motioning for him to stop and let the passengers take cover. Joseph drifted behind and yelled for the people to get off the road. To his horror, he saw the double lines of machinegun fire rip across the field next to the road and stream quickly across the truck, blowing out gas and wood planks. People fell in a neat row as the bullets cut them down. The driver was killed instantly, sending the truck wildly off the road and crashing loudly into a tree. Joseph tried to stop the bike from behind but slid and fell in the mud. Itzak had managed to hop off the bike in time and roll on the pavement. He stood up with only a few minor cuts and bruises.

Joseph told him to hide under some bushes at the side of the road while he ran to help the passengers in the truck. He fumbled with the catch on the back gate, but it finally swung open and people fell out. Loud moans emanated from the truck bed as several surviving passengers pushed or climbed over the dead to escape. Joseph helped the survivors off, one by one, when he smelled gasoline. He looked over at the fuselage and saw a series of holes across the tank, pouring the liquid out onto the ground.

"We've got to move, now!" Joseph yelled.

He quickly scanned the sky but didn't see the plane, so he rushed to pull more people off the truck. Joseph could hear the distinct sound of a diving fighter plane as it lined up for its next run. A young woman leaned on one elbow and was trying to get out of the truck, but her leg was trapped under the body of a heavy man. She struggled to pull free but couldn't. Joseph jumped onto the bed of the truck and stepped over several bodies to get to the woman.

"Please help me!" the woman cried.

Joseph moved the large man off her leg and almost threw her off the back of the truck. He didn't have time to turn but heard the *thwip, thwip, thwip, thwip* of bullets rapidly closing in. He leaped as the truck was struck again; igniting the tanks that exploded in an orange fireball. The blast catapulted Joseph in a high arc over the road and into a clump of saplings. A curious thought went through his mind as he tumbled through the air—*This must be what it feels like to be launched from a cannon.* The world went black…again.

A woman's voice woke Joseph from a confused, restless sleep.

"He's lucky to be alive. Nasty gash on his head, it is."

The woman took warm water and gently wiped the blood from around Joseph's face. His eyes fluttered open at the cool touch, and he saw a woman with a mane of silver hair and soft brown eyes smile at him. She wore a cooking apron that was too small for her ample portions. She squealed.

"He's coming around. You're a lucky tart. You would've bled to death if it weren't for your boy here. Lucky thing it was."

Joseph moaned as he tried to sit up.

"No, no, no, no," the woman commanded. "You lay right there and let me clean you up. You aren't goin' anywhere 'til we get you better."

An older man turned around from a chair.

"Basha, don't let anyone leave sick…or hungry."

Itzak sat at a table with the old man, eating a piece of fresh bread.

"You best do as she says, young man. You'll be needing all your strength to handle her cookin'," the old man said. Basha threw a wet rag at him.

"Pay you no mind to him. The old goat loves my cooking." She looked at him and barked an order, "Here, make yourself useful and bring me some fresh water. I be needing my sewing and a flask of vodka water."

The old man turned to Itzak.

"You fill the basin, I've gotta go to the cellar."

Itzak hopped up and grabbed the basin while the old man ambled out of the room.

Joseph watched as Basha shaved the side of his head. She had calloused hands, was clearly familiar with hard work. Every now and then she would catch his eye as she worked. He winced when she pulled matted hair from the wound, but it helped wake him from his shellshock.

"Sorry, love. Got to clean this up. Looks like you stuck your head in a mud puddle."

Basha took a moment, wiped sweat from her face, and tied her hair back.

"Would be lookin' more presentable but they brought you in while I was bare-assed. Name's Basha. The old goat is Erik."

"Joseph."

"Nice to meet you, Joseph. You a soldier?"

"Yes."

"Them krauts got no right scarin' all these people. We're simple folk. We don't cause no trouble with no one. Erik 'n' me been living here for forty years and never had no problem. Raised a gaggle of kids. They all left, got two boys in the army. They're in Krakow. They tell me that if the Germans ever did this crazy thing that France and Britain would be here to protect our backsides. They're our allies, you know."

"They haven't come," Joseph said.

"They'll be here soon enough. We just got to hold our own for a while."

"That might not be so easy," Joseph said. He tried to swallow but couldn't get the lump down his throat.

"You want some water? You ready to sit up?"

"I think so."

Basha helped him up to sit in a chair and she poured him a glass of water. She watched as he drank it down and held out the cup for more. She filled it and he drank again.

"You've got beautiful eyes," she said. "Don't see blue eyes too often."

"My dad's."

"Your dad must be a handsome man."

Joseph smiled. Itzak brought in the basin with clean water and Erik entered moments later, patting himself from the cold.

"Getting cold again—might snow. Clouds hangin' real low. Here ya go."

Erik handed Basha a gallon jug filled with clear liquid. Basha took Joseph's empty cup, pulled the cork from the bottle, and filled it up.

"Drink up, dear."

Joseph took a sip and had to catch his breath; it burned all the way down. Basha poured a cup for her, Erik, and Itzak.

"Erik's been making vodka for years. Tastes better than store bought."

"Mmm..." Joseph hummed as he took another drink.

"I use it for disinfectin', cleanin', and cookin'. Oh, and we drink it too. You need to drink that down. I got to sew up that cut in your head so it will heal. I can't do that 'less I scrub it real good and it's gonna hurt. The more of that vodka you get in your stomach, the less pain you gonna feel."

"C'mon, Itzak," said Erik. "Let's get you cleaned up. You nor I need to see this." Erik took Itzak by the hand and walked out of the room.

Basha lay Joseph on his side and brought a lantern close to his head. Once she finished shaving around the wound, she gave him a leather strap to bite down on. With a bristle brush, she scrubbed the wound with soap and vodka, sending spikes of pain through his head. Joseph moaned and tensed as he tried to keep from moving. When she finished, the wound started bleeding again. She deftly sewed a suture into the side of his head, closing the wound from one end to the other. She rinsed it off with vodka and wrapped a compress and bandage around his head.

"Now that's gonna drain over the next few days. You need to change it every day and keep it clean." Basha opened a small tin with white pills. She dumped some out into a napkin. "Take one of these each day. They're antibiotics and will keep down any infection."

Joseph looked up at her in wonder. "Where did you learn all this?"

"Stalin."

"The Premier of Russia?"

"The bull. He's our stud. He's always trying to get through the barbed wire to the heifers. had to sew him up many times."

Basha cleaned up the blood and laid out clean clothes for Joseph.

"These are my son's. He's about your size. I'll go make your boy something for dinner."

"He's not mine."

"Oh?"

"His father was killed during the attack. I helped him escape."

"Does he have any relatives?"

"I don't know. I don't have time to look for them. I've got to get home and warn the others."

"Where you from?"

"Rejowiec. Just south of Lublin."

"You've got a ways to go."

Erik came back in the room, drying his hands.

"Itzak is taking his bath," he said.

Joseph was impressed with the two. They had shown such kindness—a stark contrast to the events of the past few days. A part of him regretted leaving them, but he was determined to get to Eva before the Germans rolled into town.

"I've got to leave in the morning," Joseph breathed.

"You're leaving us so soon?" Erik asked, surprised.

"I have to."

Basha and Erik glanced at each other knowingly.

"It's a woman, isn't it?" Erik smiled.

Joseph stared at the two in shock.

"How did you—"

"Never you mind, dear," said Basha. "When a man does something so stupid as to risk his life, there's usually a woman waiting for him at the end."

"So I take it you're fairly set in your ways," added Erik. "Least I can do is see you to the city limits."

"Thank you."

"C'mon, woman, let's give Joseph some rest," Erik beamed. He took Basha under one arm and the glass bottle with the other and led her out of the room.

"We'll see you in the morning. Sleep well."

"Thanks…for everything." Joseph smiled weakly.

"You're welcome. Good night."

"Good night."

Joseph climbed in bed, slowly, his body aching from head to toe. His head throbbed dully, but he could live with it. The alcohol had relaxed him just enough to fall into a dreamless sleep.

———

Pepi, Joseph's older sister, was bright, determined, and fearless. Her husband, Max, was away with their daughter Malka to spend some time with her father. Max was a doctor and had an office in Rejowiec and in Lublin. He saw patients on Tuesdays and Thursdays locally, and in Lublin on Mondays, Wednesdays, and Fridays. By Rejowiec standards, the family was wealthy. They owned their own car where the majority of Rejowiets either walked or used horses. And their house was only four doors down from Eva's. They could have lived in a more upscale community in Lublin but Pepi liked being close to her parents. Max didn't mind living below his means and Pepi had taught him to appreciate the simple life. She did all the housework herself, cooked and cared for Malka. The one luxury she let him buy was a telephone. No one except the mayor and a rich mining family had phones in their houses. Max justified the cost through his profession, responding to medical emergencies. As for Pepi, aside from a few businesses in town, there was no one to call, but each night Max called from his hotel, just to check on her.

Frankly, Pepi was glad to have the house to herself. She could clean, organize, and, most importantly, declutter. Max was a packrat and never threw anything away. Once a year, she would sort through his things and if he hadn't used an item since the last sorting, it got put in the "charity" pile. She now sat cross-legged in the middle of the floor, holding up a dress shirt with a small stain on it when she heard a knock at the door.

"Perfect timing," Pepi said when she saw Eva. "You can help me sort some clothes and I already have things you can give the rabbi or your cuddly bear."

"I don't call him 'cuddly bear.'"

"Really? What do you call him?"

"Bushki."

Pepi cackled with laughter.

"Did you finally kiss him?"

"I'm not telling you. Besides, you might use it for blackmail and tell my mother. I'm already in enough trouble from the hug."

"I would never tell."

"Promise?"

"I promise."

Pepi smiled at her old friend as Eva tried to get in.

"Let me in, I'm freezing," Eva said impatiently.

"Not until you tell me."

"You see?"

"Better hurry up, you're starting to shiver."

"Oh all right. Once. Now let me in!"

"On the cheek or on the lips?"

"Pepi!"

"Cheek or lips?"

"I told you, so let me in!"

Pepi stubbornly blocked the door. "Nope, cheeky or lippy lips?" Pepi smooched the air with her lips.

"Let me in."

"Not until you tell me." Pepi smiled.

"On the lips!"

"The lips?" Pepi whistled. "You *are* a naughty girl. Did you open your mouth?"

"Pepi! Why. you—"

"Well did you?"

"No! He brought me back a rose last summer and I thought it was so sweet, I gave him a quick kiss. When no one was looking."

"That's all?"

"That's it, now let me in!"

"You're boring." Pepi moved out of the way, frowning. Eva shook off the cold as Pepi closed the door.

"You let all the heat out," Eva said, exasperated. "And why do you say I'm boring? Joseph doesn't think I'm boring. He said he couldn't sleep all night thinking about it."

"He wasn't thinking about the kiss, he was thinking about—"

"Pepi, stop!"

"You can't blame me. Wait until you've been married and had kids. Then you'll understand *wifely duties*."

"When Joseph and I are married it will never be like that. He loves me."

"You don't know Joseph like I do. I used to wipe his bottom."

"I don't want to hear about it."

"Fine, then I'll tell you about all the joys of motherhood and you can tell me if you still want to persist in this fairytale fantasy of you and cuddly bear."

"Bushki."

"Whatever."

They walked over to the piles of clothes and began sorting them.

"Won't Max get mad, you going through all his things?"

"He won't even notice, been doing this for five years. He just notices he's got more space in the closet, then fills it up with more stuff."

"I'm worried," Eva said.

Pepi sat on the floor, oblivious to Eva's words. She found what she was looking for in the pile—a stained, but elegant, dress shirt.

"If you soak this in lemon juice and hot water, I think the stain will come out," Pepi said. "Joseph will look great in it. It might be a bit large, though. Max has gained some weight since Malka. It must be the good food I've been cooking. You know they say men go through changes during pregnancy just like women…"

Pepi's voice trailed off as she lowered the shirt. Eva stared at her hands. "Eva? You all right?"

"I'm worried."

"About what, sweetheart?"

"I called my contacts in the other cities and most of the lines were down. The one that got through told me the Germans had crossed the border and then the line went down."

"Joseph's not going to let the Germans into Poland."

"That's what I'm worried about. His camp is near the border."

"I wouldn't worry," Pepi said, shaking her head. "I'm sure there are skirmishes all the time. You know boys—always picking fights to show who's tougher. It's all a show."

The phone rang. Pepi furrowed her brow as she got up to answer it.

"Hello?"

"Pepi."

"Hi, honey! We were just talking about you. Eva's here and I—"

"Listen carefully, I don't have much time," Max said.

"Wha—"

"The Germans have attacked Poland. They've broken the defensive lines and they are making their way into Warsaw as we speak."

"Oh my—"

Pepi looked over at Eva, her eyes furrowed with worry. Eva mouthed, "What is it?"

"You've got to leave. Go to Russia. Go to Pinsk and I will meet you there. A group of us are leaving tonight. We're going to drive and head to the border."

"But I want to come with you."

"You can't. The southern part of Warsaw is already under German control."

"How is Malka?"

"Here, I'll let you talk to her."

Max left the phone. In the background she could hear him say, "It's Mommy. Be quick—we've got to go."

"Hi, Mommy!"

"Hi, sweetie."

Pepi began to cry, so Eva rushed over and put her hand on her shoulder.

"Tata says we have to leave. I don't want to go without you."

"Me either, baby. But you go. Stay with daddy. Make sure he's okay. Daddy will take care of you and then I'll catch up. I love you."

"I love you too, Mommy."

Max took the phone.

"It's not fair." Pepi sniffed, trying to speak clearly. "What are we going to do?"

"You've got to leave," said Max. "There are reports of the Germans burning villages and killing families. Take what you can carry. Get the cash and jewelry from the safe. See if you can hire a driver and car, but do it quickly. You can't stay there. It's not safe."

"What about the others?"

"Pepi, listen to me. Listen carefully. There is a time to help and there is a time to run. Now is the time to run. If you wait, it could mean the difference between life and death. You have to—" The line went dead. Static.

"No!" Pepi screamed into the phone. "No, no, no!" Pepi collapsed to her knees and wailed. Eva held her and rocked slowly while Pepi wept. It was the last time she ever spoke to her husband and daughter.

5

Itzak swelled at the possibility of seeing his aunt.

"I'll take him to the records office in Warsaw tomorrow," Basha told Joseph. "We'll see if we can find them."

"Thank you for taking care of me and for watching Itzak. I'm sure they'll be worried about him," Joseph said.

"Remember to change that bandage every so often."

"I will."

Joseph scooped Itzak in his arms and hugged him tightly. He bid farewell to Basha as he climbed aboard Erik's oxcart. He threw his pack in the back and looked down at Basha and Itzak. Basha set a plate wrapped in a thick tablecloth in Joseph's lap.

"Potato pie, for later."

"Thank you." Joseph smiled.

"C'mon. Basha, Stalin's not gonna sit long," Erik said. As if hearing this, the giant bull kicked his hooves into the dirt and swayed his head back and forth anxiously.

Basha stepped back as Erik flicked his whip. Stalin looked back and eyed him.

"Chup!" Erik said. Stalin took steady steps and easily rolled the cart forward. Itzak waved from the porch as Basha joined him. Joseph waved, then turned to the long road ahead.

"We'll take a shortcut around the city. It will put us far enough south to avoid patrols."

"Are you worried?" asked Joseph.

"I'm too old to worry. I've done all the worrying for a lifetime. Let the youngsters worry. They can make a difference. All I'm concerned about is a good meal, a warm bed, and a good book."

"What about Basha?"

Erik laughed. He looked at Joseph and then laughed again.

"Gave that up years ago. The only breeding going on is making sure Stalin keeps the heifers calving."

Stalin blew out a steamy snort in reply.

"He knows you're talking about him." Joseph grinned.

"He's got more sense than all the politicians combined. They need to mind their own business. One thing I've learned from a very difficult life is not to make things worse. We got enough problems in just surviving. Let people be the way they want to be. To each his own, I say!"

"But you've helped me."

"Ah, that's Basha," Erik said. "No offense, but I'd a rolled right over ya and never thought twice about it."

"So why'd you stop?"

"Basha saw the little boy shakin' you, tryin' to wake you up in the middle of all them dead people. I told her to forget about it. So she jumped off the wagon."

"Well thank goodness for Basha."

"I say that every morning."

They rode for miles. The cart wheels bumped along with a hypnotic rhythm. It seemed normal, native. Erik, Basha, and even Stalin were part of the land. Made of the same stuff; ancient and enduring. Leaders come and go. Politics change like the seasons, but people like Erik and Basha are as stable as rocks. They don't take anything that's not theirs and they don't expect handouts. As they rode, Joseph studied the lines in Erik's profile. He emanated self-sufficiency and confidence. In any other landscape, he would seem out of place. He was tough and admirable. His clothes had been lovingly patched, repaired, and repatched so many times, his jacket looked like a quilt work of durable cloth. The story of Joseph's multicolored coat flashed in his mind.

After several hours of travel, the oxcart reached the intersection between Warsaw and Lublin.

"This is as far as I go. Follow this road south and it will lead right into Lublin."

Joseph stepped down from the cart and stood for a moment. He took off his outer coat and gave it to Erik. Erik looked surprised, maybe not as much by Joseph's offer, but that he took it. He was a proud man. Erik took off his old coat and put on the new one. He buttoned the buttons and admired the sleeves.

"It's warm. How do I look?"

"Like an aristocrat."

"Really?" Erik gleamed and sat up straight. "Hear that, Stalin? He called me an aristocrat."

Joseph laughed.

"Take care of Basha. You might think you've been put out to pasture, but she's not. I think she needs your lovin' more than ever. Ask Stalin…he can give you some pointers on the way home." Stalin grunted.

Erik smiled. "I guess I forgot she needs that too. I'll make it up to her."

Joseph shook his hand and patted Stalin's rump.

"Goodbye, my friend."

"Come on, Stalin!" Erik cracked his whip. "You and me got some talkin' to do. I need a professional opinion. Chup!"

Stalin groaned and snorted, and slowly turned his massive body around in the opposite direction. Joseph watched the two rumble off into the distance before continuing toward Lublin.

The road was barren, but he knew at the end was awaiting his ultimate prize. In the distance he heard a loud "moo" followed by Erik's hearty laughter.

Eva leaned forward in her chair.

"Father, you've got to listen to us. You've got to leave!"

"You will not speak to your father that way," Eva's mother said. Pepi tried to calm Eva down, but Eva retaliated by punching her fist into her armchair.

"They're going to kill us! We have to run!"

"Where?" Rabbi Rozenfeld stood to his feet. "Where would you have us go? Shall we go to Warsaw? Shall we flee to Russia? To what? The Russians are as crooked as the Germans. We're not safe in our own country—even the Poles hate Jews. So where are we going to go?" Eva didn't answer.

"I'll tell you where I'm going," Rabbi Rozenfeld finally said. "I'm staying right here and trusting HaShem to protect us. You have to have faith."

"But Papa!"

Rabbi Rozenfeld walked over and took her hands.

"Your mother and I have worked all our lives to build this house. I'm not talking about the wood and brick, but about our place in the community. This is all we have. There's nowhere for us to go. Even if the Germans come knocking at our door, we will stay here. This is our dream." The rabbi looked his daughter in the eye and smiled. "You are young and there are many more possibilities for your future. If you want to go, I won't stop you. But you will always find us here when you decide to come home."

"We must warn the others," cried Eva. "We have to try."

"Do what you must. Can your mother and I help?"

"Please pack my things. I've got to talk to my friends and my coworkers. I've got to try."

"Go, then. We'll pack your bags. They'll be ready when you get back."

Eva's mom shot a worried glance at her husband. Her husband met her eyes, closed his own, and nodded. Her mom held back a sniffle.

Eva and Pepi went from house to house, explaining the severity of the situation. Most families didn't believe them or simply didn't answer their doors. Some did believe. Eva's friend, Ester, believed her. She lived with her husband and two young children.

"Where will we go?"

"To Pinsk, across the river. It's our only hope. Max will meet us there."

"What about Joseph?"

"I hope he's all right. I want to believe he's all right. I haven't had time to let the worry set in. I pray he's okay."

"We need to plan what we're going to do," Pepi said.

"Let's meet at the Rynek in an hour," Ester's husband said. The Rynek was the center of town.

"We need to find transportation," Eva said.

"I'll go see if I can get Michael to drive us in his truck," Pepi said.

"Wonderful, we'll see you then."

<hr />

Joseph kept a watchful eye on the road. Now and then, trucks loaded with families and household goods passed by. The faces were always the same, however: disbelief, shock, and fear.

After several hours, Joseph's wounds began to open up again, his muscles ached, his head throbbed. He touched his hand to his head wound and his fingers came back sticky with fresh blood. Joseph quickly turned his head back down the road as he heard the approach of a large vehicle. Sure enough, an armored truck covered in a drab tarp rolled up a hill. Joseph ducked behind some bushes, fearing it might be German. As the truck drew near, he recognized the Polish Army insignia on the front and came out of hiding. He waved as the truck went by.

The truck stopped and gave Joseph a ride as close as possible to his home town.

———⟊⟊⟊———

"I don't understand it," Eva said. "No one believes us— or they don't seem concerned."

"We've tried, Eva," said Pepi "We can't wait to see if they change their minds."

Eva sat at Pepi's dining room table, drinking coffee. Their feet were sore from scouring the community.

A sense of loss fell over her Eva, and she began to cry. Pepi set her cup down and put her arm around her. She held her best friend and stroked her long hair. Eva looked up at her with wet eyes.

"I miss him. I'll never see him again. He's gone," Eva cried.

"Have I ever told you how lucky Joseph is?" Pepi asked.

Eva sniffed. Pepi gave her a lace handkerchief and Eva wiped her eyes.

"No," she said in a wavering voice.

"Have you spoken with your father about the invasion?" Eva asked.

"No, not yet. But I already know his answer. He won't leave. He's stubborn. But I want to say good-bye. Want to come with?"

"Yeah, I'm ready."

"Good, let's go."

———⟊⟊⟊———

The tannery was north of town on the main road. Joseph was so excited, he forgot about the aches and pains riddling his body. He couldn't help but run when he saw the big brick building with the tall chimney in the back.

As he walked through the building, he met the surprised looks of his coworkers. The noise of steaming machines was replaced with the celebration of Joseph's return. He moved like a magnet through the plant floor, drawing people from every corner. His father cut his conversation short with a foreman to walk to the second-floor balcony overlooking his factory floor. Joseph looked up and smiled as his dad waved him up. Joseph had to literally pull himself up the railing as the throng of friends peppered him with questions.

Joseph's dad reclined behind a large wood desk. A wall of windows let in the ominous gray light of a cloudy day.

"What happened to you?" his papa asked.

"I got shot."

The man's eyes widened, but only for a fraction of a second. "Is it serious?"

"No."

"Good," he breathed. "You here on medical leave? Go on home and your mother will make you something to eat."

"I came to warn you."

"About what?"

"The Germans, Tata. They've invaded."

"Impossible."

Joseph shook his head and leaned in. "They overran us. They're already in Warsaw."

"If the Germans invaded, there would have been a radio bulletin. There would have been an alarm. There would have been messengers."

As if to underline what Joseph had just said, in the distance a siren cranked up, then another one, closer.

"I'm the messenger," Joseph said in a low voice.

His dad looked at the tannery floor, then scanned across the room, looking for some sort of explanation. He looked up and saw his son with a clear mind. His pretentiousness and banal view of Joseph fell away like scales from his eyes. His injured son stood before him, no more, no less. He realized in that moment the torment his son had been through, so he rushed around the desk and hugged him tightly. Joseph held him too. His father pulled back and wiped his eyes.

"You have to leave, Papa," Joseph warned. "You have to run. They're killing people indiscriminately. The Polish army, it's…it's ineffective."

His dad sat in his chair and looked at the village of Rejowiec. He twirled a large star sapphire ring on his finger.

"Where will I go? I can't leave."

"They will kill you."

"Then I will die here!" his father yelled.

Joseph remained silent. His dad opened a drawer and pulled out a metal flask.

"I didn't know you drank."

"I don't."

His dad turned up the flask and winced. He exhaled. He offered it to Joseph who waved it away.

"I took this from Victor yesterday. He's always drunk." He took another drink. "Our family has always run from place to place over the centuries. First from the Romans and then from the Spanish. I can't run anymore. I won't run. *This* is my home. This was my father's home and his father's. I'm proud of what I've built here."

"But is it worth it? Is it worth dying for?"

His dad thought for a moment and looked up. His eyes lied. He was a man without options. His success chained him in place. While he would have loved to shirk his responsibilities and flee, his embarrassment stifled any thought of failure.

"I can't leave."

Joseph stared deeply into his father's eyes, pleading for him to understand the gravity of the situation. When Joseph knew his father's answer, he got out of his chair and hugged his father. The flask fell to the floor and the smell of strong whiskey filled the room. Meanwhile, the sirens wailed incessantly.

There was a sound at the door, and Joseph craned his neck over in a panic. Pepi appeared in the doorway, followed by Eva.

"Joseph!" Eva yelled.

She ran in the room and jumped into his arms. She kissed him with short pecks on his cheeks and lips, unashamed. She held him tightly and cried on his shoulder. Joseph held her closer than he ever had before. He stroked her hair AD could feel her warmth. She smelled clean. Her hair was… wonderful, luxurious. He wanted to disappear into it. She felt so good in his arms. The rules that their parents had forced upon their relationship simply dissolved in that moment—in its place was just raw emotion, pure passion. In that instant, Joseph knew what love was and he knew he would never let anything separate him from it. He was part of Eva and Eva was part of him. Together they were complete. It was meant to be.

"You're hurt!" Eva said, noticing the bandage on his head for the first time. She ran her hand over the freshly blooded wound.

"I'm okay. I'll tell you later. We've got to warn the town. The Germans are coming."

"We know," chimed in Pepi. "We've told everyone who'd listen." She looked at her father and he looked at the floor.

"We're meeting everyone at the Rynek in a little bit," Eva said. "Pepi got us a truck that will meet us there."

"A truck?" Joseph asked.

"We have to go now. They're waiting on us," Pepi said.

Pepi walked to her dad and kissed him.

"I'm sorry, honey," her dad said.

"I know. I love you. Take care of Mother."

"I will," he said. "Oh, one more thing."

Her dad opened a drawer and set a metal box on his desk. He took out a handful of bills, put a rubber band around them, and then handed them to Joseph.

"Here. Take this too. I left it to you in my will." Abram pulled the large ring off his finger and held it out to Joseph. A white star flashed in the deep blue field of the sapphire, and Joseph's eyes went wide. He had always been mesmerized by the ring, ever since he was a boy. He remembered sitting on his father's lap, turning it in the light to make it glitter.

"Dad, I can't take it. I won't take it. Because if I do, then it means you're dead. I won't do that."

Abram ran his thumb over the ring's hammered gold, then silently slipped it back on his finger.

"Then take the money and my blessing," Abram said.

"Thank you."

"You're welcome," Abram replied. "Take care of them."

Joseph hugged his father as the three walked to the balcony and down the stairs. A voice crackled over the loudspeaker.

"Attention. The German army has invaded Poland. They have already reached Warsaw and will be coming here shortly. If you want to escape, meet at the Rynek, downtown. Otherwise, shut down your stations, go home, and secure your houses. Protect your families."

Joseph looked back as his father stood on the balcony. He nodded and smiled at Joseph knowingly, as the employees on the floor erupted into anxious conversation.

6

Joseph, Pepi, and Eva rode in the hired truck. They expected only a few families to take the warning seriously, but when they rounded the corner into the main plaza, it was crammed with hundreds of people waiting to get out of town. Ox carts, horse-drawn carriages, and a scattering of vehicles waited in a parade pointed out of town. The truck drove through the crowd as citizens secured bags and bid farewell to their loved ones staying behind. The truck stopped in the middle of the crowd and Joseph climbed onto the roof. They all grew silent as he raised his hands.

"I know what a difficult decision it is for you to leave your property and loved ones behind. I would love to tell you that we will only be gone for a short time and that we will be able to come back and resume our lives, but I don't believe that's going to be possible. The Germans are making their way from Warsaw. They're cutting telephone and power lines as they move. They are burning homes, killing families, and taking few prisoners."

"Bullshit!" a man in the crowd screamed. "Your scare tactics don't work on me." The man scanned the crowd. "You all aren't seriously believing this man. He's lying! There's no attack. Go back to your houses. The Polish Army will protect us from any invasion."

"The Polish Army is useless against the Germans. They're retreating. The generals have already surrendered."

"Traitor! How can you wear a Polish uniform and say those things? Traitor! You don't deserve our trust. You're the one who defected. You're the coward who turned tail and ran. Otherwise, you'd be out there defending your country instead of trying to stir us up."

"Where's your friend? What's-his-name?" a lady asked.

"Janek?" Joseph asked.

"Yeah, Janek. He's in your unit, right?"

"Yes."

"Where's Janek?"

"He's dead. The German's killed him. And they shot me and left me for dead." Joseph lifted his bandage and the crowd murmured. "If you want to stay, then stay, but you need to find a safe place and arm yourselves. Do not hesitate to kill a German soldier. They will not hesitate to kill you."

"Don't believe this renegade," shouted the man. "He's probably waiting to rob you when you leave!"

"Shut up!" another said.

"Let him talk!"

"We want to hear Joseph!"

"Go on, Joseph; tell us what to do," came voices from the crowd.

"We can take thirty people or so on this truck, so if you don't have a ride, bring your things. We're heading to Pinsk, across the border in Russia. We should be safe there."

The crowd started moving like a living mass, sorting and organizing itself. Children and mothers were put on the truck while the elders who owned property or businesses stayed behind, yet came out to see their loved ones off.

Eva was helping an older woman climb in the back of the truck when she turned around and saw her father.

"Mother baked some cookies for your trip," said the rabbi. "She wanted to come but was too worried. I brought your Sidur and some photos I thought you might like to take with you."

"Thank you, Dad."

"Oh, and here." Her dad gave her a sealed envelope. "Don't open this until you're safe."

"Okay," Eva said.

"I love you," the rabbi said.

"I love you too, Papa."

She hugged him as tears rolled down her cheeks. Joseph stuck his head out of the cab of the truck.

"Eva, are you—"Joseph paused when he saw her father.

"Take good care of her, Joseph!"

Joseph was taken aback. The rabbi had never called him by his birth name.

"I—I will, sir."

Rabbi Rozenfeld helped Eva into the truck as the driver cranked the engine. Eva waved good-bye, and he simply smiled. Eva watched him shake and vibrate through the rearview mirror as his frame grew smaller and smaller and finally blended with the rest of the crowd as the truck headed out.

The truck had barely gone five miles when the first bombers were spotted coming in from the north. The truck squealed to a halt and everyone held their breath. The sound of distant explosions rolled over them, wave after wave, then the smoke rose over the trees.

"Go! Go!" Joseph yelled to the driver. The truck ground its gears and lurched forward, picking up speed.

No one spoke as the truck bumped along the road. If Joseph was right about the Germans, then what were the implications of those they left behind? A gloom enveloped the back of the truck, pressing inward until it suffocated the passengers. Even though the weather had cleared, the truck seemed to move with its own cloud of darkness.

Pepi stared blankly at the passing scenery while Eva held onto Joseph as if she might float away. She imagined her parents running for cover as the bombs decimated her home. She pictured the large bronze statue of Henry Rejowiec toppling over in the town square, and could hear the cries of the wounded. She thought about the man who mocked Joseph and imagined how now he wished he had jumped on the truck. She hoped her mother and father were safe. She pulled out the envelope, and read the three letters scrawled in her father's beautiful handwriting.

"Eva."

———❧❧❧———

Friedric Muller was angry. He had wanted to go with the Sixth Panzer tank division into Lublin, where he thought he could get a good dinner in a local restaurant if the idiots hadn't blown them all up. Of course he wouldn't pay for it. If the food was good, he might let them live. He might even take them on as his personal chefs. Instead, he had the unsavory job of commanding a Schutzen regiment, or forward guard, which quickly rolled into an enemy's territory with air support. He was angry because he had found nothing but farmhouses and a few factories. He was hungry.

And to make things worse, this seemed to be a Jewish community. It turned his stomach.

He had ransacked enough supplies from the Poles on his long trek from Germany. A lot of the goods he stole were of a high enough quality that he slept comfortably at night, but it didn't matter. To Muller, it all smelled like animal Scheisse.

The regiment made its way to the center of Rejowiec. Store windows were blown in and the bodies of the locals were strewn about the cobblestone. Muller held up a handkerchief to his mouth and ordered his motorcade to stop outside a restaurant whose walls were still intact.

The windows were blacked out so Muller couldn't see inside. He stepped down and looked around the town square. *Not many horses*, he thought. He opened the door to the restaurant and cursed. Daylight poured through an open hole in the back of the building where the kitchen used to be. *Imbeciles.*

"Commandant," a soldier said.

Muller turned in disgust. The soldier led him to a man leaning against a wall, doubled over in pain. The man sported a large welt over his eye, but Muller wasn't interested in this. All he saw were the man's dark features, the black vestment, and the long hair that twisted into corkscrew curls on either side of his face.

"Sehr gut," Muller said. He leaned down and lifted the rabbi's battered head with a gloved hand.

"Jew?"

The old rabbi rolled his good eye up to the commander's face.

"This *Schwein's* name is Rozenfeld," said the soldier. "He is the town's rabbi."

"I have a little proposal for you, my friend. You see, I have traveled on the back of a rickety truck which has rocked me back and forth on these godforsaken roads, and I have yet to consume a proper meal. If you will be so kind as to direct me to a reasonable restaurant, I will instruct my medic to clean you up and make you better. What do you say? Hmm?"

The rabbi faded out of consciousness, so Muller tapped his cheek with the back of his hand, annoyed. The rabbi reawakened.

"Well?"

The rabbi slurred some whispered words.

"I can't hear you." Muller leaned an ear toward the rabbi.

"Go...to...hell," the rabbi said.

Muller stood with a scowl, his lip quivering with rage. He tightened his cheek muscles. He pulled a Luger from his holster and shot Rabbi Rozenfeld in the head.

"Waste of a bullet," Muller muttered to himself.

Little did he know that the man he just murdered was a descendant of four hundred years of a rabbinical line, with hundreds of students, a judge, teacher, father, and grandfather.

"Waste of a bullet," he muttered again.

———∞———

The train of refugees stretched over several miles. They paused at several towns to warn residents of the coming terror and quickly set out again toward the border. The villagers in the towns stood in their yards watching them pass.

———∞———

Muller ordered his regiment to find a suitable place to spend the night. The mayor's home was destroyed, but there was a neighborhood with two-story homes that would do. Muller found the largest home and decided to set his operations there. It had all the modern conveniences, and although not elegant, it was comfortable.

His men corralled the locals and assigned them to troops and houses. No one resisted.

Muller took over the master bedroom with its own bathroom and posted guards at the door. He decided he wanted a hot bath, so he ordered one of the local women to bring him boiling water. She came in and out of the room with full buckets, poured it in the tub. Muller relaxed and closed his eyes with a rag over his face. The woman returned with another kettle of boiling water and poured it in the tub. Muller snapped upright, the rag flying from his face.

"Stupid! Are you trying to burn me?"

"I'm sorry," she said.

"Just be careful." Muller lazed back and watched as the woman poured the rest of the water. She averted her eyes from his naked body.

"Why do you not look at me? Am I ugly?" The woman turned to walk away, ignoring him.

"Stop!" Muller yelled. A guard now blocked the woman's exit.

"Do you know any songs?" Muller asked. The woman remained quiet.

"Oh, come now. You must know some sort of song." She said nothing, and this annoyed him. So he sat up. "You know if you are friendly, I can make our time together… pleasurable. But if you resist, then I will kill your neighbors one at a time until you change your mind. Do you understand?" he said in a soft, almost sympathetic voice.

"*SING!*" he yelled. The woman was so startled she jumped back. She was trembling so violently, the kettle rattled in her hands. Muller motioned for the guard to take it from her. "Now sing, please," Muller said with a trill.

The only song she knew was a children's song. She sang it in a shaky voice.

> The sun shines bright, the day leads to night. The owl will hoot and the baby sleeps, for the sun to rise again.

Muller leaned back and relaxed. He brushed the water with the tips of his fingers, lifted the rag and looked at the woman.

"Take off your clothes."

———⟨∾∾⟩———

The river at the eastern border was crowded with refugees. The Bug River was wide and fast moving from melting snow. Upstream, a large metal bridge spanned the river with border guards on either side. Joseph walked up to one of the crossings, packed full of people. Russian soldiers with automatic weapons stood shoulder to shoulder behind a metal barricade. An incensed Russian customs agent was overwhelmed by a crowd of Polish refugees trying to cross. He sat in a tiny metal cage and spoke through a round hole in the wall.

"…no, I can't. You aren't a citizen…No, there's no way for you to cross. I'm sorry but no," he said.

A senior supervisor stepped up to the harrowed agent and spoke in his ear. The agent immediately closed the cover on the window. He keyed a microphone.

"We are only letting Russian citizens cross the border at this time. If you have Russian identity documents, please make your way to the window. Otherwise, go back to your homes!"

The crowd yelled back in response.

Joseph returned to the vehicle. When he gave his group the news, their faces fell.

He hopped into the cabin of the truck and asked the driver to take them downstream, to a small village on the river bank. As they entered, Joseph noticed a boat tied to a home's private pier next to a boat ramp. The driver stopped the truck, and Pepi and Joseph climbed out, walked to the front door of the small home and knocked on the door. An old man opened up and eyed them with a furry brow.

"I want to hire your launch."

"It's not available. Go away."

The man slammed the door shut. Joseph knocked a second time. The door opened reluctantly.

"I said—"

He stopped short as Joseph shoved a wad of bills through the door. The man opened the door further and looked at the money. He stuck his head out to see the people on the truck.

"How many need to cross?"

"All of them."

The old man swallowed hard. "You know what the Ruskies will do if they catch me? I like my life here."

Pepi added another wad of bills into his hand. The old man smiled.

"Well, let's get the motor going, and get you fine people across the river!" The old man turned and yelled across the room while he pulled a suspender over his shoulder.

"Shimon! Top off the gas tank. We got to get moving."

The man looked back at Joseph.

"Let me get my coat. I'll meet you at the boat. I can take groups of ten, but you'll have to leave all of that junk behind. I ain't coming back for it. Lug whatever you can carry."

The women and children crossed first. The old man unloaded them at a secluded spot on the far river bank, while keeping an eye on the bridge a mile upstream. The second load went with the same efficiency.

The sun was going down, along with the temperature. Before the day's last light, groups of refugees noticed the boat ferrying Joseph's group across the river. By the time the boat made it back to the dock to pick up Joseph and the last group, a number of refugees were gathered around, struggling for a position to cross.

Joseph loaded the last of his group and hopped onto the boat with them. The cooling air caused steam to rise from the river. As they motored across, the Polish dock faded from view in the mist. They were about halfway across the river when they heard loud machines echo out onto the water. Joseph peered into the distance and saw the hulking outlines of trucks and tanks rumble past the crowded fisherman's pier.

"They're Russian," guessed Joseph. "Or maybe… they're German. I can't tell."

The group all turned to look, straining their eyes to see past the thickening fog. Soon they heard the distinct sounds of screams and gunshots echoing in the distance. Then they saw a baby carriage roll down the ramp and into the water. The mother lay dead on the shore. The carriage sank in the river and the baby floated on the surface for a moment, struggling to right itself, and then it quit moving. Its corpse floated down the river.

After what seemed like hours, the launch finally reached the Russian bank. The old man tied the boat to the shore, then got out with Joseph and looked up at him with worried eyes.

"Come on, Shimon," the man said to his companion. He grabbed a few things from the boat and looked at Joseph again. "I'm coming with you." He cut the boat loose and let it drift away

7

The small band of refugees headed up the embankment, and they could hear a loud speaker up ahead, blaring instructions in Russian. As Joseph crested the ridge, he stopped. It took a moment to process what he saw. He turned to the rest of the group and gestured for them to remain quiet. Joseph lowered himself to the ground and crawled to the edge of the ridge. Below he could see hundreds of vehicles—tanks, trucks, and transports— curled along a winding road and around a bend. It appeared as though they were waiting to cross the bridge at the checkpoint, back into Poland. Soldiers dumped canteens or half-finished cigarettes and scrambled to board their vehicles. One by one, black smoke spewed from exhaust as big diesel engines moved their burdens forward.

A captain with a megaphone stood thirty yards from Joseph on a rocky perch, yelling at his troops. He paused, sensing something behind him, and turned toward Joseph. Seeing nothing, he turned back around and continued his rant. Joseph turned to his group and pointed away from the encampment, indicating that the group needed to move away quietly.

They headed along a dry creek bed that led deeper into a wooded area and away from the Russian troops.

By now they were miles from the river. Their meager rations dwindled and fatigue set in. The few elderly people with them lagged behind.

———❧———

Eva had a contact in Pinsk, as did several others. Joseph took two men and they scouted ahead while the others rested. The three came to an ancient stone wall along the edge of the forest, climbed it, and saw smoke rising from several chimneys in the town. There was enough room for the party to wait at the foot of the wall without being seen. They returned to the group and directed them all to the wall. They decided it was best if Joseph went alone into Pinsk to find some refuge—walking aimlessly with a group wasn't a good idea, and would draw unwanted attention. Eva collected the names of three contacts and her own and wrote their addresses on a piece of paper.

"Be careful," she told Joseph.

"I'll be back soon. I promise," Joseph replied.

Joseph kissed Eva on the lips while Pepi grinned.

Once Joseph had left, Eva turned to Pepi. "Don't say a word."

———❧———

Miriam admired her reflection in Pepi's vanity mirror. She had hung her hair in ringlets, and wore her sister's beautiful lace dress—and simply looked gorgeous. How many times had she admired Pepi as she got ready using this very mirror. Miriam had always wished she could be like her older sister. And now that she was, Miriam dreaded the reflection. She had never looked more beautiful. Her spaghetti-string sequined dress accented the diamond necklace shimmering in a brilliant triangle in her cleavage. But it was all a façade. It was a fairytale from hell.

Nadja, Miriam's childhood friend—and Muller's latest spoil of war—was also admiring Miriam's beauty as she helped prepare her for Muller.

"You remind me so much of your sister," Nadja said. "Have you heard from her? Do you know if she is safe?"

"No," replied Miriam. "But whatever her fate, I am just thankful that she doesn't have to endure such a… monster.

Miriam heard Nadja gasp loudly, prompting her to turn around quickly. She looked on in dread as the dark figure of Muller stepped through the doorway. She turned back to the mirror and stared into her reflection, hoping that he hadn't overheard her.

A gloved hand pulled the hair from her ear, and Miriam swallowed hard, nervous. She breathed a sigh of relief when the hand dangled earrings adorned with a trio of diamonds. Muller pressed them to her ear and leaned in to look at their reflection together. A gaunt face with zippered teeth grinned back. *This face had only one expression*, Miriam thought. *Grim pleasure*. This was the same face she saw when he had raped her. The man was a walking nightmare, with putrid breath, and a blackened soul. She had never noticed the black goo between his lower teeth before now. It made her sick to think of those thin lips, those dirty teeth that were pressed in her mouth while he forced his way into her. She felt ashamed, helpless.

Finally, the creature spoke. "These are beautiful, yes?" Muller said. "They match your necklace." He looked at Nadja. "Put these on her."

Muller moved out of the way and dropped the earrings in Nadja's hand. She obeyed and put them in Miriam's pierced ears.

"Let me see. Turn around." Miriam turned mechanically toward him. Muller spread his grimace even wider.

"There. See? Beautiful." He took a step back. A tear rolled down her cheek.

"No!" he said. "I will not have you crying. You are going with me to attend an extravagant dinner party in Lublin in honor of the German victory. You should feel privileged that I chose you to be on my arm."

Miriam stared blankly at him. Muller blinked in frustration.

"Stand up."

She did. Muller wiped away the tear and adjusted her dress straps.

"You will be happy tonight. You will smile and be respectful. You will be my Cinderella. Is that understood?"

Miriam looked him in the eyes and nodded imperceptibly.

"Good. We will eat. Maybe dance. We'll see if the Polish know any German polkas. Then you and I will come back here and we can"—Muller licked his lips and ran his finger across her breast—"pick up where we left off." Muller breathed deeply. He kissed Miriam forcefully and immediately jerked away, grabbing his lip.

"You bitch! You bit me!"

Muller struck Miriam across the cheek and knocked her to the ground. He looked in the oval mirror and pulled his lip out. A drop of blood pooled in the tiny split. He grunted and pressed a handkerchief to it.

"You had better hope it doesn't leave a mark." He looked at Nadja. "Clean her up. And cover that cheek with makeup." He looked at Miriam. "Dammit. Get to the car. Don't make me wait." Muller left the room holding his lip and slammed the door.

"Bastard," Nadja said. "Come on, honey, let's see how bad it is."

———

Joseph pulled out the scrap of paper with the list of names and street addresses. As he made his way through the town, he casually strolled along, looking at street names and comparing them with Eva's list. He tried to blend in like a local, covering his wounded head with a hat. He paused at a sign, written in Cyrillic. *Darn Russians*, he griped. He could read some of the characters. He mouthed out each sound and eventually worked out "Kirov Street," one of Eva's contacts. Vladimir Burlaka, 107 Kirov Street. He walked past a tight row of houses huddled so close together it looked like they were trying to keep each other warm. He stopped outside Number 107.

"Yep, V. Burlaka," he said.

He pulled the bell string, and a dog immediately started to bark. He then heard a deep voice yell something and heavy footsteps pad to the door. The man was mumbling as he turned the knob. The heavy door creaked and a blast of hot air hit Joseph in the face. A man with heavy jowls, moist cheeks, and stained shirt stood in the door.

"Da?"

"Are you Vladimir?" Joseph asked in broken Russian.

"Da. What do you want?"

"I…I am a friend of Eva Rozenfeld."

"Eva? Eva! Ya, where is she?"

The man looked out the door for her with a big smile.

"She's nearby, but I need to talk to you."

"Oh." Vladimir's face fell. "I see. Well a friend of Eva's… come in."

Joseph looked behind him. No one followed. Vladimir looked too, wondering what he was looking for. He flicked his eyes back and forth under a heavy brow, shrugging his shoulders and followed Joseph inside.

Joseph thought he had been attacked when the big man slapped him on the shoulder with a fat palm.

"So tell me! How's Eva?"

Joseph stumbled to catch his breath.

"She's…fine," he said with a withering voice.

A roaring fire made the house excessively hot.

"Can I get you something to eat? Drink?"

"No, thank you."

"Well, okay. What's on your mind?"

Joseph took a deep breath, formulating his response. "The Germans have attacked Poland, and the Russians are invading as well."

Joseph paused for a moment as Vladimir casually looked around the room. His eyes settled on an old rifle leaning in the corner.

"So you know Eva? How is the rabbi?"

"Rabbi Rozenfeld?"

"Yes, Rabbi Rozenfeld, good. You'll forgive me. I had to check."

"I don't blame you."

"People are very suspicious of the Polish. Just talking to you could place me in prison. Is she okay?"

"She's fine. And another thirty of our friends are waiting just out of town."

Vladimir leaned in close to Joseph and lowered his voice.

"It is dangerous to be here. There are eyes everywhere."

"I know, but we have no other place to go."

Vladimir sighed and wiped a hand across his face. "I was afraid you would say that." He walked to the window and looked out at the street. It appeared peaceful enough with pedestrians casually walking by, busy in their daily routines.

"I don't agree with it," Vladimir said.

"Hmm?"

"The invasion. I think it's wrong. We've got our own problems. Leave the Poles alone, I say. But one man is not enough to speak against Stalin." Vladimir raised his hands, shook his head, and walked to the fire. "No one says anything since the NKVD began rounding up dissidents and sending them to Siberia. People keep their opinions to themselves if they know what's good for them."

"I understand."

"But for Eva and her father, I would give my left arm. They were always good friends and helped me many times. So what can I do?"

"We need a place to stay."

Vladimir laughed.

"Thirty people? Where can I put them? Unless I move my furniture to the backyard and someone sleeps in the bathtub. I can't fit them in here."

———✺———

Eva squeezed Vladimir's arm. He didn't look very happy as he drank from a bottle of vodka.

"Thank you for helping us," she said.

"Da, you're welcome. It's all I could do."

"We'll move the furniture back inside before we leave," Joseph said.

"Moshe is very comfortable sleeping in the tub," Eva said.

"Good, it doesn't get used that often anyway."

"Now for some food," Eva said.

"There's not much food. I have some crackers in the—." Vladimir paused as two women walked by eating the crackers. He sighed. "There's just no food."

"Then I'll go buy some," Joseph said.

Vladimir brightened. "Good. I'll go with you. There is a bar on the way."

"I don't drink," Joseph said.

"That's okay. I was going to see if I could spend the night there."

Eva kissed Joseph, then he, Vladimir, and several of the men stepped into the night air. The shock of the chill wind stiffened the skin of their faces. A woman walking her dog watched them suspiciously as they crossed the street and quickly walked to the bar. Laughter rolled into the street and then singing as a man played an accordion.

"The grocery store is around the corner. I'm going to stay here for a while. Busy houses make me nervous," Vladimir said.

"I understand. Thank you for putting us up for the night. We'll find someplace else tomorrow."

"That's fine. Stay as long as you like. I have some trustworthy drinking buddies. I'm sure that between us we can make some room for all of you. I just ask that you leave my side of the bed clear."

"We will. Thank you."

Vladimir tipped his hat, started singing, and walked into the bar. His voice could be heard booming over the music as he greeted his friends.

Joseph led several men from the group of refugees to the local food store.

One of these men, Leo, stood watch outside while the rest went in to purchase groceries. As Leo waited, a man approached him and leaned against the building.

"Cold out tonight," he said in Russian.

"Yes, very cold," Leo replied. His Russian was rusty, but he could still hold a conversation.

The man pulled out a pack of cigarettes from his pocket. He offered one to Leo, who took it gratefully. The man held his lighter out to Leo, and lit his cigarette. The man did the same with his own and took a deep drag. He let out a blue cloud of smoke in the chilly night air.

"The English cigarettes are the best. They are expensive but good. The Russian cigarettes taste like shit."

"It's very good. Thank you."

"Waiting for someone?"

"Yes, my friends are buying some groceries."

The man's cigarette fell from his hand.

"You, you're Polish! You speak with a Polish accent!"

"It's not that. I just sound—"

To Leo's horror, the man reached in his pocket and blew a whistle. Leo immediately ran into the store.

"Joseph!" he yelled.

The man continued to blow the whistle in shrill bursts. Leo looked down an aisle and saw his friends.

"Joseph! We've got to go!"

By the time they made it to the door, two policemen were speaking to the man who was frantically pointing at Leo. When the police saw the men, they yelled and drew their weapons.

"Put your hands up! Put them up, now!"

Joseph and the men did as they were told. The police put cuffs on them and stood them along the store wall.

"How did you get here?" one policeman asked. "Where did you come from?"

None of the men said anything. The frustrated policeman swung a baton into Leo's gut, who then fell on the concrete. A crowd gathered, and the woman with her dog stepped forward.

"That's them! Those are the men," she yelled. "I saw them come from Vladimir's house."

The group was taken back to Vladimir's house, where one of the policemen banged on the front door. A man opened it, and before he could say a word, the policemen kicked it in and rushed in with guns drawn. Eva screamed.

"Get on the floor. Get down!"

The refugees all did as they were told. They were all placed in restraints and taken to the police station. Some vagrants, a prostitute, and several pickpockets were released to make room for the refugees in the three small cells. The women were placed together in one cell and the men in the other two. Eva and Joseph could barely touch fingertips through the bars.

Vladimir stumbled home in the early morning hours. He thought nothing unusual about his front door being unlocked. He clambered up the stairs to his bedroom, fell on his bed and passed out. He never knew what had become of his houseguests.

8

Muller's limousine left Rejowiec late. The driver had to weave slowly around soldier convoys and prisoners marching in long lines on their way to Lublin. Miriam caught her reflection in the rearview mirror and was taken aback at how beautiful she looked—Nadja had really done a great job of covering up her bruised cheek. But that was only on the surface; Miriam's soul was bruised and no amount of makeup or expensive jewelry could cover that.

The further they drove from Rejowiec, the deeper her depression grew. Outside in the hopeless lines of refugees were her neighbors and friends. She rode in luxury while they were hobbling, beaten and broken. She glanced at Muller who reclined luxuriously, smoking a cigarette in a long black holder. She watched as the smoke curled around his head, accenting his demonic features.

"Not again!" Muller yelled.

Miriam snapped to attention as Muller sat forward and slapped the driver's seat.

"Run them over!" he told the driver.

Miriam looked out the front window. Hundreds of prisoners blocked the road as German soldiers herded them along like cattle. They did not know, but it was the March of the Dead.

"Sir, I can't," the driver said. "We have to wait until we can pass."

"Then honk the horn, fool!"

The driver honked and the guards parted the prisoners to either side. The car crept through the multitude.

"Get these people out of my way. That's an order!" Muller yelled out his open window.

"Yes, sir!"

Miriam watched out the window in disbelief, as her home had been turned into a prison camp. When she looked ahead, she nearly fainted—her father, Abram, was carrying her mother on his back. As the car passed, her father collapsed in a heap on the road. Miriam yelped, turned in her seat as a German guard kicked her mother, then jabbed her father with the butt of his rifle. Her father slowly got back to his feet, picked up his wife, and continued to plod ahead.

"Ignore them, my dear," chirped Muller. "You are now my princess. You must learn to act like it. Now turn around so we can enjoy the drive. That was your past, so leave it behind."

Miriam glared at Muller as she slipped her hand on the door latch.

"Those are my people, my family. That is my life."

"Why, you disrespectful, ungrateful little—"

Miriam flung the door open and jumped from the moving vehicle. She hit the ground with a loud *smack!*

and rolled several times. Fortunately the car had just begun to accelerate. The car stopped and Miriam could hear Muller's curses and threats. She got to her feet and ran back to her father. The German soldiers witnessing her escape didn't know what to do. Here was this elegant goddess in a fur stole, sequined dress, and dazzling jewels running toward them. Up ahead, Abram set her mother to her feet.

"Miriam!" her father exclaimed.

She kissed him and then her mother. They knelt together on the ground, laughing, tears streaming down their faces.

"I was so worried," her mother said. "I thought I'd never see you again."

Muller's car backed up and stopped. As Muller climbed out, the soldiers snapped to attention.

"Sieg heil!" they shouted and saluted. Muller ignored them. He walked to Miriam and yanked her up by the hair.

"Look at what you've done! Look at this mess. You better hope you can be presentable by the time we get to the party."

Miriam cried.

"Put her in the car," Muller ordered a soldier standing nearby.

As the soldier pulled Miriam by the arm, her mother yelled and clung to her. Before Miriam knew what had happened, a shot rang out and her mother released her grip. Miriam's mother fell back, a pool of blood forming behind her head. Muller stood before her, shaking his head. His cold stare focused on Miriam while the barrel of his Luger sent snaking trails of smoke into the bitter air.

Miriam's dad lunged at Muller who stepped back and leveled the pistol at him. Miriam dove in front of Abram and Muller was forced to lower his weapon.

"Stand her up," Muller barked at the soldiers. They pulled her up and held her dad. Her mother continued to bleed out at her feet. Muller walked up to her and tugged at her hair, yanking her head upward.

"So this is how you repay my generosity? Fine, you've proven you can't be trusted. You're no better than them."

Muller jerked the diamond earrings and necklace from her.

"There you go. You can die with them. Remember what you've given up."

Muller pushed Miriam out of the way and kicked Abram as he knelt next to his dead wife. Abram fell backward onto the pavement.

"It's your fault. You ruined everything!" Muller again leveled his gun at Abram's head. Abram didn't blink. Instead, he locked eyes with Muller, who immediately averted his eyes. That was when he noticed the ring on Abram's finger.

"The ring, give it to me." Muller said curiously, holding out his hand. Abram looked at Miriam and slowly removed the ring. He threw it to Muller, who caught it in a gloved hand. He turned it around in his fingers and admired the ghostly star floating inside the stone. Muller put it in his pocket and focused his attention back on Abram.

"This ring has saved your life for now...Jew."

Muller walked back to the car. He glanced back at Miriam, shook his head, and climbed in.

"Let's get out of this wretched pothole these people call a town," he said.

The car drove away as the guards pushed Miriam to join the other refugees. They all continued their march to Lublin. Miriam's mother's corpse was pushed to the side of the road, like an unseemly pile of trash.

—⚬⚬⚬—

"I want to speak with the commissar," Joseph said.

"He's not ready to speak with you," the constable said.

"We are refugees. We have rights."

"You are enemies of the Union and prisoners of war. You have no rights. It's just—" The constable put down his paper and looked at all the people crammed in the tiny cells. "It's just I don't know what to do with you."

"How about some food and bedding? We haven't eaten for two days."

"I'm not doing anything until I hear from the commissar. So sit yourself down and be quiet."

Joseph punched the bars of the cell with his hand.

"It's not right! We did nothing wrong," Joseph screamed.

"Patience. It'll be fine. We just have to wait," one of the prisoners said.

"I'm tired of waiting."

A short time later, the door to the station opened and a small army of older women entered, wrapped in scarves and carrying armloads of pots, blankets, and boxes.

"Mimi, what are you doing here?" the constable asked in desperation.

Women continued pouring through the door, gabbing and giving each other instructions.

"We're here to feed your prisoners," Mimi said.

"You can't do that."

"Why not? Are *you* going to feed them?"

"We're waiting for—"

"Right, you were waiting until when? Until they starved to death? Really, Sergi..." Mimi put a heavy basket on a desk. "Put the blankets over there. Where's the bread? Good. We can push those desks together and make a food line around the counters."

"Mimi!"

Mimi stopped and all the *babushkas* looked at the constable.

"What?"

"You can't do this."

Mimi's expression turned into a scowl. She reddened, slammed a box on the desk, and walked up to her husband. She said something excitedly in his ear. The constable's eyes grew wide and a worried expression contorted his face.

"You wouldn't," he said.

She grimly nodded, then whispered a few more words. He had lost all vestiges of his manhood.

"But, Mimi, I can't," he pleaded.

"Then open the women's cages."

"They aren't cages, they're jail cells."

"Cages, cells—what's the difference?"

"They would escape."

"Lock the front door." Mimi turned to the ladies in the cell. "Would you try to escape if we let you out to eat and feed your men?"

The voices all barked, "*NO!*" in staggering unison.

Mimi turned back to the constable.

"You have their promise."

"But, Mimi."

Mimi stared at him, put her hands on her hips, and pointed at the cell door. The constable put his head down and unlocked it.

For a moment the stress of being a prisoner abated. Cultural differences and politics didn't hold a candle to the universal act of kindness. The Jewish women assisted the babushkas in preparing dinner plates and serving the men. Lively conversations picked up and laughter peeked through the reality of their confinement. The group of refugees ate their first good meal since they left Lublin. They were able to bathe and spread out warm blankets to arrange sufficient sleeping mats. Hot coffee was shared after the meal. Promises were made to bring more food the following day. Good-byes were exchanged and the ladies were locked back in their cells. By the time the babushkas left, even the constable seemed to be in a better mood. Few words were said as the exhaustion of their flight from Poland sank in. They rested better than they had in days.

———∞∞∞———

Miriam and Abram couldn't believe the efficiency of the Germans. A work camp had already been established in a Lublin suburb, but more incredible was the concentration camp being built on the outskirts of the town in a large field. Prisoners had already framed a long building destined to become barracks for stationed guardsmen. A double fence of electrically charged barbed wire ran around the perimeter. One guard house was completed near the main gate and others were still being erected.

Miriam and her neighbors were put to hard labor. They were all given gray prison uniforms, and yellow patches shaped like the Star of David to denote their Jewish lineage. During the day, they worked long hours building the concentration camp, referred to as Majdanek, which was the name of the county. The original design called for a capacity of 30,000 prisoners. In reality, before the war was over, it would house more than 120,000.

As the facility neared completion, Miriam and Abram began to feel the sting of the food shortage. At first, sufficient food was available at the labor camp, and life was about as good as any prison could get. But as the population increased, the Germans refused to increase food supply, so many of the prisoners began starving to death.

Each night, after the lookout watched the German guard leave the vicinity of "D" Block, the prisoners engaged in a flurry of activity. Mattresses were overturned, inseams and hidden compartments were freed of their treasures. Prisoners ate what little food they could smuggle in, while others delighted in washing their bodies with small soaps and lye.

Tonight was special, however, as it was Rosh Hashanah. Smuggled foodstuffs were organized and yarmulkes were distributed among the inmates. Abram wore his talis, a prayer shawl, and opened his machzor, or prayer book. For that moment, the barracks had been transformed into a sacred place. The prisoners' faith tied their hearts together and brought relief as they recited memorized prayers to HaShem.

"Blessed are You, Lord our God, King of the universe, who has granted us life, sustained us and enabled us to reach this occasion."

"Amen," they all said in unison.

Abram unwrapped a small bundle he had kept hidden for some time. It was a small shofar, a ram horn trumpet. He felt the trepidation of being caught as he sounded the horn, but he could not help it. He had to feel the elation of hearing the shofar again. Its sound resonated back through the ages to the destruction of Jericho, when HaShem commanded the Israelites to blow the shofar, to absolve them of their sins and herald in a new year. Abram held the little shofar to his lips with shaky hands and blew.

Once Abram completed the ritual, the prisoners immediately gathered their things and scrambled to hide them.

"Hurry!" the lookout said. "He's coming."

They all jumped in their bunks as the door opened.

"Quit making noise and go to sleep!" the guard yelled. He slammed the door closed. They spoke of their joy into the early morning hours.

"Get up! Get your things together," the constable yelled at Joseph and his group of refugees. "You're leaving today."

Suitcases, rucksacks, and cloth-bags that had served as beds were quickly organized and repacked. The mood was upbeat among the prisoners, as it had been three days of cramped incarceration. The babushkas returned each day to feed them, but the last time they had left quickly and hardly said anything at all.

"Where are we going?" Joseph asked.

"I don't know. Probably to a refugee camp where they can properly process you," the constable said.

The group was shocked when Soviet soldiers showed up and loaded them onto an open cattle truck. The truck rattled through the streets, and passersby stopped what they were doing to watch the military escort with its cargo of prisoners. As they approached the train station, they saw another group of Jewish Poles in the same situation. Some of the group recognized the other refugees but most were from other villages. They all retold harrowing experiences of their escapes but none seemed to know what was going on.

A steam engine thrust billows of gray smoke high as it pulled into the station. A long string of cattle cars stretched behind the locomotive. Prisoners in the cars yelled out family names at those gathering to get on board. The questions were always the same: "Have you seen…?" and "Do you know where they took…?" Many of these questions remained unanswered.

The group from Rejowiec was stuffed onto a partially filled car. Women and elderly were lifted unceremoniously, with hurried shouts from the guards. Young boys ran from car to car, dumping honey pots. Others filled buckets with fresh water and handed them to waiting hands. The wood corral doors were slammed closed, but before the train moved, soldiers stuffed loaves of bread through the wood slats. A Russian guard with a rifle rode in each car.

Pepi sat next to a young woman who seemed quite upset that she had been touched so rudely by a soldier. She whispered something to her female companion sitting next to her. They stared as Eva and Joseph entered the car and sat on their luggage. A soldier walked by and rapped a stick on fingers sticking out of the car.

The train piped a note and the box cars shuddered. A loud clank rang out as the brake released, followed by a long hiss as the engine put the train into motion. Slowly the station slid by through the thin slats. Steel squealed and screamed as the engine was rewarded with acceleration. The smell of acrid smoke and soot flowed over the train and into the cars. Many of the refugees grabbed cloths to cover their faces or tucked their noses in their undershirts. Cold wind blew through the cars as the train picked up speed.

Pepi looked at the woman sitting next to her. "Hi, my name is Pepi," she said, reaching her hand out. The woman looked at her outstretched hand as if it were ridden with plague.

"Anna," was all she said.

Pepi looked at her hand to see if there was something wrong with it, then tucked it back under her coat sleeve.

"It's getting cold," Pepi said.

"Cold. Hmph! This is warm compared to where we're going," Anna said.

"I thought we were going to a refugee camp."

"Refugee? You mean slave labor camp."

Pepi's eyes widened. "And where is that?"

"Siberia."

Pepi shot a worried glance at Joseph.

"We're all going to die in Siberia," Anna said, and let out a psychotic laugh.

⌖

The train rolled on through the vastness of the Russian Steppes as its whistle echoed out into the plains. Most of the passengers had fallen asleep, or were lost in their own mind-numbing depression. When Eva woke up, her face was cold. She stood up, stretched her cramped joints, and stepped over several sleeping bodies toward the privy. It wasn't much—the small compartment was a rudely cut cubby hole in a wood ledge that jutted out from the wall. In the center of the floor was a wood bucket. She turned to sit and noticed several sleeping men facing the toilet. She carefully slid her panties down and squatted over the hole, all the while watching the men suspiciously. As she began, she saw several men peek their eyes open. They were unabashedly watching her. She wanted to yell and tell them how evil they were, that they should show some respect and give her privacy. She wanted to call out for Joseph. She wanted to be home in her own bathroom. As she finished, she pulled up her panties, stood up, and kicked the closest man to her.

"Depraved ingrates," she muttered. The others chuckled as she made her way back.

The next day, the train stopped at another station to pick up more prisoners and refuel. Honey pots were emptied and fresh water was filled. Surprisingly, hot potatoes were thrown in the car, and the prisoners rushed to grab what they could. Joseph had fond memories of butter and cheese garnishes; even still, his potato was the best he had eaten in days. He was thirsty and gathered three tin cups to dip into the water. However, when he got to the bucket it was frozen over. He chipped the ice with the edge of his cup and broke off several chunks. He returned with the cups of ice and gave them to the girls.

"Sorry, but it's frozen."

Eva and Pepi tucked the cups under their coats and waited for the ice to melt.

After another day and night, the train stopped at a distant outpost. The small shack shone in the night dimly, with a single light from a window. Eva could barely discern a potbelly stove aglow inside. A stooped man came out and went down the line, speaking to the guards in each car. When the man left, the guard turned to the prisoners.

"If you like, you can leave the train and stretch your legs. Stay away from the guardhouse. When you hear two blasts on the whistle, return to your car. If you're thinking of running, go ahead. The closest city is a hundred miles in any direction. You will die of exposure long before you can make it. You have a half hour."

The door slid open and everyone rushed from the train. Around them was a windswept alien landscape. A sea of snow stretched as far as they could see. Snow devils blew over vast ridges. The light from the shack created long orange shadows over the drifts. Groups of people huddled together on the lee side of the shack, and allowed themselves to enjoy this moment out.

After a half hour, the whistle sounded twice, and the refugees boarded their cars again and settled back into their corners. Joseph's heart sank into the cold darkness as they headed north and further away from home.

We have lived in numberless towns and villages;
in too many of them we have endured cruel suffering.
Some we have forgotten; others are
sealed into our memory,
A wound that does not heal.
We value those men and women who had the courage to
stand outside the mob, to serve us, and to suffer with us.
May such times never come again.

—A daily prayer, "Gates of Prayer,"
Hebrew Prayer Book

9

A German soldier yelled commands to a line of workers building the foundation for what they called "The Retinery." Men were laying brick around a wood frame, and the concave supports held large metal cylinders with a flue on one end and a large door on the other. They were constructing huge ovens.

Abram worked twelve-hour days pierced by few breaks to drink water or eat a crust of bread. He had lost sixty pounds since his internment, and his skin now hung loose on his bony frame. His eyes were rimmed with dark sockets, and his cheeks were gaunt.

Miriam worked in the kitchen. She earned extra rations repairing clothing but Abram refused to eat them.

"Daddy, you've got to eat something. I saw you give your food away," Miriam said.

"I will give my food to whomever I wish, and you can't stop me."

"But you're wasting away. Look at you."

"I'm fine and much stronger than you. I've lifted brick."
Abram broke into a coughing fit that left him gasping.

"See? You're not well. You must eat."

"I'll eat when I'm dead."

"Daddy, don't talk like that. Don't ever say that. Not even kidding." Miriam broke down and cried, and Abram held her.

"It's all right," he said.

"It's *not* all right. It's not. Not if you won't eat. I don't understand. I don't understand."

"I'm not hungry," Abram said simply. Miriam looked up at him with wet eyes. She watched as his eyes drifted into thought.

"It's Mom, isn't it? You're not eating because of her."

Abram's mouth went slack. His eyes rolled around hers. He smiled and coughed again.

"You wouldn't understand."

"I want to understand. Make me understand."

He looked at Miriam and moved a strand of hair from her face.

"You look so much like her. You've got her eyes."

"Daddy…"

"You don't remember. But when you were a baby, there was a terrible snow storm. Rejowiec was buried under several feet of snow. At first it wasn't so bad. I didn't have to work and I got to spend lots of time at home with you kids. Problem was the snow didn't melt. And to make matters worse, it snowed again. No one could go to town—all the businesses were closed anyway. We had a pantry full of food. So guess where the neighbors came?"

"To you."

"Well, more to talk to your mom. And she fed them. All of them. We had to cut back, but she made sure they had something to eat."

"And you're doing the same."

"Maybe you're bright after all."

"But these people wouldn't do the same for you."

"It doesn't—" Abram coughed again. Miriam held a rag to his mouth until he recovered. When she took it away, she noticed a spittle of blood. She gasped. "It doesn't matter," Abram repeated. "They're still our neighbors. If your mother were here, she'd do the same thing."

"But, Father, you've got to eat. She wouldn't want you ill."

"I know. I miss her."

"I miss her too."

Abram lay back again and drifted off in thought. Miriam held him in her arms. His eyes refocused and he leaned up.

"Get me the shirt," he said. He pointed to a rolled up shirt at the foot of the bed. Miriam retrieved the bundle and gave it to him. He carefully removed his shofar.

"I want Joseph to have this when I'm gone."

"Please don't talk like that."

"What? Should I make believe that I'm getting better? I wish I had that much faith. Maybe you're right. Without your mother, there isn't much for me to live for."

"Papa, stop it! You're scaring me!" Miriam's face was red with anguish.

"Shh," her father said as he pulled her to his chest. "I don't believe for a moment you're scared. You stood up to that beast, Muller. I think you've grown stronger, if anything. This place is designed to eat people." He brushed the hair from her face. "It's just about eaten me. I hope and pray it doesn't eat you. You've got a chance. And if you find a way to get free, run. Okay?"

Miriam nodded and wiped her nose.

"So give this to Joseph when you see him next." He put the shofar in her hands. "Tell him he was right. We should have gone with him and Pepi. If I'd have listened, you wouldn't be here and your mom would be alive."

"You don't know that. You don't know what happened to the others. They might be gone as well."

Abram looked into his daughter's eyes. His pupils couldn't hold their focus for very long; the strain was too great. He closed his eyes and smiled, allowing a tear to stream down his cheek.

"No…no, he's fine. So is Pepi and Eva. I just…I just know they're fine. That's why I want you to give this to him. Try for me."

"I will."

Abram leaned back on his bunk and closed his eyes. "I'm…tired. Just need…to take a little nap. Then I…then I'll feel better."

"Okay, Papa. Get some sleep. I hope you feel better. I love you."

"I…love you…too."

Miriam kissed her father's forehead, sniffled, and pulled his covers up to his shoulders. She wrapped the shofar back in the shirt and took it to her own bunk, where she lifted the mattress and removed a single line of stitching. She tucked the shofar into the pocket and then sewed it back up. That night she had a dream about her mother.

She woke up and went to tell her father about how vivid and real it seemed. When she got to him, he had already gone to be with his wife. Miriam just stood there. Tears rolling down her face. "Sh'ma Israel," she prayed for her Papa, a prayer in Hebrew to honor her father.

———

After weeks of grueling delays, the train began unloading its human cargo at several final destinations. Periodically the train would stop and guards would pull refugees from the cars. There was more room now in Joseph's carriage, but he felt the bite of the cold wind more than ever, now that he was sharing less body heat.

The group was jarred awake as the brakes screeched against the railing. The light through the slats in the car was a diffuse white, as though they had stopped inside a giant cotton ball. The cattle door slid open as the guard stood and stretched. A ramp was put in place for the passengers to exit, which was strange until Joseph walked out into the light. The train was sitting in a snow channel dug out by the engine. The ramp was the only way to reach the platform. The guard blocked the doorway as Joseph helped Pepi and Eva to their feet. Men were shouting at the station and brushing snow away. Joseph watched through the doorway as a guard placed a tiny wooden desk on the platform, followed by another that brought a folding chair. A small man with a tiny hat and glasses sat down and placed a briefcase on the table. He opened it and removed a stack of index cards and several pencils. His mustache twitched when he moved his eyes from one refugee to the next. He pulled out a stack of papers and placed a paperweight on them, then turned to the guards who were engaged in conversation. Once he tapped the pile, the guard signaled the boxcar guard.

"Let's go, one at a time."

Joseph went first and waited as Eva and Pepi joined him in front of the desk.

"You are a family?" the little man asked.

"Yes," Joseph said. "This is my sister and my wife." Eva shot him a surprised glance.

"Your names?"

"Eva," she began to say.

"Mitsen," Joseph interjected. "Eva and Joseph Mitsen. And this is Pepi Mitsen."

Pepi and Eva looked at each other with raised eyebrows.

"Birthdates."

"Eva, May 5, 1920; Pepi, March 10, 1916; and me, Joseph, April 5, 1920."

"Hometown."

"We are from Rejowiec. Poland."

"What is your skill?"

"Excuse me?"

"What kind of work do you do?"

"Eva is a teacher, Pepi is a seamstress, and I am a mechanic."

"A mechanic?"

"Yes, in the army."

"Hmm." The little man wrote something on the margin of the page. "Do you know how to fix engines?"

"Yes. It was my job to maintain the generators."

"Really? We have need of your talent." The man wrote three serial numbers on three blue cards along with their names. In the upper corner he wrote a number, then slid the cards across the desk.

"You will be treated fairly if you aren't lying. Welcome to Siberia. Get on the truck and when you get to the camp, the ladies will go to Cabin 11 and you'll go to Cabin 12. Do you understand?"

"Yes."

"Next!"

The guards ushered them to a long platform covered in scraps of bark mixed with tree limbs and snow. A small crane hovered overhead. Joseph deduced it was used for loading logs onto train cars for shipment to southern regions.

Just then, a large flatbed truck rumbled up. There were no sides, only vertical poles spaced every few meters apart, and a deck covered in a layer of fresh snow. One by one, Joseph helped everyone up. The refugees sat on their suitcases and bags with their backs to the wind. Once they were loaded, the truck rolled along a bouncy dirt road. Soon they were in dense forest, with tall evergreens and ancient hardwoods. It was strikingly beautiful. A herd of reindeer watched the truck amble by. The driver honked at them and they bounded away.

Joseph reflected on the primitive nature of this place. They were a very long way from civilization. The truck hit a rut and a woman sitting on the tailgate bounced in the air and off the truck. She fell hard and took a moment to get to her feet. A guard sitting on the bed roared with laughter, and the truck didn't stop. The woman ran in a desperate attempt to catch up but tripped in the slush. The guard nearly fell off himself, he was laughing so hard. No one else was laughing. The refugees on the truck encouraged her to run. When Joseph realized what was happening he went to the rear to talk to the guard.

"Stop the truck," he said.

"Sit down, Polack," the guard said. The woman was growing tired, slowing in her pursuit. So Joseph jumped off the bed. The guard swung his rifle around, but Joseph didn't care. He ran to the woman, scooped her up in his arms, and brought her back to the back of the truck, lifting her to the waiting hands of several men. Joseph then grabbed an upright pole and pulled himself up.

"Don't do that again," the guard said. "If they can't keep up it's one less mouth to feed."

Joseph leered at the guard and returned to Eva's side. He was determined to never forget the man's face.

The truck passed a sawmill complex, where logs had been stacked in huge piles, all covered with tarps. They then passed several rows of logs curing in the wood-yard, and the long, flat-topped tin sawmill. The sides were open and Joseph saw a long chain track and the biggest saw blade he'd ever encountered.

After another few miles, the truck stopped at a camp. Thirty or so cabins were hunkered around a dirt plaza, each made from roughhewn planks. All of them were adorned with shoddy tin roofs and a chimney. An outhouse sat between every fourth cabin, and a gravel area served as a parade ground.

So this is one of Russia's famous labor camps, though Joseph. He also realized that this was their new home, thousands of miles away from their past in a remote, desolate wilderness where no one would ever find them. All they had now was each other.

Eva put her arms luxuriously around Joseph's neck.

"That was a very brave thing you did, jumping off the truck to rescue a damsel in distress, Mister Mitsen."

"The guard didn't appreciate it."

"No, but such bravery…it's very romantic," Eva cooed.

"She wasn't bad-looking, so I thought I should help."

Eva hit him on the shoulder.

"I wasn't talking about her."

"Who then?" Joseph looked confused.

Eva rolled her eyes and gave him a brilliant smile.

"Would you jump off a truck for me?"

Joseph turned his eyes upward and thought about it. Eva frowned.

"Of course I would." He tried to kiss her but she leaned back.

"You know, we're *not* married yet."

"I know. I said that so we wouldn't get separated."

"Is that all? I thought you were dropping a hint. I like the sound of Eva Mitsen."

"I like it too. We'll have to do something about that."

"Like what?" Eva asked.

"Like get married."

"Here, in this place?"

"Why not? I'm sure Pepi would organize everything."

"Hmm. Are you sure you want to marry me? Maybe the woman you saved would be interested. Are you sure you'd rescue me?"

"Next time we're in the truck, I'll have Pepi push you off. Then I'll rescue you."

Eva couldn't help but laugh. "Will you carry me too?"

"All the way back."

"Okay, but only if I accidentally fall off." The door of the cabin opened and Pepi peeked her head out.

"You'd better get in here before lights out," she said.

"Good night, Eva Rozenfeld." Joseph laughed.

"What happened to Eva Mitsen?"

"You'll have to wait for it."

"I hope it doesn't take too long."

"It won't."

"Come on, you two. Stop the puppy love chatter," Pepi said, clearly disgusted by this public display of affection.

"I love you," Joseph said.

"I love you too."

Pepi pulled Eva by the arm. Eva blew Joseph a kiss and he caught it.

"You both make me sick," Pepi said. She yanked Eva in the door and slammed it closed. It opened again after a moment.

"Good night," Eva said.

"Good night," Joseph said.

"Stop it!" Pepi said. She pulled Eva back and slammed the door again.

The snow had stopped and the sky was clear. Thousands of stars twinkled in the vastness, and Joseph found himself content.

"Thank you, HaShem," Joseph said under his breath.

The guard in his cabin gawked as Joseph hopped up the steps two at a time.

"Was about to come looking for you," he said.

—ᴓᴓᴓ—

The prisoners were taking their evening break, and most used the time to wash their hands in expectation of dinner. No matter how meager the rations, when you were hungry, any food looked good. Miriam borrowed a shard of broken mirror from her bunkmate to examine her reflection. She could tell she had lost weight as she looked at her face. Her eyes had receded into her head, and her cheeks looked thin. Her gums had grown darker, her tongue was cracked. She brushed her hair and it came out in clumps.

The new showers had just been completed and she looked forward to a good scrubbing. Since her transfer from the labor camp in Lublin, she thought things would be better in Majdanek. The buildings were new and there was more room. The labor camp in Lublin had housed Gypsies and reeked of sweat and urine. Majdanek smelled better, although the bedbugs and lice had come with her.

"Guard!" someone yelled.

People scrambled, stashing their smuggled goods. A game of chess was quickly ended and stored. Miriam returned the mirror to her bunkmate who promptly slid it under the loose lamination of the bed frame.

"They've got dogs!"

The soldiers entered with German shepherds on tight leashes. The dogs barked and snapped at the prisoners as they passed each bunk. The prisoners stood frozen at the foot of their beds as the guards randomly dumped the contents of cubbies on the floor. They kicked through the piles and took anything they wanted. A dog growled and a man screamed. The sound of a scuffle distracted the other guards.

"Knife! He's got a knife!" a soldier yelled.

A dog had been loosed on a hapless prisoner. The man lay on the ground and screamed as the dog bit his arms and legs. The German guard seemed to enjoy watching the man thrash about, helpless under the sharp fangs of the beast. The other guards approached and pulled the dog away. The soldier who had released the dog held out a dull piece of metal.

"I found this in his shoe."

The other guards dragged the bleeding prisoner away. They never saw him again.

Two guards returned later with their dogs and continued their search. When they got to Miriam she recognized one of them. She had repaired the buttons on his coat. He recognized her too. With a quick glance he passed her by but his dog resisted. He tugged on its leash but it wouldn't move. The guard looked in Miriam's eyes, then slackened his grip on the dog. The frenzied animal shot forward and pawed feverishly at the corner of her mattress. It tore out the threads and a small rip opened up. The guard knelt behind the dog and pulled gently on the seam. He reached in, touched something solid, and pulled out Abram's shofar. He puzzled at it for a moment and then stood. He looked at the other guard who was several rows away. The guard looked back.

"Did you find something?"

The guard looked at the shofar in his hand and then at Miriam's horrified expression. Then something amazing happened. He looked back up.

"No, nothing. Must have been a rat," he told the other guard. He shoved the shofar into Miriam's trembling hands.

"Hide it better next time," he said softly. Then he continued searching the rest of the barracks.

10

Pepi worked in the laundry room, washing the prisoners' uniforms and bedding. Next to the kitchen was the warmest place in the camp. Eva worked in records, keeping track of all new internees, and also ordered food and supplies. She made friends with several other female prisoners who comprised the office pool. The camp commandant was a forgettable elderly tradesman who also doubled as the manager of the sawmill. He rarely made appearances in the camp office, preferring to spend his time supervising the mill operations. And a good thing too. The mill was a dangerous place for unskilled workers.

The atmosphere at the office was almost genial, were it not for the gray prison uniforms and the remoteness of the place. It almost felt like a normal job. During their frequent breaks, the office pool ladies would reminisce about their homes, or their men. When Eva talked about Joseph, the other women always paid close attention. This was better than lurid gossip because it was happening right there in the camp! Eva would relay the latest love struck platitude to responses of "How romantic!" and "That's so sweet!"

Unbeknownst to Eva, however, Pepi and Joseph were putting together a grand wedding ceremony. Everyone in the camp seemed to know about it, except for Eva. Leszek, a prisoner who shared Joseph's cabin, happened to own the only concertina in the camp. The guards let him keep it because he would play for them at their parties. He was asked if he knew any wedding songs and the rumor spread from there. Suspicions were further raised when Pepi approached one of the female prisoners to see if she might trade clothing and food for a gold ring.

A few days later, four guards rushed unannounced into Cabin 12. Joseph and Fima (his bunk mate) were roused from their sleep at gunpoint and taken to a metal building used to store trucks and a tractor. Joseph was held in a front storeroom while Fima was taken through a door into the garage. The trucks' engines were started to mask any noise.

Fima had been gone for a half hour before the door to the garage swung open. A semi-conscious Fima was dragged out of the front door, badly beaten. His entire body was covered n bruises and welts, and he moaned softly, trying not to show the pain. Joseph was taken in next.

As the two guards dragged Joseph into the garage, he recognized the man waiting to meet him. Two guards threw him forward and he landed on his hands and knees.

It was the guard who had laughed when the girl had fallen from the truck. Joseph had learned his name since the incident. Uri.

Uri leaned against a tractor, smoking a cigarette. He had taken off his coat and dress shirt, and was sweating visibly under his white undershirt. He had clearly worked himself up over Fima, not showing any mercy on the old man. Uri wiped his face and motioned for the soldiers to bring in Joseph with a nod of his head. After Joseph was placed into a solitary metal chair in the middle of the room, the guards took a few steps back, crossed their arms, and leered.

Uri walked up and blew smoke in Joseph's face.

"I heard you were planning a wedding."

Joseph looked at him but kept quiet. "Me and the boys wanted to celebrate with you. We thought we'd throw you a little bachelor party." Uri clenched the cigarette in his teeth and held his arms out to the laughter of the guards. Joseph looked at the floor.

"Would you like a cigarette?"

"I don't smoke."

Uri paced around him.

"Come on. You have to loosen up. It's *your* party. We want you to have fun." Joseph still didn't speak. "Who did you say was the lucky woman?"

"I didn't."

"Eva," a guard said.

"Eva? Ah, the beauty at the office. She's very nice. A very good choice. So what kind of ring are you going to get her? I'm sure somebody has a nice ring of some value. But you can't afford a ring, can you?" Uri walked around the back of the chair. "Tsk, tsk, tsk." He paused. "But you could trade something of value, maybe a pocket watch?" Joseph looked up with a puzzled glare as Uri walked around front.

"I know you took my watch and were going to trade it for a wedding ring. I want it back, now."

"I didn't take your watch," Joseph said defiantly, as he watched Uri.

"Looks like we've got another hold out," a guard said.

"Looks like it. But this one's a soldier. He thinks he's better than the Russians," Uri said.

"I don't know, Uri. He looks pretty strong," a guard said.

"Him?" Uri laughed. Uri kicked the back of Joseph's chair, sending it forward onto the floor. "Tell them that Russians are stronger than Polacks." Joseph cringed in the dirt, but said nothing. He simply stood up and brushed himself off. He then picked the chair up, dusted it off, and sat back down.

"See? He thinks he's stronger than you. Fifty rubles says you can't take him," the guard said.

"Fifty? Hear that, Jew-boy? They bet me fifty rubles that you could beat me up. Tell them they would waste their money. Tell them I would win." Joseph remained silent, and Uri slapped him. "Tell them!" Uri flicked his cigarette butt away. "Stand up." Joseph stood. "Now defend yourself, Polack." Uri kicked the chair away, and it crashed against the wall with a clatter.

"If I hit you, you'll kill me," Joseph said.

"No, no, no. Let's call it repayment of a debt you owe me. Fifty rubles will buy me a new watch. Even if I beat you senseless, I won't kill you. I might mess up that pretty face of yours though. Your fiancée might lose interest. Maybe she would like a Russian instead of a puny Polack. I'd make her squeal in bed."

Joseph clenched his fists and took a step forward.

"That did it," the guard said.

"Fifty rubles?" Uri asked.

The guard pulled out some notes and threw it on the ground. The other guard matched him.

"One hundred rubles! Looks like you've made some friends. Well then, I'll have to show you all."

Without warning, Uri swung a backhanded fist at Joseph, connecting with the side of his head. Stars exploded across Joseph's vision and his ears rang. But he quickly shook it off. The guards were now yelling at him to fight. Joseph smiled as Uri goaded him, then he charged Uri, picked him up, and slammed him into a tool rack. The tools flew across the floor and the guards laughed. Uri dumped a box of screws off of him and got to his feet.

"That was sneaky," Uri said. "I like it." Uri got within striking distance and swung a hook, but Joseph knocked it away with a swipe of his hand. Uri swung again and Joseph knocked it away again. Uri's face was ready to explode in a burst of pulsating veins.

"You fight like a little girl, slapping my fists away," Uri said.

"Then start fighting like a man," Joseph said. The guards were now chiding Uri.

The brutish Soviet growled and swung a wide haymaker. Instead of knocking it aside, Joseph ducked and countered with a fist into Uri's exposed side. He heard a satisfying "Oof!" from Uri as the air was knocked from his lungs.

Uri stumbled back and braced against a tractor tire. The guards quickly dropped their smiles as Uri grabbed a tire iron.

"That was a lucky shot. You'll never beat a Russian."

"Because Russians are cheats and cowards. You couldn't even fight your own wars. You had to let the Germans do your dirty work."

Uri screamed and ran at Joseph with the iron bar held high. He swung it at Joseph's head, but Joseph leaned out of the way and caught the forward momentum of Uri's arm. He tucked Uri's outstretched arm under his and lifted. A sickening *SNAP* reverberated in the tin garage, reflecting the shock on Uri's face. He screamed in agony and the tire iron clattered on the dusty floor. Joseph took his free hand and pounded Uri's face. His yells pulsed as Joseph's fist cut into his mouth repeatedly. Joseph almost twisted Uri's arm out of its socket when he looked back and saw one of the guards' fists plow right into his surprised face.

He awoke hours later, maybe days. He couldn't tell. He could only see out of one eye. The other was swollen shut. He had a terrible headache and the side of his chest burned with every movement.

"Doc," a fellow inmate, used to have a thriving practice on the outside. He had just arrived from Warsaw, but his presence had immediately been a godsend to the other prisoners. The camp doctor visited only once a week and it was up to the inmates to take care of each other on his days away. Doc had impressed the camp physician so much that he was given access to the infirmary to treat minor injuries in his stead (under a guard's supervision, of course).

He first saw Eva after she had peppered him with questions about Joseph's condition. When Joseph was lucid again, Doc decided to meet with him.

"You're lucky," Doc said. "I thought you'd punctured a lung, but it's only a cracked rib."

Joseph tried to speak but his mouth was stuffed with cotton. The doctor took one swab out, and it was covered in blood.

"What happened?" Joseph asked.

"The guards jumped you. You're lucky to be alive."

"You're not the first person to tell me that. Where's Fima?"

Fima stepped up with his head wrapped. "You look how I feel," he said.

"I feel terrible."

Fima smiled.

"There's someone waiting outside to see you, if you can make it to the door," Doc said.

Joseph struggled to his feet with their help, and the guard sneered as he limped by. He stood in the doorway and squinted at the bright sunlight and instantly heard a familiar squeal. Before he knew it, Eva had grabbed him in a bear hug.

"AHH!" he cried in pain.

She immediately let go of him.

"I'm sorry. I'm sorry!" she screamed. "What did they do to you?"

"They gave me a bachelor party and I think I won a watch."

Eva punched him in the arm. He cried out again.

"I'm sorry. I didn't mean to. It's just. This…this isn't the time to be funny. I was worried to death, and they wouldn't let me see you."

"I won't be funny anymore. It hurts too much."

Eva looked at Doc. "Is he going to be all right?"

"We'll keep him wrapped up for a couple of weeks and he should be fine. Although I wouldn't recommend any fights for a while."

Uri approached when he saw Joseph descend the steps to the infirmary. Joseph didn't see him until the Russian bear was right on him. Joseph instinctively withdrew. When Eva saw Joseph's reaction she knew Uri had been the man responsible for his injuries. So she did the only logical thing she could think of—she threw her body over Joseph's to protect him. He screamed in pain…again. Uri did nothing; he simply stood and watched this display. His arm was in a cast, hidden under his coat, and his jaw was wired shut. Unsightly black stitches ran from his lip and up his cheek in the shape of a question mark. Uri puffed the last of his cigarette and flicked it away. He laughed as Eva pushed against Joseph, even through his painful protests.

"Don't worry. I'm not going to hurt him," Uri said through clenched teeth. "I just want to talk to him."

Uri motioned for Joseph to follow. They walked far enough away so the others couldn't hear.

"You're lucky. I found my watch. If you tell anyone you beat me, I'll kill you. Understand?" Uri poked Joseph's rib. The pain almost caused him to black out.

"I won't say a thing," Joseph choked.

"Good. I'd hate to make her a widow." Uri motioned to Eva. Spittle dripped from the corner of his mouth.

"Have a nice wedding!" Uri yelled to Eva, then hobbled away. Joseph limped back.

"What did he say?" Eva asked.

"He wished you a nice wedding."

"Wedding?"

Joseph looked Eva over with his good eye. She was enraptured. Even beneath the layers of bandages she could see the shimmer of a tiny blue planet.

"Will you marry me?" Joseph asked.

Eva's heart leaped.

"Here in a hard labor prison camp? Yes! Yes!"

She hugged him again. He yelled in anguish.

"Oh, I'm sorry! I'm so happy. I've got to tell Pepi. We've got so much to do." She stopped in her tracks. "I've got to get a dress." She bounced on the balls of her feet and hugged him again while lost in thought.

"Yow!"

"I'm sorry! I love you!" She kissed him. He winced when she ran to the other cabin. "Sorry," she yelled over her shoulder.

Doc came out to the steps.

"Why are you yelling so much?" he asked.

"She was showing me how much she loved me."

Doc smiled. "I'd hate to see when she's angry at you."

11

Eva had been waiting for the right time to open her father's letter. Every time she took it out she cried. But with the wedding imminent, she decided now was the time. As she tore the edge she caught a brief whiff of his favorite cologne. She removed three folded parchment pages and immediately recognized his tight, meticulous print.

My dearest, most beautiful, treasured and beloved special daughter,

This is the most difficult letter I have ever written. How does a father say farewell to his daughter? It's probably best not to dwell in the past but the present. It's hard to think of you as an adult. I can still see you as a little girl playing with my wool tzitzit while I worked at my desk. But when I saw you this afternoon, I realized for the first time that you might no longer be that little girl, but a very independent and mature woman. I'm not sure when it happened but I blinked and you were grown.

I also realized my job as a father was nearly complete. I had but one more task, however: to find you a good husband. You'll have to forgive me, I can be so focused on the details that I miss the larger picture—your happiness.

Your mother took me aside this morning and had "the talk" with me. She wanted to make me understand that in your heart, you had already chosen a mate. I was content to brush it off as childhood infatuation, but when I saw your intimacy with each other, I knew it was true love. You didn't even have to speak. Just by your actions, I could tell you adored each other.

I thought of all the good things I knew about Joseph. When you know someone for a long time you can take things for granted. He's a good man and I know he will be a great father. I just wish he took his Jewish heritage more seriously. So I give you my blessing on you marrying *if* Joseph abides by a few rules:

1. He finds a rabbi to perform the ceremony according to Jewish law laid out on the following pages.
2. He honors the Shabbat and the high holidays.
3. He attends synagogue each week.
4. He teaches my grandchildren in the ways of Judaism.

I pray HaShem's blessing on you. That He will give you many children. That He will open many opportunities for Joseph and give you both a long, happy life. That you would lean on each other for strength in difficult times. And that Joseph would only have eyes for you.

As HaShem guided and protected the children of Israel, may He guide and protect you. Amen.

Take care my dear, sweet, loving daughter, and know that wherever you go we love you with all our heart, our LALA!

—◦◦◦—

Fifty people were jammed into Cabin 11. Evergreen boughs were festooned over the main aisle between bunks, and a wedding tent, or huppah (canopy) was made by draping Joseph's tallit (prayer shawl) across four broomsticks tied to the ends of two bunk beds.

Eva was beautiful. Her hair had been braided and worn in a bun. Her head was covered in a sheer veil made from a curtain lining. She wore a full-length white dress, skillfully tailored from used nurse outfits. Pepi had even found a pair of matching white shoes for her. Joseph wore a black suit patched together from several donations. Eva even found an inmate rabbi who offered to perform the ceremony, according to her father's instructions.

Neither Eva nor Joseph could stop smiling throughout the ceremony. Their fondness for each other permeated through-out the entire gathering. Nothing—not imprisonment, the harsh conditions of Siberia, nor the cruel mistreatment from their captors—could dissuade the infectious joy they felt at that moment. Joseph gave her a simple gold band, and then stomped the glass with everyone yelling "Mazel Tov" (good luck) and broke out in a song played on Leszek's concertina. Everyone brought something as a wedding gift: cookies, a tin of candies, a handkerchief, a candle. It all added up to a random assortment that seemed perfect for the occasion.

There was a long banging at the cabin door. The singing stopped and the note on the concertina sagged. Someone opened it. Uri stood in the glow of the cabin lights, wearing street clothes. And for the first and last time, they saw him without his rifle.

"Can I come in?"

Joseph stepped forward.

"Sure. Please, come in."

Uri walked in and the inmates parted for him. He walked straight up to Joseph, reached under his coat, and grabbed at something. The guests collectively gasped.

"I came to give you this, and to tell you congratulations," Uri said as he pulled out a bottle of vodka. The crowd breathed a sigh of relief.

"Thank you," said Joseph as the festivities resumed. "Please join us."

Uri accepted a cookie and then joined in the singing and dancing among the inmates.

Eva and Joseph kissed, and Pepi couldn't help but cry. For a moment there was a respite from their circumstances. It wasn't the end of the world but the beginning of something new. Two had become one. Childhood friends had become lovers. Man and woman had become husband and wife. Eva's father would have been proud.

12

It was an early February morning, and the snow had fallen for two days without stop. Pepi struggled through a waist-high drift to Cabin 12. She beat on the door, waking the guard, who eventually opened up and squinted into the blinding light reflecting off the snow. He saw the concern in Pepi's eyes and let her in. Most men were still asleep in the warm room. Pepi found Joseph polishing his boots. He was shocked to see Pepi, since women weren't allowed in the men's cabin.

"What's wrong?"

"It's Eva. Come quickly."

Joseph pulled his boots on and grabbed his coat and hat. He got permission from the guard and tromped into the snow.

"Too cold for sex," the guard muttered.

The guard at Cabin 11 burst out the door past them.

"Get her out of there, the smell is making me sick!" he said.

Eva had just thrown up in a bucket. She looked up at Joseph with a half-smile, a dribble of bile still clinging to her lip.

"Hi, honey," she said weakly.

"She's been sick all night," Pepi said. "Help me get her to the infirmary."

"I'm sorry to get you out of bed," Eva said, wiping her mouth. She tried to sit up. "It's just—" she gagged and threw up again in the bucket.

"Now! Out! Get her out! Throw that bucket outside!" the guard yelled. He was standing in the doorway with a rag held to his mouth. He fanned fresh air with the door.

They carried Eva between their shoulders through the deep snow to the infirmary. They were lucky because the deep snow had made the road to the station impassable and the camp physician couldn't leave until it was clear.

By the time the doctor ushered them into an examination room, Eva was dry heaving. The doctor was irritated with Pepi trying to comfort Eva, so he chased Joseph and Pepi out. They waited in the hall and looked out the window as it started snowing again. Pepi took her brother's hand and held onto his arm.

"She'll be fine," she said.

"I don't want her to get sick, I don't want to lose her," Joseph said.

"Maybe you should pray. You did agree to become more religious. No better time than the present." Pepi patted his arm.

Joseph cleared his throat, gave Pepi a wary eye, then looked out the window to the overcast sky.

"Dearest HaShem, creator of the universe. Please heal my wife. Please don't let her be sick. We haven't even had a chance to enjoy life together as free people. Please don't let her die. Amen."

Pepi smiled and hugged him.

"Not bad. A little overdramatic, but not bad for a first try."

Just then they heard a scream. Joseph charged into the exam room. Eva was still sitting on the table with her hands drawn up to her mouth and *she was smiling.*

"What is it? What's wrong?" Joseph asked.

"Nothing's wrong," Eva said, still smiling.

Even the doctor was smiling and this was beginning to annoy Joseph.

"What then? I don't understand."

"I'm—I'm pregnant."

Pepi squealed with delight and did a little jig before she hugged Eva. Joseph's jaw dropped as the news set in. He grabbed Eva off the table and spun her around.

"Careful!" Pepi yelled.

"Oh yeah! Right." He set her back on the table. "I'm going to be a father!" he yelled.

"Would you like to hear?" the doctor asked.

"Hear what?"

"The baby."

"Yes!"

The doctor placed his stethoscope on Eva's abdomen and moved it around. He pressed down and stopped. He took off the earpieces and handed them to Joseph. Joseph listened to the tiny pulsing heartbeats of his baby and laughed. A tear ran down his cheek.

When the trio exited the clinic, Joseph spun off the top step, spread his arms out, and fell backward into the snow.

"Thank you," he said, looking at the stars.

———⟨∾∾⟩———

Miriam made a nest of sorts with her clothes spread over a pile of dead grass. It wasn't comfortable but it was better than the hard ground. Her neighbors were new arrivals, clutching their belongings and sitting in similar nests. Most were Jews but more and more were Russian soldiers captured by their old allies. When Stalin realized he'd been duped by Hitler, he had decided to change sides. Millions would die because of his arrogance.

Miriam knew what happened to the prisoners that sat between Barracks 4 and 5. They were to be "sorted." After two days, even more prisoners arrived. Once the enclosure reached capacity, it would begin. Water was scarce and food scraps of bread were thrown into the cages like they were animals. People tend to act the way they are treated. The stronger men fought over the morsels while the weaker women and children went without. She knew she had been sentenced to die, she just didn't know when.

As the days wore on, Miriam lost weight as her body ate itself to survive. She was forced to drink filthy water even though an outbreak of typhus had claimed the lives of hundreds of workers in the Russian enclosure. The smoke from the ovens never stopped. Night and day they burned corpses, yet the prison was still over capacity, so the Germans stacked the bodies in piles, poured fuel on them, and set them alight. Whenever the wind blew the smoke from the pyres, she gagged.

One night she sat awake, shivering uncontrollably. She looked out of her tiny window and saw a dark figure scurry across the enclosure to the far fence. The man threw his coat over the electrified barbed wire and carefully separated two rows with sticks. He then crawled through them carefully, resting his body on his thick coat. He balanced on an angled brace that held several rows of electric wire running horizontally off the ground. He then removed his coat from the inner fence, walked across the brace, and laid the coat on a row of wire on the outer fence. He separated the strands and could see freedom through the wires. He only had to place one more stick. Unfortunately, a spotlight had swung along the fence and caught him right in its sights. He paid no attention, staying focused on his task. A whistle soon blew and guards yelled, but the man kept working. He eased down and carefully started between the strands. He heard footsteps approach and someone yelling at him to stop. But he ignored them. Just a little further and he would escape. Suddenly, a gunshot echoed out over the camp, and the man immediately went limp, dropping onto the lower strand of wire. His body then rolled back between the fences and fell onto the rows of electrified wire. A sickening buzz filled the night air, and the man screamed, still alive from the gunshot. The man's body twitched as it was electrocuted. The next day the man was still on the wire, his frame swaying gently in the passing wind.

Miriam felt terrible. She couldn't sleep or get comfortable. One moment she was shivering from fever, the next she was sweating profusely.

Every morning, a young girl from Lublin would bring news about the war and mail from loved ones. The guards seemed to think she was harmless as she stood on the outside of the fence and threw the mail over. If they tired of her, they would yell and she'd scamper away until the next day. Some of the prisoners didn't trust her, saying she would throw the letters away and steal anything of value. The truth was that she was part of a well-organized resistance and was the only way for many prisoners to stay in touch with the outside world.

Many families in the camp realized that they would never leave, so they buried what heirlooms they had with them in the enclosure. Better to return them to the earth than for the Germans to benefit from them.

Miriam decided that she didn't have much time left before the camp claimed her as well. She found an old document and turned it over to write a letter. Her writing was shaky, erratic, but thankfully still legible. When she finished, she folded the letter and wrote, "Joseph Mitsen of Rejowiec." She waited until the next morning when the little girl came by and threw the letter across the fence. The girl walked over, picked it up, and looked at her. Miriam pulled out a gold ring she had hidden and threw it to the girl. The girl caught it and went on to collect other mail.

As the day carried on, Miriam's fever got worse. She wore everything she owned, yet she still couldn't stop shivering. She wasn't hungry or thirsty. The others stayed away from her, fearful of becoming infected. She suffered in silence, curled upon the ground, alone.

———◦◦◦———

The day of the sorting had arrived. The Germans lined the newcomers up and marched them to a holding area in front of the showers. Their belongings were thrown in piles and they were forced to strip. Every man, woman, and child stood naked, huddling together. Commandant Erich stood behind an assistant with a list of names, and they called each prisoner forth, one by one, to be inspected by the commandant. If they appeared healthy enough for work detail, then they were sent to the showers on the left. If they were sick or otherwise weak, they were sent to the showers on the right. The shower on the right didn't dispense water, however. Rather, it spewed poison gas that killed each prisoner who entered. In front of Miriam, a man was separated from his wife. She cried and tried to join him, but was promptly quieted with a bullet to her head. Their little girl cried over her dead mother and was eventually pulled back by other prisoners when the guard threatened to shoot her too.

Miriam's fever was higher than ever. Cold sweat oozed out of her pores, and she had trouble walking toward the Camp Commandant Erich. To Miriam he looked like a squat demon that spoke with a shrill voice. The commandant recognized Miriam's face, yet was appalled at her thin body. Her ribs stuck out and the bones of her hips stretched the thin skin tightly over them. She frowned, her head held low. The guard shook his head and guided Miriam to the right. To the *gas-poisoned* showers. *To die.*

> If you were a Jew in Europe during the Holocaust, you had to believe in miracles.
>
> —David Ben-Gurion,
> the first prime minister of Israel

13

"**G**et up!" Uri yelled. He kicked Joseph's bunk. "Generator 3 is down. Fix it. Now."

"Yes, sir," Joseph said with half-open eyes. Joseph got dressed and stumbled out of the cabin door. It was dark out but a full moon was up. He had his flashlight but decided it was bright enough to navigate by moonlight. Batteries were hard to come by and he might need it to repair the engine.

The moonlight gave everything a gray-blue tint as it reflected off the snow. A soft wind blew but the only sound was the crunching of snow under Joseph's boots as he trekked the mile or so down the road to the generator shed.

Trees creaked in the breeze on both sides of the road. The camp had originally been the end of the line on an old logging road, and a dense growth of hardwood forest had overtaken much of the area. When Joseph cleared the first turn from the camp, he was completely alone, isolated among trees that were taller than any building he'd ever been in. He felt small and insignificant. In the daytime, the forest was full of life and beauty, but at night, especially with a full moon out, the ominous pallor made him nervous. He tried whistling and thinking of the news he had heard earlier in the day.

I'm going to be a dad.

He felt better and realized he was clenching his fists. Soon the war would be over and he could take Eva and Pepi home. He hoped it could be soon enough to have the baby in Dad's house with the family gathered. That would be wonderful. Life wasn't so bad despite the war. He relaxed and imagined all the things he and his child could do together. He didn't care whether it was a son or daughter.

He picked up the pace and began whistling a favorite tune. His lips were cold and he struggled for the high note on the chorus. To his surprise, it sounded true and clear. To his horror, he had stopped whistling yet the note persisted—a wolf's howl.

Was he too far to turn back?

A chill ran through him as he listened to the howl trail off. He thought he saw movement off to the right in the corner of his eye. Something was keeping pace with him behind the trees. He flicked his light on. Nothing. Must be nerves. He laughed and felt a bit childish, but left the light on—just in case.

He flicked the light around the woods, trusting his instincts that something was in fact out there. His hands were clammy, his heart pumped. He stopped momentarily and shot the light toward what sounded like a twig cracking beneath someone's feet. He swore he saw a silvery shape slide behind a tree. But there wouldn't be any wolves this close to human settlement, would there? He was almost to the generator shack now. He could hear the rumble of generators 1 and 2. But he could also hear a rumbling from *behind* him. Growls. He quickly turned and shone his light against two reflecting orbs, staring right at him.

Joseph froze. He thought of grabbing a stick but he knew it would take too long. The wolf snarled fiercely, then pounced, immediately latching onto Joseph's arm. The thick padding of his coat protected him for the moment but the wolf's tight grip furiously shook his arm, tossing the flashlight into the snow. Joseph thought the beast was going to pull his arm from its socket, it pulled with such determination. He could now see the monster's ridged nose and gleaming teeth. Gathering strength, he pulled the wolf in an arc to his chest and jammed his thumb into its eye socket. The wolf yelped loudly and broke its vise-like grip. Joseph took this brief moment to dart into the trees. He could hear other wolves approaching now, tracking him in the dark. Branches slapped his face as he bungled blindly forward at a full run through the thick brush. A branch nearly clotheslined him, but he managed to catch the limb and climb up it. He found another low branch closer to the tree's trunk and pulled himself up higher. He was about to ascend higher when a wolf leaped up and managed to latch onto his dangling boot. Another leaped and found a loose tail of his jacket, its weight pulling Joseph back down. By sheer strength, he was able to stay on the branch. Luckily, the canvas of his coat ripped in a wide strip, dropping the wolf off his back. The wolf on his boot was more tenacious. It snarled and growled and wriggled at his foot. Joseph slowly reached down, maintaining his balance, found the shoelace knot, and pulled on the lace. The knot loosened, and he was able to wiggle his toes and twist his foot until the boot, wolf and all, fell back toward the earth. Joseph pulled himself up further in the tree, beyond the reach of the frenzied monsters below. The branches were much thinner now, so Joseph stayed close to the trunk, hugging it tightly.

The wolves orbited the tree for nearly an hour before giving up. Joseph's hands were asleep from clinging to the trunk for so long. He waited until he thought it was safe to climb down, but as soon as he set foot on the ground, a wolf pounced on him. If he had been less wary it would have pulled him from the tree. He beat harshly at the wolf's head, finally dislodging it from his leg. This time the wolf drew blood, so Joseph decided to climb back up and stay in the tree until dawn.

He tied the arms of his jacket around the tree trunk, creating a tight sling for himself. The wolves could now smell their prey's blood, and refused to leave. Looking down, he could see where he had dropped the flashlight, beaming into a thicket. He watched it for a while, and then drifted off to sleep.

"Hey Jew!" a voice called out. Joseph opened his frost-covered eyes. It was Uri and another soldier. "What are you doing up there?"

Joseph's voice was weak, but he managed to mutter the word, "Wolves." His body shifted backward, untying the jacket harness from the trunk, and he fell right out of the tree. He landed at Uri's feet, and instantly blacked out.

⚬⚬⚬

"This is the second time they've brought me your unconscious body," Doc said. He leaned in with a flashlight and checked Joseph's pupil response. "How you feeling?"

"I don't know," Joseph said.

"Are you in pain?"

"I don't think—" Joseph tried to sit up. "Uh, yeah. I'm pretty sore."

"Your toes on one foot are frostbitten. I don't think you'll lose them, though, just some skin. A word of advice—don't climb trees with your shoes off."

"Thanks. It was not my choice.

———◦◦◦———

Pepi learned from other prisoners that her husband and daughter have died of starvation.

Pepi mourned for several weeks. Her normally boisterous personality had been gutted. She went to talk to the prisoners often after this news, gleaning as much information from them as she could about the final days of her husband and daughter.

———◦◦◦———

A few weeks later, the camp commander ordered all prisoners to collect at the flag in the middle of the square.

"You have one hour to gather your things and meet back here. Leave your bed linen. Leave your blankets. Put all your things in one of these duffle bags." The commander nodded and soldiers threw armloads of canvas bags on the ground. "One bag for each person. Anything that doesn't fit will be left behind. We are moving you to another camp. One hour!"

"All right," shouted a soldier. "Let's go! You heard the commander. Grab a sack. Move it!"

Eva, Pepi, and Joseph picked up their bags and returned to their cabins. An hour later, several flat-bed logging trucks were lined up around the square and the prisoners were loaded up. The trucks convulsed forward toward the tiny train station, and the prisoners were loaded without incident.

"At least it's pointed south," Joseph said. "I can't handle any colder weather."

The cars they were in weren't the cattle cars they arrived in but passenger cars. They were old and worn, but they were designed for human occupants. Most importantly, they had heat. The prisoners stowed their bags under their bench seats and overhead lofts. They settled into their seats and faced one another, in shock. Soon water, milk, potatoes, and bread were brought around for everyone.

The train lurched forward and the "prisoners" ate their food, looking out the window comfortably, as the station slid into open country.

Joseph said a prayer while the ladies listened.

"Hear, O' Israel. HaShem is our God, HaShem the one and only…"

—◦∾◦—

The Warsaw Ghetto was a walled enclosure in the center of the city where over 450,000 Jews from the surrounding area were kept by the Germans.

Muller was called in to assist in putting down a rebellion. He thought it would be relatively easy to contain the resistance, but Jewish resolve was greater than he expected and even with several thousand troops, they waged battle in the streets from house to house, block by block. The Germans burned everything as they advanced.

After he had finally managed to get the situation under control, fifty thousand Jews lay dead. Muller retired to a hotel, exhausted and not very happy. He had just received orders to head to Krakow, to put down another rebellion on the outskirts of town. Resistance fighters had raided a weapons depot and destroyed a fuel station.

Muller hated Poland more and more. He considered the Poles the same as the Russians—ineffective country bumpkins. Everything he saw confirmed in his mind the depravity of the country and he longed for a vacation to a villa in the Alps.

His train headed south from Warsaw. The pause in the action gave him a moment to think. Although he outwardly professed an anticapitalist stance and aligned every comment to the party doctrine, he secretly admired the American West, particularly the lifestyle of the cowboy. He had his cowboy boots specially shipped all the way from a company in Texas. Whiskey was something he learned to drink from the movies as well. He fancied himself a European type of cowboy, and identified himself with their struggles. For his next purchase, he wanted a pair of Colt Peacemakers. He had a cowboy hat but could only wear it in the privacy of his room. As he looked out the carriage window he swilled his shot, slammed it down on the table, and made a face—just like they did in the movies.

A worried officer entered his private suite.

"You don't knock?" Muller exclaimed.

"Excuse me, Herr Muller," the nervous man said.

"What is it?"

"There is a communiqué from Berlin."

"Go ahead."

"Allied forces have invaded Germany and all commanders are ordered home to defend the Fatherland." Muller looked at the officer with a drawn expression. "Commandant?"

"Uh, yes. From the Ministry?"

"Coded and priority."

Muller sighed.

"Your instructions, sir."

"Acknowledge and confirm. Reroute our destination and inform the engineer."

"Yes, sir." The officer turned to leave.

"Sergeant!"

"Yes, sir."

"Keep me informed on enemy troop movements. I want to know where they are and where they're going to be. Let me know if there are any changes in their position as we get closer."

"Yes, sir. Will that be all?"

Muller thought for a moment. "I want to speak to a loyalist when we arrive in Krakow."

The officer smiled as he nodded his head knowingly. "Looking for a young woman? I have a friend who knows where to get the very best."

"Maybe, but I'm more interested in a counterfeiter."

"Counterfeiter? For money?"

"Documents."

"Ah, I'm sure I can find someone, sir."

"Good. Keep it private."

"As always."

Muller nodded. The officer left.

"That's it. That's the end," he said to himself. "They wanted to get rid of me by sending me to the front. But they couldn't kill me. I survived. I am alive and rich!"

The train pulled into Krakow Station and Muller suddenly noticed a stunning blonde looking back at him, lying on a beach under a parasol. He blinked a few times and realized he was looking at an old billboard promoting a vacation on a beautiful beach.

14

February 1945

The prison train pulled away from the transfer station heading southeast. Joseph and his family had been traveling for two days. A middle-aged man moved down the aisle with his duffle bag and asked if he could sit with them. He had a big beard and an even bigger smile. He stowed his bag and sat next to Pepi.

"Until this year, I had never been on a train," the man said. "I lived all my life in a small town. I had no need to go nowhere. I know my parents have never been on a train. Name's Ludek. Where are you coming from?"

"Siberia," Joseph said.

"And I thought it was cold here. You glad you took the offer?"

"What offer?"

"We weren't given an offer," chimed in Eva.

"Ah, they probably knew you wouldn't want to stay in Siberia."

"I don't understand," Joseph said.

"What did they tell you?" Ludek asked.

"They told us to get on the train. We were going to another camp."

"You're right. They didn't tell you anything. You know where we're going?"

Joseph shook his head slowly. Ludek laughed. "Kazakhstan." Joseph looked at Eva as she grabbed his hand. "Specifically, Alma-Ata, the capital city."

"Why so far away?" Pepi asked.

"The Russians have lost much of their labor force in the war, and there is no one left to make weapons. We are going to Kazakhstan to make guns."

So that's the answer, thought Joseph. The Russians were conscripting prisoners of war for service in their factories. They had run out of warm bodies. It's easier to force prisoners to work than to entice skilled labor from other countries. Joseph looked out the window as he let his mind drift.

I thought we were fighting the Germans, he thought. Why are the Russians doing this? There has to be a better solution. How is it possible that simply being a Jew causes all of these problems? It isn't like the Jewish people are a threat. My father wouldn't hurt anyone. Hard work—that was his motto and that was what he lived. Are people jealous? Do they feel that Jewish people are jeopardizing their livelihoods? There's some truth that Jewish people stick together and prefer to do business with one another, but doesn't everyone? I'm sure most social groups or cultures take comfort with those they are most familiar with. Did we do something extraordinary to deserve this persecution? Is it really that hard to leave us alone? If the war started with Poland, why were the Jews singled out? Shouldn't it be the Poles versus the Germans?

Joseph realized that Ludek was still talking about his family or something. He wasn't really listening.

What about Eva? And now I've got to take care of Pepi too. What kind of world waits for us? What will my child inherit? I'm going to do everything I can to make sure he doesn't have to face the fears that we have. But should I teach him to be suspicious of everyone? Should I show him how to plan an escape route from every situation, how to defend himself from attack? What happened to peace? What happened to generations living and working in the same community, in the same house? Maybe it's always been an illusion. Maybe it has always been an unattainable goal; a dream seen through rose-colored glasses. But don't others have that dream to some degree? Don't they have a place, a country they can call their own? Why can't we have our own? I want to play with my child in open spaces without worrying about our safety. I want him to learn respect and to love all people. I don't want to have to teach him to fire a gun or how to kill a man with a knife. There has to be a better way. I'm responsible for that little life growing inside of Eva. What he or she becomes is my new charge, and right now I don't have many options. It's just not the right time. HaShem blessed me with Eva and He's kept us alive through monumental challenges. Not everyone was so lucky. How can I protect another addition to my family? If we didn't have this war, if I was back home in Rejowiec, if I was surrounded by my family and friends… but I have nothing. I have nothing to give. I can't even provide a home! All I have are my hands, my mind, and my love. Is it enough?

Eva squeezed his arm, jerking him out of his reverie.

"You all right?" she asked.

"Yeah. Sorry, just thinking."

"About what?"

"About our future, about the baby."

"Me too. As long as we're together, we'll be fine. HaShem brought you back to me when I thought you were gone. So I know without a shadow of a doubt that no matter where we go, whatever we face, He is there. And He will make a way for us, for all of us. We just have to believe. We have to trust Him."

Eva turned around in her chair and took both of Joseph's hands in hers. "Do you know why Papa wanted you to be more religious?"

"No."

"He wanted you to have the peace and confidence he had in his own life. The things I saw him stress over were always things I thought were silly or unnecessary. Then I realized as I grew up that he never neglected issues of the heart or faith. He took those very seriously, but big things like money or sicknesses he treated almost inconsequentially. He'd say, 'I've already prayed about that,' and that was the end of it. Funny thing was he was usually right. Things did take care of themselves, almost miraculously.

"He would say that we always had to address the core problem, not the symptoms. A small fire is easy to put out. But if it's ignored, it can grow into a conflagration that destroys and can't be controlled.

"You know, he spoke of you often!"

"He did?"

"He knew I loved you. He tried to put the fire out a few times. Each time he tried, it grew stronger. He was worried you would hurt me. At least that was his excuse. He might have been testing me. If I was intent on being with you, if he could just make sure you were strong in your faith, he would have done everything HaShem required of him."

Joseph looked into the dark pools of her eyes. He was moved by what she said. He felt there was a divine protection over him.

"Are you psychic?" he asked.

"Only with you. You start to know when things bother someone when you've known them all your life."

The trip stretched into weeks. Eva became more uncomfortable as the baby grew inside of her, and Pepi knew that the limited daily nutrition provided by their captors wasn't enough. She had seen babies aborted prematurely if the mother didn't get enough to eat. She wasn't about to lose any more of her family members, even unborn ones.

A guard made his daily rounds and brought them their meal rations. Pepi stopped the young man in the aisle and said, "Excuse me, the woman in the cabin is pregnant. She's really eating for two. Is there any way she can get more food?" Pepi smiled sweetly and put her hand on the man's shoulder. His face flushed and he swallowed.

"I'm sorry, but the rule is one tray per person. That's all I'm allowed."

Pepi looked back in the cabin where Joseph and the others were eating. She held the guard's arm and took him to the end of the hall and into an alcove. He followed along without resistance. She unbuttoned her blouse, then looked up to the guard and smiled. She took a gold chain and gave it to him.

"Are you sure you couldn't give us an extra tray?" The guard tried to speak, but his mouth was dry. She stroked his hair.

"I…uh, I guess one tray more would be all right." He pulled another tray from the cart and handed it to Pepi. He started to say something and she put a finger on his lips.

"Shh. I'll see you tomorrow, okay?"

He nodded.

Pepi fixed her hair, put on a big smile, and took the tray to Eva. She was surprised and looked incredulously into the hall.

"Who gave you that?"

"The guard."

Eva gave her a doubtful look. Pepi ignored her and sat next to Ludek.

"I was going to eat your meal if you didn't come back," Ludek said. He laughed.

"Thank you for waiting," Pepi said. Eva narrowed her eyes, studying Pepi suspiciously.

"What did you do?" Eva asked. Joseph caught the tone in his wife's voice and suddenly looked up from his meal.

"Look, just eat the food, okay?" Pepi stammered.

Eva rolled her eyes and started to eat. Pepi shot a curt smile at Joseph and started eating.

"Thank you," Eva said.

"You're welcome," Pepi replied curtly.

Eva devoured the rest of her food without a word.

The following week the train stopped at several stations on their journey south. As they made their way across Kazakhstan, they passed groups of nomads living in yurts, with herds of sheep, goats, furry oxen, and diminutive stocky horses.

The flat land eventually gave way to lakes and rivers, and soon the train was circumnavigating large bodies of water. It took the better part of a day to pass around them. But once they were clear, Joseph kept his eye on a looming mountain range rising like teeth in the south. In the air, he and Eva could clearly see snowcapped peaks. After another day, they had finally arrived— Alma-Ata. Russian troops herded them through a busy town as the city's pedestrians watched. The weary Poles entered an industrial zone marked by factories and smokestacks, where the trucks pulled into a camp named MEHYLUVKA. Eventually they came to a stop in front of a platoon of intimidating soldiers.

One by one, the trucks were discharged and the prisoners huddled together with their belongings. The soldiers parted at the approach of an immaculately dressed officer, the kind that reveled in bobbles and accoutrements to impress. Every bar, every award (and a few he bought) bedecked the breast of his uniform. It was a statement of pride in a commandant who found approval in the reflected impression of others. He was a stout man with red cheeks and a bulbous nose. He jingled when he walked.

"Welcome to Kazakhstan," he said with a booming voice and magnanimous gesture. His teeth were immaculate.

"You will sign in at the tables. Families can remain together, but singles are to be separated. We don't want any problems, if you know what I mean." The commandant smiled to himself. "You will work in the factory over there." He pointed with two hands across the lot to a two-story building bristling with chimneys. "In exchange, you will be given two meals a day and a comfortable place to sleep. There is running water in each cabin. The bathhouse is over there. Please tell the officer at the table of your particular skillset and educational level. If you treat us with respect, we will reciprocate. If you cause problems, it's really very simple. Just remember the golden rule. Do the work assigned to you. Be where you're supposed to be. If you do that, you will find your time here almost pleasurable. If you are thinking of escape, I wouldn't advise it. We offer a generous reward to the good citizens of Alma-Ata for the return of prisoners. So if you plan to run, make sure you dress like the people, maybe put some makeup on to darken the skin and cover the head." The commandant smiled as he mimed hiding a turban. Some prisoners laughed. "And most important, don't speak to anyone. Your accent will give you away." He looked over the newly arrived crowd. "Are there any questions?"

No one said anything.

The commandant fluttered his hand and bowed. He turned and walked into a single-story house which served as an administration building. Joseph, Eva, and Pepi approached the table.

A soldier wrote their names in a book, and Joseph was officially a prisoner of war. These same men were responsible for the deaths of his friends and family. That was when he noticed the rose in a vase on the check-in table.

The cabins were… nice. The walls were insulated. There were electric outlets and diffused overhead lighting. The walls were freshly painted and the beds had real mattresses and feather pillows. To top it off, each bunk had its own sink and mirror. They couldn't believe the marked improvement in their accommodations.

"This is weird," Pepi said. "It's like they're trying to be nice."

"Like a funeral home," Joseph said.

"There's no razor wire. The fence looks like something a cow might push over. Did you look at the gate?" Eva asked.

"No," Joseph said.

"It hasn't been closed in a long time. There are thick clumps of grass growing in front of it. You can't close it. And there's no guard stationed in the cabin." She looked out the window. The trucks rolled by with most of the soldiers aboard. "There. See? They're leaving. There's practically no security."

"Maybe the citizens are all the protection they need," Pepi said.

"No!" exclaimed Eva. "You believe the commandant? That frilly loudmouth was all show. You still don't get it. This isn't a prison camp. It's a labor camp. This place was never intended to house prisoners. It's for employees.

This is a factory. Remember, Ludek said they didn't have enough men to keep things running."

"That's why we're here," Joseph said.

"Better than the snow," Pepi said.

"They're treating us better because they want us to stay," Eva said.

"Then we're leaving as soon as possible," Joseph said.

"After the baby," Eva responded.

Joseph agreed, but in his heart he knew that involuntary servitude was just another way of saying prisoner. Even slaves worked in the most beautiful places and drank from golden vessels. They were now a higher class of slave, but still slaves. They would have to leave if they ever wanted to truly be free.

Pepi worked on a stamping machine. She loaded cut pieces of flat stock onto a dye, pressed a button, and a hydraulic press stamped down and formed the metal into part of a gun grip. The monotony of the work was a pleasant distraction, as it made the time pass by quickly for the first time since she learned of her family's fate. The concentration of not getting her fingers caught made her forget her circumstances. At least for a while.

Eva worked in the office. She handled orders and shipping schedules. It was easy work for her, as she excelled at tedium. She got to know the commandant on a personal basis—Nicolai Yanin was his name. He stayed in his office most of the day and had few visitors. Eva thought of him as an eccentric. Every so often, he would spend hours organizing binges, stripping the furniture and scrubbing everything clean, then putting it all back in place.

Commandant Yanin became quite fond of Eva. As she began to show, he brought her treats from home or would insist on her taking breaks to put her feet up. And the questions, the never ending questions—How do you feel? Do you think it's a boy or a girl? Are you gaining weight? Do you feel sick? Are you sleeping?

At first, she thought they were cute and innocent, but as she got nearer to term he seemed obsessed and needy. Joseph was grateful for the extra care, however. He met her at lunch break, but often fretted about her during the day. When Eva mentioned the commandant's growing interest in her pregnancy, he brushed it off to innocent concern for her wellbeing.

—⁓—

The next day, the commandant came into the cabin. He knew that Joseph and Eva would be at work and Pepi would be getting up soon for her shift. She was alone. The commandant stood at the foot of her bunk and watched her sleep. She seemed so peaceful. A slight curl to her lips…she might be smiling. *These Polish Jews are beautiful people*, he thought. He cleared his throat, prompting Pepi to flutter her eyes and groan in her sleep. She stretched and popped open an eye when she realized someone was standing there. She gasped and drew up the covers.

"I'm sorry, I didn't mean to wake you," the commandant said.

"Uh…no…I was…I was just resting." Pepi sat up and scooted back with the covers. She ran her hand through her hair and brushed it back with her fingers. She took a deep breath and looked up with squinted eyes. "What time is it?"

"Ten thirty."

"Hmm…I have to get up for my shift."

"I thought I might talk to you before you left." The commandant looked at the bed. "May I?"

"Sure." Pepi drew up her feet. The commandant smoothed the covers and sat down with both hands on his knees.

"I noticed your friend is pregnant. We had a few children that were born in this camp, but they all died here…due to the poor food, sickness, and poor medical services. I am interested to adopt your fiend's baby. I will pay them, let them live here under better conditions, give them more food until they have to return to Poland. I know the baby will not survive here otherwise."

The commandant brushed his sleeves, turned, and walked out the door of the cabin without another word. Pepi watched him leave, then fell back on her pillow. She shivered. She was very confused. She tried piecing the conversation back together, thinking she hadn't heard correctly. Later that evening when Joseph and Eva returned, she told them about the strange visit.

"I think he asked for your baby."

"He what?" Eva asked.

"He said he wanted adopt your baby," Pepi explained the conversation.

"That's…that's weird," Joseph said.

"I'm not sure. He was nervous and he didn't make any sense."

"There, you see?" Joseph looked at Eva. "Our baby is so special, people want him even before he's born."

"It's a 'she,' and it's not very funny."

Just then, a soldier opened the door and entered with a basket. He walked up to Pepi. "Are you Pepi?" he asked.

"Yes."

"This is from the commandant." He set a basket on the table, nodded, and left. The three of them circled the basket and leaned over it. Pepi lifted the top. On a checkered cloth rested a small note.

Dearest Friends,

Please enjoy the treats in celebration of your upcoming baby.

Sincerely,
Nicolai Yanin and Anatola

Pepi unfolded the cloth. Inside was a loaf of bread, cheese, grapes, a can of milk, and a bottle of vodka. Joseph stared at Eva.

"I guess he's serious," he said.

"I promise I will do everything I can to make sure you and your baby survive."

"Thank you," Joseph and Eva both said in unison.

"You're all I've got," Pepi smiled.

"We'll make it together."

15

"A thousand Deutsche Marks," Muller asked. "I could buy a car for that!"

The short man he was talking to collected the fake passport and visa before walking away. Muller scowled.

"Wait! All right, I'll take them." Muller pulled a long leather wallet from his coat pocket and opened it. He removed bills, counting them as he placed them in the man's waiting hand.

"Seven hundred, eight hundred, nine hundred, one thousand." The man handed over the documents. Muller opened them, and ran his fingers over the new Swiss passport. *FREDERIC MILLER* was printed in bold type across the top.

"The corner of the photo is folded."

"Where?" the man asked.

"Right here." Muller pointed to the edge of the picture.

"Aw, that's just a little crumple. Nobody is going to say anything about that."

"For the cost, it should be perfect."

The little man grew frustrated. "Fine, give it back to me and meet me here tomorrow. I'll have it fixed."

Muller thought for a moment. "Never mind. This will do," he said.

"I thought so. It was a pleasure doing business with you, Mr. Miller." The little man laughed, stuffed the money in his pocket, and walked away.

Muller looked over the documents. They were exquisite—maybe too perfect. He crumpled the pages and rubbed them on the wall. *There, that's better.* He tucked them into his pocket and scanned the quiet street. He had told his staff he was going out to eat and find a prostitute. He wouldn't be back to the army base until the following day. That should give him at least a twelve-hour head start. It would take them even longer to mount a search. By the time they figured out that he'd defected, he'd be out of the country. Muller walked to the back alley to where he had stashed his bags. He opened a paper bag containing his military uniform. He fingered the silver eagle on his hat and looked over the medals he had collected for his Nazi service. He was making a decision he couldn't undo. Once he started down this path, he couldn't turn back. He was leaving his old life behind.

His family members lived outside of Berlin. He didn't think they would live very long once the Allies started their bombardment. This was who he had been, not who he was—the old him, the military career man. The reliable officer of the Third Reich—the same Reich that tried to kill him by sending him to the front lines.

"Screw them," he said resolutely.

He picked up the bag and stuffed it under a pile of rubbish. He then grabbed his suitcase and walked to the Krakow train station.

Muller boarded the train and quickly found his seat in the first-class cabin. He hung up his jacket, stowed his bags, and leaned back in his chair. He glanced out the window, pretending to tie his shoe. He was relieved when the train started moving.

—◦◦◦—

Eva typed a letter and the camp procurement officer dictated it to a recording. She didn't notice when the commandant stood in the doorway to his office and watched her work.

"Eva," he said, startling her. "I'm sorry, I wonder if I might have a word with you in private." Eva looked around the office. A few people were going about their duties, but no one paid her any attention.

"Sure, I guess so." Eva walked into his office and he closed the door.

"Please sit. Make yourself comfortable." Eva sat on the edge of the proffered chair.

"Can I get you anything? Juice? Milk?"

"Water would be nice. Thank you."

"Are you sure? Milk or juice would be better for you…I mean, in your…condition."

"Juice, then. I'd like some juice."

"Excellent." The commandant walked to several pitchers filled with different colored liquids. "Grape, plum, or apple?"

"Grape, please."

He filled two glasses and brought one to her. "The fruits are brought up from Afghanistan each week. They're delicious. Try it." Eva drank her juice. It was good. "You know, I could get in trouble if they found out I gave you special consideration."

Eva abruptly pulled the glass from her lips and set it on the table.

"Oh, but no, don't worry. Drink up. Nothing will happen. It's our little secret. I just…I just wanted you to know how I could benefit you." Eva was confused, but went back to the tasty juice. The commandant sat on the edge of his desk and crossed his legs.

"Joseph, your husband, is a handsome man. Those blue eyes can be seen halfway across the compound." The commandant laughed.

Oh my God, Eva thought.

"Do you have anyone with light-colored eyes in your family?" the commandant asked.

"No, I don't think so."

"Hmmm…so there's only a fifty-fifty chance the baby will have blue eyes."

"I…I guess so."

"Have you considered how difficult it will be to raise a child in a place like this?" The commandant fluttered his hand and Eva nodded. "The food is limited. The weather is unpredictable, and there are no supplies like diapers or nursing bottles. I have to be frank. I don't think the chance of survival is very good for your baby. There, I've said it. What do you think?"

Eva paused, started to speak, but hesitated. The commandant took off his jacket and laid it across his desk.

"Don't be nervous. I'm not going to punish you for being honest. I want your opinion. I'm genuinely worried about you and your baby."

Eva set her empty cup down. "I think…I think I will do everything I can to protect my baby. People have had children under worse circumstances and they have survived."

The commandant frowned. "We have had babies die here before. Right here. It's not uncommon. Sometimes the mother dies because there isn't adequate medical care." The commandant sat into a chair next to Eva. He scooted close and took one of her hands in his. She marveled at how well-groomed his nails and skin were.

"Did Pepi speak to you about my proposal?"

Eva didn't say a word.

"Well, never mind. Here's what I propose. If you would let me adopt your baby, I will take you and Joseph out of here immediately to come live with me and my…partner. We'll provide the proper nutrition for you and register you with the best hospital in Alma-Ata. I will pay for all of it. You can have your baby born in a hospital with doctors and nurses on call to help you through the delivery. You can nurse the baby while you recover at my villa, with your husband. You will live in safety and comfort and your baby will be healthy."

"What do you mean?"

The commandant cleared his throat. "After you give me the baby, you will return here. That is fair, no?" Eva stared at him with shock.

"Oh, I'll make sure you get extra rations, clothing, a private cabin. Money?" The commandant crossed his hands. "I'll make your life much better. You will see. What do you say, hmm?"

"Well, I, uh—"

The commandant cut her off. "I tell you what, don't say anything now. Tell me later."

That evening, back in the cabin, Eva told Joseph and Pepi about the strange conversation with the commandant.

"Maybe he is really worried about the baby," Joseph said. "He does have a point—and we would be living in better conditions. Maybe we should think about it."

Pepi hit him so hard in the arm it knocked him off the chair. He laid on the floor, rubbing his sore arm while Pepi stood over him.

"Joseph Mitsen! I can't believe you would actually... ugh!" She kicked him in the leg. "That has to be the stupidest thing you've ever said."

Joseph alternated between rubbing his arm and thigh. "But we should think about it."

"I have thought about it." She kicked him again, and this time he deflected it. "We've thought about it and there's no way we're giving up our baby!"

"It's not your baby."

Pepi got on her knees and began punching Joseph. When he blocked his stomach, she hit him in the chest, and vice versa. All the time she yelled, punctuating the strikes with her forceful words. "I'm...the...baby's...aunt! I have...rights! I have a say so!"

Eva pulled Pepi off of Joseph. She was still swinging, her hair in disarray and Eva stood between them.

"I'm the father and I think we should consider what the commandant has to offer," Joseph said, smiling.

Pepi yelled and ran toward Joseph. Joseph grabbed Eva and held her like a shield against the circling Pepi. "Ha! You won't hit a pregnant woman," Joseph said.

"No, I won't, but when you let go of her I'm going to give you such a beating." Joseph stuck his tongue out at his sister. Pepi yelled and tried to reach around Eva.

"Pepi, stop!" Eva yelled.

"I'm going to knock those teeth out of your head!" Pepi screeched. She tried to side step Eva, but Joseph rotated his wife into the face of the storm.

"Stop it! Stop it, the both of you!" Eva's legs went weak and she fell back into Joseph's arms. Immediately the brawlers ceased their attack.

"Eva! Are you okay?" asked Pepi.

"We're sorry, Eva!" Joseph helped her to the bed.

"Can I get you something?" Pepi asked. Eva opened her eyes and smiled.

"I know how to play the sister too," Eva said. Pepi hit her with a pillow. They laughed.

"What's wrong with the commandant? He's always been nice to me."

"Of course he's nice to you. He likes you, but not in the way you think," Pepi said.

"What are you talking about?"

"Oh come on, you're not that blind."

"What?"

Pepi looked at Eva with a drawn expression. Eva raised her eyebrows and broke into a huge smile. She chewed her thumbnail.

"The commandant is a man lover. He's a homosexual, his life partner is another man," Pepi said to Joseph.

Joseph looked with his mouth wide open. "Nah, no way."
Eva and Pepi nodded their heads in unison.

———⌾⌾⌾———

Eva cried out as all the muscles in her abdomen stretched outward. "Time it!" the midwife, Leja, barked at Pepi. She tossed her old wristwatch at Pepi and returned her attention to Eva. "Breathe deeply, honey. You're doing great."

Eva sweated through a grimace. Her hair was matted in dark ringlets on her forehead.

"This isn't a very flattering position to be in," she growled.

"Once you start having kids, you're going to have a lot of strangers looking at your hoo-hoo. Might as well get used to it," Leja said. Eva cried out again.

"Five minutes," Pepi said.

"Hang in there, sweetie. Your cervix is dilating." Pepi squeezed Eva's hand.

"How's Joseph?" Eva asked between gulped breaths.

"He's fine. He looks a little nervous, but the boys are watching him. He's ready to hold his baby," Pepi said. She patted Eva's hand.

"I'm going as fast as I can." Eva cried out from another contraction.

"They're coming faster," Leja said

———⌾⌾⌾———

A healthy baby boy was born at 8:00 a.m. the following morning. Joseph sat next to Eva's bed, holding his son. The baby's tiny hand grasped Joseph's finger, and he leaned over and kissed a very tired Eva. She rolled her eyes up to look at him and slowly smiled.

"What's his name?" Pepi asked.

"Haim," Joseph said. "Haim means 'life' in Hebrew. HaShem has brought life in the midst of death."

Joseph entered the tiny cabin with a cloth bag. A gathering of people crowded the room to witness and celebrate Haim's briss, or circumcision.

"I looked all over," Joseph said.

"Did you find it?" Eva asked.

Joseph unwrapped a bottle of wine. Eva smiled.

On the eighth day, baby Haim was circumcised according to Hebrew law. Eva healed quickly and had soon returned to work at the office. The commandant remained aloof, still smarting from the rejection of his offer. Joseph made Eva a portable crib from a wicker laundry basket, which she kept next to her desk.

16

On May 8, 1945, Eva ran from the office shouting, "It's over! It's over! The war is over!" She burst into the cabin where Pepi and the baby were napping. "It's over, Pepi! We can go home! The war is OVER!" Eva yelled over Haim's cries.

"What? Are you sure?"

"I just heard it over the radio. The Germans have surrendered. "Stay with Haim—I've got to tell Joseph!" Eva exclaimed. She ran across the yard to the factory where Joseph was testing a switch. Eva nearly tackled him, sending machine parts into the air.

"What?"

"The war is over! I just heard it on the radio. We can go home!"

Joseph picked up his wife and cried. He twirled her around and then brought her down for a much needed kiss.

Joseph then turned to the other workers and cheered, "We can go home! The war is over!"

He threw his hat in the air, and the others gathered to see what was causing so much joy in such a bleak place.

As the news spread, the production lines were halted and people danced on the worktables.

That afternoon, the commandant called all prisoners to the flag.

"I know that you have heard that the war is over. I am just as excited as you, but I am unable to release you until I receive orders from the Kremlin. So I give you the joy of congratulations, but ask you to return to your duties and proceed with your work as if you have heard nothing. When I hear something, I will inform you of our next course of action, but not until then. Do I make myself understood?" A roll of grumbles and murmurs swept through the crowd. "Good, you may return to your tasks."

—⁕—

After several weeks, relief agencies sent vans to the camp. Doctors from the Red Cross climbed out and set up shop, examining all the inmates and outprocessing them to their countries of origin.

Joseph and his family stood in the line marked by a hand-written POLAND sign. One by one, each prisoner spoke to an official seated behind a desk. He took names, hometowns, next of kin, contacts, and other pertinent information.

Joseph felt lighter on his feet as he approached the desk. For the first time in years, he felt a semblance of relief.

"What's your destination?" the officer asked. Joseph laughed. He hadn't thought about where he wanted to go. He had been carted against his will to destinations thousands of miles away and now someone was asking where *he* wanted to go? Glorious!

"Sir?"

"Ah sorry," Joseph swallowed anxiously. "Rejowiec. Outside of Lublin."

The man typed some information on a card. "Sign here, and here." The man pointed to two blank lines on the card. Once Joseph signed his name, the official counter signed below it and stamped the card. "This is your temporary ID. Keep it with you at all times. If you lose it, you'll have to stay where you are and you won't be able to get any refugee services."

"Thank you very much." Joseph shook the man's hand, a smile stretching his worn face. The official was surprised at first, but Joseph's enthusiasm and infectious smile warmed his heart. Even Haim got a card.

Two weeks later, the transport trucks were loaded with refugees and taken to Alma-Ata's train station. The commandant never showed his face in the time leading up to the evacuation until Joseph and company got ready to board the truck.

"This is for Haim," the commandant said. "It's not much, but we wanted to give you something." The commandant handed Joseph a small black box. Eva slowly reached out for it and opened it. Inside was a small, silver locket in the shape of a heart on a silver chain. On the outside was an inscription, "WITH LOVE." On the inside was another inscription: "FROM UNCLE YANIN AND ANATOLA." On the other half was a picture of the two men smiling.

"Thank you," Eva said, her voice unsteady. "It's very nice." She kissed the commandant on the cheek and Joseph shook his hand. The commandant grabbed him for an uncomfortable moment and revealed a pained expression. Pleading. When he let him go, the commandant wiped away a tear. He pointed back to the office, and Joseph and Eva turned to see Anatola in the window, waving sheepishly. Eva took little Haim's hand and waved it back. Anatola blew a kiss and smiled. The family boarded the truck, and the commandant fluttered his hand in the air. He watched on until the truck turned the corner onto Main Street.

17

The voyage home took several weeks, yet their hearts remained exuberant throughout. The other liberated refugees from Poland on the train shared all they had—drinks, snacks, music. Prayers of gratitude were offered up as the Jewish refugees thanked HaShem for their freedom. Some of the passengers recognized others who had boarded the train along several stops bound for Poland, and rejoiced in their tearful reunions. Joseph couldn't help but notice, however, one very terrible reality—there were much fewer refugees on the way back to Poland than those who were taken out at the start of the war.

Joseph rationalized all of this as he looked out the window and watched the world pass by. Seated across from him was his beautiful wife and son. Son? He had been surrounded by death and loss, yet he was bringing home so much more life than he had started with. He watched Eva and the baby as they slept. Eva looked older now; not in a bad way, but more mature. The chubby cheeks of her youth were gone and she looked more distinguished. Her nose was more slender and defined. Small creases now ran down the corners of her eyes, forming shadows across her still creamy skin. He wondered how he must look to her. He certainly felt older. His body nagged and barked at him from the abuse he had taken in the past few years, but he no longer cared. He shifted in his seat and his back popped. It was so loud, the baby twisted in Eva's arms, then returned to his dreams. The peacefulness and hope Joseph felt for Haim was in direct contradiction to the raw stress they had been under for so long. Something in him was beginning to relax, yet a part of him continued to doubt, searching in vain for a deception.

He realized then that he never really fit the definition of a "refugee." A refugee is someone fleeing from political oppression. "Refugee" didn't convey the level of anguish or horror he had witnessed, or what he had overcome. They weren't refugees, they were *survivors*!

—◦◦◦—

No one waited to greet them at the Lublin platform. For whatever reason, Joseph had expected some sort of amenable gesture for the return of their neighbors and compatriots, but there was no one there. Had they all died? Had they all been captured? Could they have been the first to return? Still, surely someone had survived and was concerned with what had happened to the three of them. If anything else, just to share their story with someone to hear firsthand accounts of the other side of war. Someone must have wanted to know where they had been and what they had been through, but no. The porter helped unload their baggage without as much as a raised eyebrow.

The refugees stood on the platform in shock. The train puffed away and what should have been a feeling of elation was one of a disappointing anticlimax. Joseph, Eva, and Pepi all waved good-bye to the passengers they had shared a compartment with for the past few weeks, then gathered their belongings and started walking down quieted streets.

Their happy recollections of home quickly evaporated as the small group made their way through Lublin's quiet, cracked streets. Telltale signs of the war's fury were etched on the buildings and faces of the few inhabitants still alive. The fog of war often referred to the smoke drifting between battle lines, but here it meant something else. Where the streets once bustled with cheery men and women, folks now hurried to their destinations with downcast faces.

Russian patrols rode by periodically, but they paid little attention to Joseph's group as they passed through town, shocked at this nightmarish version of their home. Some buildings were boarded up, others were burned out. But the majority had been reduced to rubble. All signs of the Polish government had been removed or defaced. Joseph recognized the old church on the edge of town, one of the few buildings still fully intact. The castle had been burned and part of the roof was missing. Joseph caught a glimpse of a new structure in the distance—a tall brickwork chimney in what used to be an open field.

That shouldn't be there, he thought. He would have remembered seeing the sixty-five-foot tall tower that resembled the chimney at his father's tannery. Joseph led the others to it and as they approached, they could now see the barbed wire, guard house, and barracks. Apparently, the Germans had built a concentration camp on Lublin's doorstep. A chill ran down Joseph's spine as he realized what had caused the horror in the faces of those he passed in the streets of Lublin.

Joseph was drawn to the front gate. A thread pulled him closer and closer, even though his mind was screaming for him to run away.

Take Haim and run as far away from this place as possible!

But Joseph couldn't resist the pull. He walked straight up to Russian soldiers guarding the front gate.

Eva wanted to follow, but Pepi pulled the sleeve of her blouse and stopped her. As Joseph approached, a Russian soldier flicked his cigarette butt away, and swung his machine gun around in Joseph's direction.

"Hey Jew! You're not allowed in here."

Joseph didn't even register the soldier's warning.

"Stop! Turn around or I'll shoot. I mean it! I'll kill you dead in front of your family!"

Joseph kept his eyes on the chimney and walked forward until he ran into the barrel of the machine gun. Joseph rubbed his face and looked down. He looked back up with a puzzled expression and gazed blankly into the guard's eyes. But something drew his attention upward. The tower summoned him.

The chimney. What was the chimney used for?

He gently pushed through the checkpoint, ignoring the guard entirely. The guard watched him pass through and scratched the back of his head.

"You're a big pussy," his fellow guard said.

"Shut up."

Joseph walked involuntarily through the grounds of the camp, where men in uniforms mulled around him and a backhoe dug a giant pit. The smell of putrid flesh hovered over the field like heavy smoke. The workers all wore masks, but Joseph could hear their muffled moans floating all around him; smooth seams of swirling ethereal fabric. Joseph could see the tortured souls of the dead wandering about, looking for something. He heard their cries and saw the pained expressions of their suffering.

"Thousands…thousands…thousands. They are all gone. Thousands," Joseph mumbled over and over.

He approached the looming chimney. It looked like a giant cannon, as though the Nazis were trying to shoot heaven itself. Joseph stopped in front of a huge cast iron door and placed his hand on the metal. It was still warm. After a moment's hesitation, he lifted the heavy latch and pulled the door open. It cried and squealed, fighting to keep its secrets hidden. A thin waft of moist smoke rolled out and up. He looked into the gaping maw at the blackness that retreated as the sunlight crept inward. Joseph stood in the doorway and gazed into the giant black furnace. His eyes passed over unfamiliar shapes sticking out of the ashes. Slowly, they coalesced into ribs and skulls. He reached out and grabbed a handful of ash, then slowly opened his hands and let the ash blow through his fingers, away on the wind.

He began sobbing, deep, uncontrollable convulsions of grief. He dropped to his knees with his fists to his eyes. Ashes and tears mixed, then ran down his cheeks. It was now clear—crystal clear what had happened here. He understood their horror. He understood their pain.

He would have felt the same had he stayed. He felt the pressure of the lost souls around him. They were consoling him. It wasn't his fault. He did what he could, he saved those he could. Even *they* were proud of him.

Joseph sat in the dust and wept. Two guards lifted him by the arms like a limp bag of flour and escorted him back to the gate. Pepi, Eva, and Haim waited for him, concerned. Eva hugged him, sharing the ashes on his cheek; a purification that echoed back to covering one's self in sack cloth and ashes. They huddled together while the Russian cleanup crew drifted in slow motion around them. It began to rain.

They started to walk to their home town of Rejowiec.

—◦◦◦—

The tannery was quiet. All the windows were broken with boards nailed over the lower rows. The big, double metal doors at the main entrance were chained and padlocked. "ZYD" (Jew) was spray-painted in big letters on the metal sign.

Eva sat at the side of the building and nursed Haim as Joseph and Pepi crawled through the broken window. Pigeons flew through the rafters, stirring eddies of dust and feathers in golden shafts of light. The machines had been removed and hundreds of bolts protruded from the concrete. The large bleaching vats and tanks were gone. Wires and debris were scattered across the floor.

They climbed the metal staircase to the second floor offices and passed several opened office doors. Most of the chairs and desks were gone. At the end of the hall, his father's name had been scratched off the door. Joseph pushed it open, and a pigeon darted by, startling them. Papers were strewn about all over the floor. His father's cash box lay open and empty, and his safe was missing entirely. Log books, notes, schedules, and account records were thrown carelessly about.

Joseph found one of his father's favorite fountain pens and put it in his pocket. He lifted a stack of magazines and newspapers, and a black pocket memo pad fell out. Joseph recognized it immediately. His father had always kept it with him. Inside were the names, addresses, and phone numbers of all his father's suppliers and clients. Joseph felt a twinge in his spirit. It could have been a draft through one of the shattered windows, or maybe his mind was playing tricks on him, but he felt as if he was *supposed* to have found the book.

Joseph turned to Pepi and handed her the little black book. She opened it and ran her fingers over her father's curly queue handwriting, as if she could touch him through the pages. At the back of the cabinet, pushed up against the wall, they found their father's siddur. After searching a little longer, they went back downstairs and joined Eva and Haim outside.

—◈◈◈—

Joseph stood outside his house and stared. It was strange to see it again. Someone had kept the lawn nice and cut. It had a new coat of white paint and the wooden steps and railing had been replaced. He walked up, opened the door, and went in. Pepi and the rest trailed behind. The furniture in the front room had been moved out, replaced with entirely new furniture. Joseph set his bag down with a thump and heard a dog bark and scamper down the stairs. It yipped from the bottom stair through the banister.

"Mama!" Joseph yelled up the stairs. He heard heavy feet thump their way down the hallway. An older woman carefully looked around the edge of the banister, saw Joseph and started screaming. "Alek! Alek!" She stomped her feet. "Alek!"

The backdoor opened and closed. A man wearing a thick coat and a fur hat with curious rabbit ear flaps walked through the kitchen carrying a hammer.

"What is it? I was just fixing the—"

Alek stopped short when he saw Joseph.

"What are you doing in my house?" he asked.

"Your house? This is *my* house. Who are you?" Joseph replied.

"I bought this house fair and square, now get out!" Alek stepped forward and lifted the hammer in a threatening manner.

"You're the one who's going to leave."

Joseph stood in front of the stranger, but Eva grabbed Joseph's arm and said, "Stop, Joseph, things have changed. Let's go. There's another way to do this." The older woman snapped up her dog and petted it to quiet it down. It continued to growl in her arms. Joseph looked at her and then back at Alek.

"This isn't right. This is *my* home. My family has lived here for sixty years." Joseph walked right up to the man with a clenched jaw and the old woman screamed. Alek raised his hammer, ready to strike, but Joseph maintained his gaze into the man's eyes. The hammer trembled in

Alek's hand, and Joseph snatched the hat off Alek's head. Alek cringed.

"This is my papa's hat," he said evenly. He shook the hat at the man. "We'll be back. Start packing." Joseph turned and shoved the hat on his head. The little dog started barking again.

"Shut up!" Joseph yelled at the dog. It jumped from the woman's arms and ran up the stairs to hide.

Joseph and the others walked onto the porch, slamming the door behind them.

"They can't do this," he yelled.

"I know, I know. Let's head to Mayor Zikowski's office. If he's still there, he'll straighten everything out," Eva said.

Pepi and Eva's houses were also occupied by strangers. Seems times had indeed changed. They headed for town, walking down Rejowiec's Main Street. Repair work was being done on some buildings, while others were being demolished. The mayor's office had scaffolding across the entrance, where men were installing new windows.

Plastic covered the furniture as the interior was being prepped for a fresh coat of paint. Mayor Zikowski's office was down a long hallway toward the back of the building. Eva opened the large wooden door and immediately noticed a new brass plaque, yet to be engraved. Inside the room, Joel, her associate from the tax collector's office, sat behind the mayor's desk, dictating a message to a young secretary.

"Eva?" Joel asked, unsure. He stood up with a startled look.

"Joel?"

"You're back!"

"Where's the mayor?"

Joel didn't answer immediately. When he did, he held his head low. "So many things have changed."

"What's going on?"

"Things are different now."

Eva handed Haim to Pepi, then walked up to Joel and grabbed his shirt with two fists.

"You're right things have changed! Strangers are living in our houses," Eva started, shaking Joel. "We've been through hell and just returned to find out that Mayor Zikowski has sold our property out from under us!" Eva pushed Joel backward who tripped over his chair and landed on his back on the floor. Eva grabbed the chair and effortlessly flung it out of the way. The secretary screamed as Eva grabbed Joel by the collar.

"I want some answers! I want—"

Joseph grabbed Eva by the arm and pulled her off Joel. "Let me go!" Eva struggled and boxed Joseph on the ear.

"Eva!" Joseph yelled. Eva went limp at the sound of his voice, then looked up at Joseph's calm blue eyes. She fell into his arms and cried, breathing deeply. Joseph massaged his ringing ear.

"What's going on, Joel? Where's the mayor?" Joseph asked.

"I...I'm the mayor," Joel said. Eva darted a look at Joel with such hatred that Joel had to step behind the secretary, using her as a shield. "It's true! I'm the mayor."

Joseph held Eva tightly to keep her from advancing on Joel.

"Joseph, let me go," she said calmly. Joseph relaxed his grip.

"Leave him alone," Joseph said. He turned to Joel. "Where is he? What happened to him?"

"The Germans. They…crucified…him. Out there." Eva, Pepi, and Joseph stared in disbelief. "Like I said, things have changed. You've been gone for years. We thought you were dead."

"Well, we're not dead, and we want our homes back," Pepi said. "We have deeds. We also have records of ownership right here in this office."

"The records were all burned by the Nazis," Joel said. He stammered on about how the Nazis had broken in and torn everything up. While it was true that the Nazis had carved a path of destruction through Poland, the local Poles had also used it as an excuse to settle an old hatred they carried against the Jews, which still exists today. They assisted the cruelty of the Nazis by stealing or destroying Jewish businesses, schools, and homes. The atrocities of the war never ended. The Nazis were a convenient scapegoat for many Poles' anti-Semitic attitudes.

A crowd of people had gathered outside the town hall. Pepi looked out the window.

"Joseph, I think we have trouble," she said.

"Hey, Jew, come on out here! We want to talk to you!" a man's voice yelled through the glass. Joseph went to the window and looked out. The men brandished weapons— pitch forks, shovels, batons. Joseph recognized some of them.

"We've got to go," Joseph said. Eva glared at Joel who ducked back behind the secretary. Joseph walked out first and stood on the porch facing the town square.

"You should have never come back, Jew!" a man yelled.

"They should've killed you along with the others," another screamed.

"We don't want you here!"

"You'd better leave or we'll kill you!"

"Yeah!" the crowd agreed in unison.

Joseph pulled Eva and Haim close behind him, followed by Pepi. He boldly descended the steps to the pavement and stood in front of the armed men with Haim in his arms. He stared out at them with a set jaw and yelled, "Back off!"

The men, startled, swiftly glanced at each other, then parted and opened a path through the middle of them. They said nothing, but watched with suspicion as Joseph and his family walked across the square with heads held high. They turned down the main street and out of town— the same street he had helped people to escape.

As they reached the outskirts of Lublin, a truck pulled up alongside them. Joseph stopped.

"Joseph! Joseph!"

Joseph turned and set his bags down. A man jumped from the cab of the truck and came around the front. David, his old work buddy, ran up and hugged Joseph.

"They told me you were back! Hi, Eva, Pepi."

"Hi, David!" Pepi said, embracing him tightly.

"I heard what happened. We thought you were dead."

"Almost."

"Is this your…son?" David asked as he looked at the bundle in Eva's arms.

"This is a miniature Joseph," Eva said. She brushed a fly away. Haim giggled.

"Rabbi Rozenfeld would have been—" David stopped short when he realized Eva had lost all color in her face. "You haven't heard?"

"No," Eva said.

"He was killed. I'm sorry Eva."

Eva gasped. "When?"

"The night after you left. The Germans—they came and…and they killed most of the older or sick Jews. The rest they sent to Lublin." Eva lost her balance as her knees gave way. Joseph grabbed her for support.

David turned to Joseph and said in a low voice, "They also sent your father, mom, and sister to Lublin. I saw them being escorted by a German detachment. I heard your brother Jacob went to the death camp in Auschwitz, and your kid brother was shot in bed. He was in a cast with a broken leg when the Germans came here."

Joseph darted his eyes downward. He was angry. He already knew in his heart that his parents, siblings, and those who were left behind didn't make it, but it seemed cruel to hear about it so directly, so informally, so coldly. When a soldier is killed in action, there is a process, an official respect associated with the job. Joseph protected this community. He had warned them and even managed to save some. He could have saved more. Joseph surprised himself with his own realization…the Poles here were happy the Germans invaded. They hated the Jews and this gave them all the excuse they needed to clean out the Jews once and for all. They were no better than the Nazis, at least some of them.

"And how did you manage to evade the death camps?" Joseph asked David. "You're Jewish. Why weren't you in Lublin, too?"

"I, uh…I hid. I ran to my uncle's house. They didn't find me."

"Where's your uncle?"

"They took him."

"So you kept the house, the property, and his truck? Good for you."

"It's not like that."

"Oh really? I didn't see the crowd threatening you."

"They don't know."

"They don't know what?"

"That I'm Jewish."

Joseph narrowed his eyes. He could feel the rage boiling inside of him. "Ah, so if I told them, your little secret would come unfurled and you'd be run out of town too."

"Yes. You're right."

Joseph looked at David for a moment, then shook his head. He started walking again and left David standing there.

"I knew you'd be back!" David yelled.

Joseph stopped. "I knew it. Do you know how much I worried about what I would say when I saw you again?"

David approached Joseph. "Of all the people in all this death and destruction, I knew you'd be back. I knew they couldn't kill you. It's not some magic formula, it's not even luck, it's because you always do the right thing and HaShem blesses you for it. I was never like that. I'm a coward. I was jealous of you. The way people looked up to you. When you got called away to the army, I was glad. Now I could get your job. I might've even had a chance with Eva, but I couldn't even bring myself to ask her out. Nothing changed for me. Yet your father put up a picture of you in the lobby and even read the letters you sent to the employees. And your relationship with Eva grew stronger. It didn't matter what happened, you were always blessed!" David's voice grew thick, and tears began streaming down his face.

"I stayed in that house and hid under a bed when they came to get me. I heard my uncle's screams as they beat him, asking where the rest of the family was, but he never told. Do you know what hell I've been through? I thought about killing myself. I even had the gun pointed to my head, but I couldn't pull the trigger. I was afraid of the pain."

Joseph narrowed the gap that separated the two of them. With a swift punch, he popped his old friend right between his teary eyes. David stumbled back.

"*That* is for turning on your heritage and your family."

Joseph clocked him in the cheek this time, now sending David reeling on his back. "That was for betraying our friendship. I trusted you!" David lay on the ground, gasping for breath. Joseph looked down at the pathetic creature, now sobbing uncontrollably in a fetal position. He hesitated, then extended his hand to help him up. David looked up, a trickle of blood running out of the corner of his mouth. Joseph's face showed anger.

"I forgive you," he said. "Give us a ride to Lublin, will you?"

David slowly nodded, incredulous, then cautiously took Joseph's hand and got to his feet.

———✦———

They made the drive back to Lublin mostly in silence. David hardly looked away from the road. His face had swelled where Joseph had smacked him, and now and then, he'd spit a dark red liquid out the window. Joseph looked at him and smiled, then turned to the window to watch the familiar countryside pass them by. The land hadn't changed at all, but the people had. The same farms, intersections, streams, hills, and valleys, all laid out as if nothing had changed at all. *It's just dirt*, he thought. *How could something so simple cause so many problems?*

———✦———

Joseph, Eva, and Pepi stood outside the Majdanek concentration camp. The guards wouldn't let them go in, and were much more reactive to Joseph's attempts to get through. So Joseph opened his father's prayer book at the front gate and read.

"Blessed are you, Lord our God, King of the universe, who causes the bonds of sleep to fall upon my eyes and slumber upon my eyelids and who gives light to the apple of my eye. May it be your will, Lord my God and God my Fathers, to let me lie down in peace and to raise…" Tears were streaming down his face.

Joseph closed his father's siddur and crossed his hands. He looked at the fence surrounding the gate. People had left photos of loved ones lost, and a Star of David made of cardboard, by a child, was covered with glitter and bouquets of roses. They weren't the only survivors. Others had lost family members, all across Europe. There were others who felt the same way Joseph, Pepi, and Eva did, who were suffering still from the ongoing persecution. Joseph would find these survivors. He would join with them to rebuild their lives. Together they could get through this. Together they could give each other emotional support.

The three headed off to the refugee office printed on the back of their ID cards. There they would be able to get some answers.

———✤———

"We're relocating all Jewish families to Wroclaw," the officer said.

"Where?" Joseph asked.

"Wroclaw, in the old German territory. It used to be called Breslau. It's a big city and you can find work there and a place to live."

The officer gave them train tickets, food coupons, and a little money then sent them to the nearest shelter. They spent an uneasy night, and then boarded the next train to Wroclaw. The stress from the trip was taking its toll and they all slept most of the way. Even little Haim was exhausted. When they got to the refugee office in Wroclaw, the officer took their information and assigned them an apartment in one of many identical block houses that lined the southern part of the city. After getting lost, they finally found their street—21 Mickewica Street.

"Seventeen, nineteen, twenty-one—That's us," Joseph said. The three looked up at a plain, four-story brick building. "203, up the stairs. It should be a two-bedroom apartment," said Joseph.

"It will do for now," Eva said. She kissed Joseph on the cheek. "It's ours and it's safe." She put her things down and set Haim in his basket on the floor. Pepi called out from the kitchen. "I found some cleaning supplies and a scrub pad. Nope, hold on. Dead rat, not a scrub pad."

A shirtless young man showed up in the doorway. "Hallo, neighbors!" he shouted. "Welcome to Wroclaw!" He staggered in with an unlit cigarette clinging to his lip. It bobbled as he spoke.

"My name is Ritz and my girlfriend, Hilda is"—Ritz turned around like he had lost something—"passed out. I'll bring her over to meet you sometime." Pepi walked out of the kitchen with a dead rat dangling by the tail.

"Oh!" exclaimed Ritz. "You found Charlie. I wondered where he went! Haven't seen 'im in weeks." Ritz turned around and squinted with one eye open and pointed across the hallway. "My apartment is right over there."

"Joseph, Eva, and Pepi, and Haim," Joseph said, pointing to each member of his ensemble.

Ritz shook Joseph's hand, then hugged Eva and Pepi and bent over to look at Haim. "Cute lil' bugger. Haim… Ha-im. You must be Jewish! Even better. My real name is Hans, but everyone calls me Ritz, seeing as my favorite song is, 'Putting On the Ritz.' My friends are unstable."

"We do need some food," Eva said.

"And a bed and blankets and dishes and chairs and…a scrub brush," said Pepi.

"Come, Joseph, I will take you to the stores," said Ritz.

———⟊⟊⟊———

Joseph and Ritz walked through several winding blocks. He took him through the stores district, furniture district, and finally through the market. Along the way, several pedestrians recognized Ritz and he introduced Joseph to them. Joseph wasn't used to city life—he had grown up in a more rural and isolated community. Even though Ritz was about his same age, Joseph felt old and inexperienced in Ritz's carefree attitude. He didn't realize it at the time, but Ritz was the perfect tonic to pull Joseph out of his funk. He was shy at first, but Ritz taught Joseph to relax.

Soon Joseph was making small talk with people he had never met before. He copied the laidback style in which Ritz composed himself. He watched as Ritz would touch a person on the shoulder, double squeezed a hand shake or looked straight into a person's eyes with a disarming smile. People genuinely were happy to see Ritz. Joseph thought this might help him overcome his shyness of being in a new city, but he soon discovered something more important. Ritz was the consummate businessman.

Ritz would ask Joseph what he needed, then he would go to a shopkeeper and do his little routine, always coming out with a discounted price, better service, or even free delivery, and it worked every time.

By the time the men got back, many of the items they bought had already been delivered. Haim was sleeping in a new crib and the apartment was filled with the smell of cooking food. Ritz helped unload the groceries.

"Thank you for your help," Joseph said.

"Don't mention it. We've all got to look out for each other," Ritz said as he closed the door behind him.

The following day was warmer. Joseph decided to honor HaShem and went out in search of a synagogue. Joseph wore his yarmulke as he walked the same streets he had walked the day before. People he had met the day before with Ritz now avoided him and muttered racial epithets. "Dirty Jew," an older man yelled from his shop door. Everywhere Joseph went, he felt the hatred of the citizens. *All of this is because I am wearing a yarmulke?* The few people who would speak to him didn't know of any synagogue in Wroclaw. Disheartened, he headed home.

As he walked home, he noticed an old man wearing a floppy cap. Joseph wouldn't have thought much of it, except he could see the edge of a woven yarmulke sticking out from under it.

"Excuse me," Joseph said, rushing up to the man. He gently touched him on the back to get his attention. When the man turned and saw Joseph's yarmulke, he looked alarmed and glanced quickly around. He pulled Joseph into a nearby alley.

"The young have to be more…discreet in the city," the man said.

"Why?"

"Because Jews are still persecuted here."

"But the war is over. I have nothing to be ashamed of."

"It has always been like this. If you want trouble, mind up and walk around with that." The man pointed to Joseph's yarmulke. "Then see what happens."

"I've already run into it."

"Then you know what I mean. You should take it off when you go out. At least hide it under a hat." The man took his hat off, revealing a yarmulke. "What can I help you with?"

"I'm looking for a synagogue."

The man laughed. "You won't find one. You think they are listed in some book? HaShem has blessed you by leading you to me." The man looked around. He spoke in a quiet voice and leaned in close to Joseph. "I know where one is. It's very secret, so we don't have problems."

"I understand."

"There is a shul at 30 Mickewica Street, on the second floor. There's no numbers on the door."

"Mickewica? That's across the street from us."

"I told you HaShem has blessed you!" The man shook Joseph's hand and smiled. "So I'll see you there for Shabbos?"

"I wouldn't miss it."

"Good. Nice meeting you." The man turned and walked away, whistling. Joseph looked on at the retreating man.

"What's your name?" Joseph called out. The man only waved with his back toward him and kept on walking. Joseph put his yarmulke in his pocket and walked home. No one even noticed him the rest of the way back.

Joseph told Eva and Pepi about the shul across the street. They didn't believe him, but warned him to be careful as he went to investigate. 30 Mickewica Street looked virtually the same as his own apartment building. A nondescript door opened to a hall and staircase, but unlike his building, the second floor was only divided into two apartments. One door was labeled 201, so he knocked on the door with no number. No one answered. He knocked again and heard footsteps. A peephole slid open.

"Yes?" a man asked in a squeaky voice.

"I was told there was a synagogue here."

"Who told you that?"

"Well, the man didn't give me his name. He just gave me the address."

"What's your name?"

"Joseph Mitsen."

"Come closer." Joseph leaned toward the door.

"A blue-eyed Jew? I don't think so." The peephole slammed shut. Joseph knocked again, waited, and then knocked again.

"You are persistent, I'll give you that. Now what do you *really* want?"

"I told you, I'm looking for a synagogue so my family and I can worship. I'm a Jew. We were taken to the Russian labor camps during the war. My family was killed at Majdanek in Lublin."

The peephole slid shut, and the door was opened just a crack. An old man looked at Joseph and made a sour face. He was thin with an arched back and thin, silver hair. He sported a full beard and bushy eyebrows that looked like they might crawl away on their own. Joseph noticed a tallit draped over his shoulder.

"Please come in." He swung the door open wide. "We've had problems here before, so I hope you will forgive my suspicious nature. We have to take precautions."

Joseph entered. "I understand." He followed the man down a narrow hallway that opened into a beautifully decorated room. The altar was adorned with expensive, colorful fabrics, and a golden Star of David was emblazoned on a plaque. The Torah Ark—the container containing the Torah scroll—was covered with palm trees and pomegranates. A silver menorah sat on a beautifully carved table of dark wood.

Joseph was speechless. He stopped to take it all in.

"It's amazing," he said.

"Welcome to my shul. My name is Rabbi Shlomo." The rabbi extended a hand and Joseph noticed he was missing a pinky. Joseph shook it. "I, too, was in a camp," Rabbi Shlomo said grimly. He pulled up his sleeve and turned his forearm over. Several numbers were tattooed on his wrist. Joseph told him about his adventures and his family miracles that had brought them to the apartment across the street.

"We have fifteen families that worship here. Some are survivors like us. Everyone has lost someone they loved to the brutalities of the war. You will meet them all when you come Friday night for Sabbath."

An older woman entered with a tray with coffee and baked rolls. Joseph was struck by her beauty. She displayed class and grace, despite her age.

"This is the love of my life, Rachel," said the rabbi. "She's the reason I was able to survive the camp. Whenever I thought about giving up, I just thought about her and my spirit was lifted. She was a doctor, you know? Smart *and* beautiful." Rachel served the coffee and set the tray down.

"So what are you going to do for work?"

"I used to work for my father's tannery, but I guess I'll have to find a different job."

"Hmm, jobs are hard to come by, especially for Jews." Rabbi Shlomo looked at his wife. "Rachel, what were you telling me about the new business committee?"

Rachel hesitated in front of Joseph. "The Polish government is encouraging growth in private businesses. The communists want to show that they can be good entrepreneurs as well. They were just speaking about it last week, inviting new applicants to register at their local business console."

"Have you thought about opening up your own business?"

"I haven't really thought about it, but it's not a bad idea," Joseph said.

"With HaShem's blessing, I have no doubt that you would be successful."

The rabbi took a sip of coffee and leaned toward Joseph. "I will pray for you tonight and you will see."

"I can get the application from work tomorrow," Rachel said.

"That would be wonderful."

They spoke for a little while longer and Joseph thanked the rabbi for his time. As he crossed the street to his own building, his heart grew lighter. He nearly floated across the street, thanking HaShem for his blessing.

⟞◦∾◦⟝

Joseph told Eva and Pepi that he had found a synagogue and that the rabbi's wife might be able to help him start a business.

"Start a business?" Eva asked. "Shouldn't you worry about finding a job first?" She walked over to him and put her arm around him. "I'm glad you're excited. It's wonderful to see the fire in your eyes again, but I just don't understand."

Joseph turned and held her hands. "Think about it," he said. "Who's going to hire a Jew? Even if I could hide who I am and get hired, once they find out, that would be the end of it. The stipend that the refugee office gives us can barely feed us."

"But *you* opening a business?" Pepi asked.

"Why not? Papa did and he did very well."

"*That* was before the war. *That* was when our neighbors at least acted like they liked us. And *that* was Papa. Not you." Pepi turned from the window. "Have you ever even run a business before?"

"I watched over it when he took trips."

"You went upstairs, closed the door to the office, and fell asleep in Papa's chair."

"That was only once and I was sick. You've never run a business either, Pepi."

"Who do you think helped him set up the books?" Pepi asked.

"I don't know. I was only a kid when he started the tannery."

"I know. While you were out playing cops and robbers, I was organizing Papa's books."

"Okay, okay. You're smart. You seem to have all the answers. What do you think I should do? Huh?"

"I think…"

"Yeah?"

"I think you should start a business. Why not? You've got nothing to lose and then when it all goes up in flames, you'll come crawling back and I'll watch you get a real job."

Joseph curled his lip and mocked Pepi.

"What would your business sell?" Eva asked.

"*A fashion store?*"

"In Wroclaw?"

"What should we call it? Joseph's Styles?"

"No, no. Polish Princess." This was met with laughter.

Joseph sat with a single brow under a dark cloud. "Are you two done?"

"So what makes you think you could make this business successful?" Pepi asked.

Joseph pulled his father's black address book from his pocket and held it up. He waved it at Pepi and she rolled her eyes.

"I didn't see any clothing stores nearby."

"Especially ones that carry leather goods."

"Have you seen how the German women dress?"

"I thought we were old-fashioned in Rejowiec."

"Do you remember that one store that would custom dye leather to match your dress?"

"Yes, I had a pair of shoes dyed, and a purse."

The ladies paused and turned on cue to look at Joseph bouncing Haim on his knee. Then they looked at each other.

"Honey, so…if you were thinking of doing this, how would you go about doing it?" Eva said. "I'm sorry, we were just having a little fun."

Joseph explained how he would use his father's old contacts and suppliers for the raw materials and specialty items. He would find a building for a storefront and have Jewish refugees sew or make the items to be sold. He told them how the rabbi's wife was going to get the information for a business permit from the Polish government.

Late the following day, someone knocked at the apartment door. It was the rabbi. He brought a welcome basket of freshly baked bread and the application that

Rachel retrieved from work. Eva made him a cup of hot tea.

"You have to fill out the application and take it to a *naczelnik*, or city official. He will be your guide through all the paperwork to get the necessary stamps and signatures for your business permit. He's like your advocate lawyer. If he likes you and thinks your business is profitable, he will put tremendous effort behind securing your permit."

"And if he doesn't like me?" Joseph asked.

"Then you have to give him some incentives."

"A bribe?"

"Precisely."

"How much of a bribe?"

"Well there's the cash bribe and…"

"There's more?"

"Well, it's customary to offer a percentage of the profits."

"He takes the profits too? How much?"

"A friend of mine pays 40 percent."

"So what are we supposed to live on? How are we supposed to grow?"

"Well, that's why I said he is your advocate. As your business grows, he becomes more indispensable by securing more government resources, including suppliers, shippers, marketing, and protection for your trade in a specific area."

"He's a crook," said Joseph flatly.

"You need to be aware of how you speak about the officials. They carry the respect of the people."

"You mean they keep the people in fear."

"That may be, but if you want to succeed you must heed my advice. Maybe this isn't such a great idea. The government is different now and—"

Eva interrupted. "It's fine. I'm sure Joseph will be a darling and everything will work out fine."

The rabbi stood. "Okay, okay. I'll leave the application with you. The address is on the back."

"How much of a cash bribe should I take?"

"Two thousand zloty should be a good start."

"Two thousand? Are you kidding? I—That salary is for ten months' work."

"That will be fine; we'll get the money for our *naczelnik*," Eva said. She put her hand on Joseph's shoulder in a comforting gesture.

"Very well. His name is Janusz Kozlowski."

"Thank you, Rabbi Shlomo," said Eva. "We'll keep you informed."

The rabbi placed his hand on Joseph's shoulder and said, "I pray HaShem blesses you in starting your business; that He gives you the words to inspire Advocate Kozlowski. Amen."

Eva said, "Amen," but Joseph didn't. The rabbi cocked an eyebrow. Eva elbowed Joseph.

"Ah-men," he grunted.

Eva opened the door for the rabbi, and just as he was about to leave he turned and said, "Don't forget—we start Shabbos prayers at 6:15 tonight."

"We'll be there," Eva said.

"Thank you, Rabbi," Joseph said breathlessly.

After the rabbi left, Joseph took a seat. "We'll never make any profit if we have to give it all away to the government's cronies. What happened to taxes? Isn't that enough? Why don't they just put a man at the checkout to collect the cash directly from the customers!"

"Joseph—" Eva started.

"Forty percent! Is he kidding? That's ridiculous! It's highway robbery! It's insanity! They're all a bunch of criminals! I ought to give Naczelnik a swift kick in the seat of his pants!" Joseph panted, his face red. Eva calmly stepped toward Joseph and took the application from his hand.

"That's exactly why you're not going."

"What?"

"I am."

"You!"

"Me. Why not?"

"You? You're…you're a woman."

"And I'm an attractive woman."

"Yes, but—"

"And I know how to get what I want. I got you, didn't I?"

"Yes, but—"

"But nothing! If you go to the meeting, you're going to blow the opportunity before it starts. And he's a Naczelnik."

"Who is?"

"The man I'm going to see. It's a title that deserves respect, which I always give."

"Like when you nearly took Joel's head off? He's probably still having nightmares."

"He deserved that."

Joseph rubbed his ear where Eva had smacked him in the mayor's office. "But it was my idea to start a business."

"It was, but now it's *our* idea, and you need my help."

"But—"

Eva flashed her eyes and Joseph visibly shrank.

"I didn't tell you how to be a soldier. I didn't tell you how to do your job at the tannery, and I won't tell you how to run your business. But I will tell you that I know how to deal with bureaucrats better than you. I've had plenty of experience negotiating with them in Rejowiec and Lublin, and I know I can do this."

Joseph looked at her. Her eyes were ablaze with determination. Her hair was mussed and framed her head like a mane. Her breasts quivered at her excitement. Joseph quickly realized that she had overwhelmed him with lustful passion. Eva had never stood up to him like this before. He scooped her up and carried her to their room.

The next morning Eva dressed in the only decent dress she owned, put on a little makeup borrowed from Pepi, and slipped on Pepi's shoes. She kissed Joseph good-bye, took their only savings and headed out the door with the completed application. Eva stirred uncomfortably. Naczelnik Janusz Kozlowski had given her directions to his personal residence. He seemed genuine enough and was surprised when Eva brought him the application. He was even more surprised when he realized that she was negotiating terms for starting a business.

"We can't give you 40 percent of the profits yet. We're just starting up and it would stagnate growth," Eva said.

"Don't think that all goes to me," Janusz said. "I don't get my cut until the taxes and fees have been paid. I only make 15 percent by the time it gets to me."

"There's no way we can pay you directly?"

"No. That would be difficult."

"But there is a way?"

"Well, maybe. If...if I sponsored the business."

"What do you mean?"

"If became a silent partner."

"Oh."

"Then I would handle the transactions for myself. Political officers have certain benefits."

"No taxes or permits?" Eva said.

"Let's just say they are reduced."

"I'll bring you 20 percent of the profits each month in cash."

"Cash? Hmm..." Janusz paced the floor and stopped. He turned. "You sure he'll make money?"

Eva nodded.

"Thirty percent," he said.

"Let's split the difference. Twenty-five percent."

Janusz thought for a moment, then smiled. "Twenty-five percent then."

Janusz typed a modified application and added his name to the document. He signed it and pulled a copy apart for Eva. "Give this to Joseph. He'll be able to rent business space with the document. Come back in a week and I'll have your permit."

"Thank you," Eva said.

18

Joseph found a small storefront that had once been a tailor in Wroclaw's center, just two kilometers from his apartment. The sign on the storefront said LEATHER GOODS in big block letters. He hired Jews from the synagogue to make purses, belts, shoes, boots, wallets, jackets, and vests. He ordered supplies from the companies and individuals in his father's little book.

———

Two ladies opened the front door to the store and entered. They were admiring a purse trimmed with blue leather and shiny brass buckles.

"I've never seen anything like it."

"It's beautiful."

A young man dressed in a neat pressed shirt stepped up to the women. "Can I help you?" he asked.

"Where do these come from, young man?"

"We make them…here."

"You're kidding! I thought these had to be imported. They look so…luxurious."

"Thank you."

"How much is this bag?"

"Twenty zloty."

"Twenty? Do you have one in green?"

"I think so. Let me check in the back."

The man walked to the back. Several women were busy stitching leather goods together while Joseph and some men cut patterns.

"Do we have any green in the Parisian?"

"I can make one if they can wait a little bit," an elderly woman said.

The young man went back to the sales floor. The ladies were surprised by the length the store would go to fill a request. When the green purse was brought to the counter, the lady set the blue one next to it.

"I'll put the blue one up for you."

"No, you won't. I want both of them. I had to carry it around to keep other people from buying it. When will you have more inventory?"

"We should be restocked by next Tuesday."

The women paid for the purses and promised to come again. The next Tuesday, a dozen women waited outside in a cold breeze for the store to open. When Joseph opened the door, they rushed inside and quickly snapped up the trendy handmade leather goods. Joseph had to officiate a tug-of-war between two babushkas over a sequined belt. He was only able to stop the dispute after promising to make the other woman a matching belt.

The store offered unique fashion accessories in an area where creativity and expression had been shunned and repressed. Now that the war was over, people were ready to put the past behind them. There was a dividing line—everything in the past was part of the old generation, and everything thereafter was filled with youthful anticipation. There were practical reasons as well. With the loss of so many men on both sides, there were fewer bachelors for the picking, yet many more girls were reaching maturity and looking for mates. This bred fierce competition and women were looking for anything that would set them apart from the herd. Fashion filled that need.

Word spread and the local leather suppliers were not able to keep up with demand. Joseph was forced to leave the city to look for suppliers that could fill his orders. The problem was that Joseph was just beginning to know his way around Wroclaw and traveling seemed too heavy a burden. Joseph also had a psychosis about trains; he preferred not to take them, but he had no choice.

He kissed Eva good-bye, grabbed a sandwich that Pepi made for him, and headed to the train station. People mechanically disembarked and boarded trains as they tried to keep to their schedule. Joseph was confused just watching the activity. The ticket agent's explanation wasn't much more helpful.

"Take the Rabin Line to the south terminal and the East Express until you get to Kraztka. When you come back, take the West Line, but when you get to the terminal, the Rabin Line will be down for the evening so you'll have to go north to Draslaw, and then take the Special Line to get back to Wroclaw. Do you understand?"

Joseph just stood and nodded, dazed. He looked down at his ticket, which was a list of abbreviations, numbers, and times. He pictured himself walking alone in the frozen wastes of Siberia, and physically shivered.

"Joseph!" a voice called out.

Joseph turned and saw his neighbor, Ritz, walking toward him wearing a railway uniform.

"Ritz! What are you doing here?"

"I work here. You didn't know? Guess I never told you."

"Maybe you can help me out. I'm a little confused."

"Let me see." Ritz took the ticket and looked it over.

"Ah, you're going to Kratzka, I know a great restaurant there. Go there often. We get free travel if there's space. You want some company?"

"That would be wonderful," Joseph said, relief washing over him.

Ritz spoke with his supervisor and soon they were on the train together. As the train jostled about, Ritz patiently explained how the city transit schedule worked. He also gave Joseph insight to each of the destination cities. Joseph took extensive notes. Ritz turned out to be a well spring of knowledge. He told Joseph the areas to avoid in certain cities, the areas and attractions that he shouldn't miss, and even gave him contact info for friends of his where Joseph would spend the night for little cost at some of the more remote areas.

Soon Joseph became a master of the city railways. As he became more experienced, his travels took him further from home. At first he would miss connections, but soon he was able to efficiently travel long distances and still make it back in time for dinner.

There were two types of leather that Joseph could purchase—legal and illegal. The legal leather was stamped with a tax seal, which nearly doubled the price. Unstamped leather was available on the black market. While Joseph typically used stamped leather, sometimes the kind he needed was only available unstamped. These expeditions made him the most nervous. He had only been stopped once by a government inspector who had set up a checkpoint at the main terminal. Fortunately, all the leather he carried had the proper stamps. This taught him to wrap his unstamped leather around his belly under a loose shirt and coat.

Each Shabbat, Joseph and his family attended services at the hidden synagogue. The other fifteen families faithfully attended as well. As Joseph looked around at the congregation, he took comfort in the fact that he was grounded again. Some of the other members worked for him and he had gotten to know them very well. It wasn't difficult establishing close friendships, as they were bonded by the atrocities they had all suffered during the war. It was an unspoken bond, however, as the community remained focused on healing rather than looking back. Sometimes, though, during a private moment when few others were around, Joseph and another member from the congregation would let their guards down briefly to examine their scarred souls. Joseph personally treasured these moments the most. It reminded him that he had not come through this alone. Each time a difficult memory was brought before uncritical eyes, he received a medium of healing—a little balm of Gilead to soothe the rough edges and turn the memory into an image instead of a point of agonizing pain.

So they healed. They healed each other. The racism and hatred still ranged around them, forcing them to keep their ancestry a secret, but they had each other and when they were together they were safe and they worshiped HaShem for it.

———◦◦◦———

Joseph's business was taking off. He didn't trust the banks, however, so when Eva went to pay Kozlowski with young Haim in tow, Joseph stayed home and hid his cash behind the metal grill of the fireplace stove. It made sense for Joseph to do this. They never used the stove since Eva bought a nifty electric heater. Eva never lit the stove because she hated having to turn on the gas and stick a burning match into the grill. Besides, no one would ever think to look in the stove for money.

One morning, after a rainy night, it was very cool in the apartment. While Joseph went to work, Eva decided she would dry out the wet clothes from the previous day. She surmised that the best way to do this was to heat them from a nice hot fire. Besides, it was drafty in the apartment and she didn't want Haim to catch a cold.

Eva found the book of rarely used matches and turned on the gas. She winced as the grill woofed and the gas ignited. She was begging to enjoy the warmth of the smoke seeping from around the fire box. Soon, thick smoke poured out. She shut off the flame, but the stove continued to smoke. By now the whole apartment was filled with a thick, dark cloud, so Pepi took Haim to Ritz's while Eva opened up the windows to the street. She poured a bucket of water on the stove until it eventually steamed itself out.

She had just gotten the apartment back together when Joseph got home. He smelled the smoke when he opened the door. His eyes immediately darted to the stove.

"You didn't," he said.

"Didn't what?" Eva asked.

Joseph ran to the fireplace and snapped off the metal cover. He pulled out the wall panel where he had put the money.

Eva watched him and cocked an eye. "I was just about to tell you that there was something wrong with the stove. It smoked up the whole house today."

Joseph yelled as he pulled out a fistful of charred bank notes. He could see the mocking image of some dead Polack leader on the face of the bill, which crumbled in his hand. He turned to Eva with a black streak across his cheek.

"You! You did this."

"It was cold. I lit it the normal way. I didn't do anything differently."

"Not that! THIS!" Joseph held up two handfuls of ash and shook them. Tears welled up in the corner of his eyes.

"What is that?" Eva asked in frustration.

"This…this is all I have worked for. This is all I've earned. This was our savings. This was going to be a birthday present for you. This was going to be a vacation."

"You put the savings in a stove?" Pepi asked as she walked in. "Of all the idiotic things I have ever heard you do, Joseph Mitsen, this has to be the dumbest yet. What were you thinking?"

"I thought—"

Eva cut him off. "I'll tell you what you thought. You didn't think. If you had thought anything, you would have trusted me with the money and I would have secured it."

"But I—"

"But nothing. From now on you bring me all the money home and I will make sure it stays safe. I surely won't put it in a stove."

"But—"

"No. You won't pin this on me. This is not *my* fault. It's *yours*."

Joseph thought for a moment, looking at his black hands. "I guess it wasn't a very good idea." Pepi cackled from the other room.

"No, it was a stupid idea," Eva said.

In total, Joseph lost a year's earnings. Some bills were salvageable, so they were able to start anew. Joseph's clothes smelled like burned paper for weeks afterward, acting as a constant reminder of his mishap.

Eva watched their money from then on.

19

Joseph decided to walk home from work one evening. He passed the park and thought of bringing Eva. Suddenly he caught some movement out of the corner of his eye. He didn't turn he could tell who had just hid behind the tree near him. Pepi.

Joseph was about to call out to her when he noticed a second figure—a short, skinny man carrying what looked like Pepi's scarf in his hand. He was looking wildly around and breathing hard. Pepi looked around the tree at the man, then ducked behind it. The man saw her and crept slowly toward the tree. Something in Joseph's head sounded an alarm, so he walked quietly, out of sight, toward Pepi. When the man rounded the tree, Pepi screamed and took off running.

"Come back here! I'm not done with you!" the man yelled as he ran after her. He caught up to her and grabbed her coat. She fell with a squeal and the man jumped on top of her, holding her down in the grass. The man was about to say something more, but was cut short of breath by a kick in the ribs. Joseph grabbed the man with his brute strength and threw him ten feet in the air. When he landed, the man moaned in agony. Joseph looked down at him and pulled him to his feet.

"You want to attack women?" Joseph yelled. "This is what you get!" He punched the man square in the jaw, spinning him around and back onto the grass. Joseph was about to hit him again when he felt Pepi's hands tug on his arm. He hadn't realized she had been yelling his name and telling him to stop.

"Stop, please!" she pleaded.

Joseph looked at her in the middle of his fury. "Are you all right?"

"Yes, but stop! I can explain."

"I saw him attack you."

The man gurgled something at Joseph and raised his hand. Joseph drew back to strike him again. Pepi grabbed his arm.

"NO!" she begged. "Stop, he's my boyfriend."

Joseph took a moment to process what she said. The man wriggled his fingers in a wave.

"You? You're her boyfriend? Why was he chasing you?" Joseph asked Pepi.

"We were playing. It was all in fun." Pepi dropped to her knees and cuddled the injured man in her arms.

"When did you get a boyfriend? Why didn't you tell me?"

"I don't have to tell you everything that happens in my life."

"But—"

"But nothing. Just because you think that you control everything and like to boss us around, doesn't give you the right to."

"But—"

———∽∽∽———

Motel cautiously shook his hand. "I'm Motel—*Ma-tuhl*. Motel Filin. Nice to... meet you."

"Eva knows about him?"

"Yes."

"And she didn't tell me?"

"Why should she? She knew you'd try to stick your nose in my business and if you didn't approve, you'd interfere. I'm not under your control. I'm not your child, and frankly I'm older than you, so if anything you should respect me."

"But I do."

"How? By beating up my boyfriend?"

"But I didn't know!"

"Go home, Joseph. Just go home."

"But—"

"Go home. You've done enough today."

"Pepi."

"GO! I'll see you later."

"Bye," Joseph said sheepishly. "Nice meeting you, Motel." Motel smiled and gave a curt wave, Pepi glared at her brother and turned to nurse her new love. Joseph walked away in a fog.

That night Pepi came in late. Joseph waited for her.

"I waited up," he said.

"You didn't have to," Pepi said shortly. She put her coat on a table and took off a pair of gloves.

"Eva told me everything."

"I'm sure she did." Pepi walked to the kitchen and got a drink of water.

"I'm sorry, Sis. How's he doing?"

Pepi looked up into the blue eyes of her brother. She sighed. She couldn't stay mad at him.

"He's fine."

"I'm sorry."

Pepi hugged him. "I know. I should have told you, but I wanted to know it was for real."

"What do you mean?"

"He asked me to marry him."

Joseph was astonished. His thoughts sped ahead of his mouth, resulting in a series of grunts and mutters.

"What did you say?"

"I said yes."

Joseph couldn't decide whether he was happy or sad. "But he lives thirty minutes away by train or bus."

Pepi nodded again. "I can't stay with you forever, Joseph. I have to move on."

"I–I just didn't expect it so soon."

"Soon? It's been three years. How long do I have to wait before I can go on my own?" Pepi massaged her brother's shoulders. "I love Malka and Max. That will never change, but Max would want me to move on. I'm not getting any younger and I still want to have a family."

"We're your family."

"I want my own family. I want *my* life back. I want to go back to what I had before."

"Are you sure he's the one?"

"Motel is kind and generous. He's creative and makes me see the world through his eyes. It's beautiful."

"So when will you leave?"

Pepi stepped around in front of Joseph. "In a few weeks."

"So we'd better go over to Rabbi Shlomo's first thing in the morning."

"I thought we'd get married where Motel lives."

"Nope. Papa wouldn't have wanted that. If you're going to get married, you're going to do it right. I promised him I'd look out for you."

"Fine, I'll get with Eva and we'll plan it together."

"You have to?"

"I do."

"Okay. I'm going to bed. I'm exhausted."

"Good night then." Pepi walked to the door of the bedroom and turned. "I love you."

"I love you too." Joseph smiled as she went in the room and closed the door. Joseph sat, looking out of the window onto the yellow glow of the street lights below.

"Protect her please, HaShem," he pleaded.

―∽―

The wedding was officiated by Rabbi Shlomo and generously attended by the synagogue's full congregation. Pepi was radiant and smiled so much her cheeks were sore. Motel made friends quickly and even his short stature seemed to enhance his loyal personality. It was instantly apparent that he was enraptured by Pepi.

Ritz bought them train tickets as a wedding present and Joseph, Eva, and Haim saw the newlyweds off at the platform.

"Thank you for everything," Pepi told Joseph. "I wouldn't have made it without your help. Thank you for showing me that what I thought was the end, was merely the beginning of the next chapter in my life. I'm so happy."

"Take care, sis. Write me often. It may be that HaShem has more planned for us. Enjoy your honeymoon and don't be too hard on Motel. His ribs are still sore."

Pepi hit him in the arm, then hugged him. With tears running down her cheeks she kissed him.

"I love you, brother."

"I love you too."

Joseph hugged her tightly and finally she broke away and dabbed her eyes. She hugged Eva and then picked up Haim and kissed him.

"Bye, bye, Aunt Pepi," Haim said.

"Goodbye, my special person," she said. She put him down, tussled his hair, and then boarded the train. She waved good-bye from the coach window. Eva and Joseph watched as the train pulled out of sight.

———

Eva spent more time at home with Haim now that Pepi was no longer there to take care of him. Being a mom suited her well and she could still keep track of the business accounts when Haim slept.

One morning, Haim woke with bright red cheeks and a flushed face. His normally large eyes were lidded and he moaned continuously. She felt his forehead and he was burning up. She filled the wash tub with cool water and lowered him into it. He screamed when he touched the surface and tried to climb up her arms. Carefully but forcefully, she pushed him into the water.

"It's all right. This will make you feel better."

"It's c–cold," Haim gritted. His teeth were chattering.

"You have a fever. I need to get your body temperature down quickly." Haim cried. She set his tiny body in the ice-cold water. He shivered and moaned. Eva wet a rag and dribbled cool water over his head.

"Shh… It's okay. You'll feel better." There was a knock at the door.

"It's open!" she yelled. Ritz stuck his head in.

"Hello?"

"Ritz, I'm in the kitchen." Eva turned when Ritz appeared.

"Hey, I just wondered if Joseph was going to be home for lunch. I wanted to give him the newest schedules. He said he'd also help me install a ceiling light."

"He's still at work. He didn't say he'd be home, but I sure do need him."

"What's the matter?" Ritz asked. Haim moaned again.

"Haim's sick."

Ritz kneeled and brushed the hair from Haim's eyes. "What's the matter, kipper? Mom says you don't feel so good." Ritz looked up to Eva. "He doesn't look so good. You want me to get Joseph?"

"Would you?"

Ritz ran out of the door and to the shop. Joseph came home to find Rachel, Rabbi Shlomo's wife, helping Eva.

"I think he's got scarlet fever or some kind of an infection," Rachel said.

"Is that bad?" Joseph asked.

Rachel took them in the other room when Haim fell asleep.

"Your son is very sick. There has been an outbreak of scarlet fever and many people have already died from it."

"Oh no," Eva gasped.

"What can we do?" Joseph asked.

"We need to get him an antibiotic—penicillin. But it's hard to find. There's a shortage in the hospitals."

"How can I get it? I'll do anything," pleaded Joseph.

Rachel put away her stethoscope and looked at Joseph with a grave look. "Come by the synagogue tonight and speak with Rabbi. He might be able to help."

"I'll be there."

That night at the synagogue, Rabbi Shlomo escorted Joseph to his small office. "Rachel told me about little Haim." He poured a cup of tea for Joseph. "The penicillin you need is very hard to obtain. The hospitals get the vials in each week and the nurses and doctors often steal some of them to sell on the black market. It's expensive and there is no guarantee that it will be available."

"What about the other sick people in the hospital? That means some of them don't get the medicine they need?" Joseph asked.

"Yes. Even the hospitals have been forced to buy their own medicine on the black market, driving up the price."

"I'll pay whatever I have to."

"Well, Joseph, it will take money to start. If you will give me 400 zloty, I will send someone to the source and see if they can produce the medicine." Joseph pulled out a pink roll of bills and counted off 400 zloty.

Rabbi Shlomo and Rachel came to see little Haim. Rachel pulled out a needle and syringe that looked like a dart, and Joseph rolled up Haim's sleeve. Rachel shook her head.

"No, this has to be given to him in the tuckus." Haim cried as they rolled him over and exposed a cheek. Rachel broke a brown vial of clear liquid, inserted the needle, and filled the syringe. She cleaned his skin with an alcohol rub and pushed the needle in gently. Haim screamed and tried to wiggle away, but Joseph and Rabbi held him tightly. Eva couldn't look. She couldn't stand to see her baby in such pain. After a few moments, Haim calmed down and fell asleep.

"The fever will get worse, as the antibiotics begin fighting off the infection, but after a few days we should see some results."

Joseph and Eva bid the two goodnight and stood holding each other while they watched Haim sleep restlessly. Each day, Rachel and Rabbi Shlomo came to the house to administer the shots. Each day Joseph gave the rabbi 400 zloty. Soon Haim started feeling better and within two weeks was fully recovered.

Eva felt awful. She was barely able to see Haim off to preschool before she felt so dizzy she couldn't stand up. It was her turn to ready the tea and snacks for the ladies of the synagogue. They met every Tuesday morning. The most she could do was crawl from the bed to the bathroom down the hall. She had just exited the stairwell when she heard the voices of the ladies coming up the stairs. They nearly tipped over her.

"Eva! What's wrong?"

"Let me help you."

"Oh my dear, let's get you back inside," the ladies said in sequence. They easily hoisted her up by her armpits and ungracefully lugged her to the sofa in the apartment.

"Get her some water," one woman said.

"I need a cool rag too," Rachel added.

"I'ma–I–I–ma sorry," Eva said. She retched twice. Eva held her hands on her mouth.

"Bring a pan, quick!" Rachel hollered. No sooner than it was put in front of her, Eva dry heaved into it.

"How long have you been like this, dear?"

"I didn't feel very well yesterday, but this morning I woke up feeling terrible."

"She doesn't have a fever," one of the women said after feeling Eva's forehead.

Rachel studied Eva carefully, and a look of suspicion crept across a wry smile. "Eva, have you had your period this month?"

Eva looked up with red eyes. "Uh…no, Now that you mention it."

Rachel's face widened, her smile stretched under cherry blossom cheeks. Eva looked back to Rachel with an astonished look, which rolled over to beaming smile. Rachel nodded enthusiastically.

"I'm pregnant?"

"We'll have to give you a test, but you've got all the symptoms."

"I'm pregnant! We're going to have another baby!" Eva began to cry. The other women hugged her and cried along with her.

———⁂———

When Joseph made his way through the front door, he was surprised to find Eva dressed in one of her most expensive gowns, with Haim next to her. He was dressed elegantly as well, and she had even combed his hair. The Sabbath candles were lit on the table and everything was ready. Joseph kissed Eva, confused, and tickled Haim. They had never dressed so nicely for the Sabbath, but Joseph decided to play along.

"What a beautiful family. I am forever grateful to have you both in my life. Let me go wash up and change my clothes. I'll be right back." Joseph came back and Eva sat, beaming at him. He looked over his clothing and adjusted his tie.

"What? Did I spill something?"

"No," Eva said with a rising note.

"What is it then? Why are you smiling?"

"I don't know. I'm just happy to see you."

"I'm a little creeped out, to tell you the truth." Joseph took a sip of water and said, "Mrs. Feldman passed me on my way home and she was smiling too. I told her good evening and she laughed. It must be something with my haircut. I told the barber it was lopsided."

"Your hair is fine. It looks good on you."

"Are you sure? I think it's shorter here."

Eva reached out her hand and squeezed his. "It's fine. I love you very much."

"I–I love you very much too," Joseph said.

"Before we begin, would you mind if I said a prayer?" Eva asked.

"A prayer. Sure! Go ahead."

Eva took little Haim's hand in hers and also held onto Joseph's. "Dear G-d, thank you for watching us and protecting our family. Thank you for the Sabbath. Thank you also for my husband whom I love very much." Eva squeezed his hand. "And finally, thank you G-d for little Haim and for the baby. Amen."

"Amen," Joseph said. It took Joseph a moment to register what Eva had just said. "Wait. Baby? What baby?"

Eva looked up with a huge smile.

"You're...pregnant?"

"Yes," Eva said, nodding her head.

"You're pregnant! Ha ha!" Joseph jumped up and danced around the table, and Haim clapped his hands, giggling. Joseph pulled Eva to her feet and danced with her. "We're going to have another baby!" Joseph was crying, and this made Eva cry. Haim saw both his parents crying and puckered out his lip, whimpering.

"No, no, no, my boy! We're not sad." Joseph picked up Haim, who grabbed his daddy's neck and laid his head on his shoulder. "We're happy. You're going to have a little brother."

"Or sister," Eva added.

"Or sister," Joseph echoed.

20

L ife was good. At least that was what Joseph thought as he whistled a tuneless melody and sang a cheery "Good morning!" to everyone he passed. He was to be a father…again. His store was doing well. He was on top of the world and nothing could shake him from his perch.

"Good morning!" he exclaimed to an old man.

"Morning," came the flat reply.

A two-step, long step.

"Good morning!" he shouted to two elderly matrons who were caught off guard by the outburst of cordiality. They turned to each other and giggled like school girls. Joseph added a swagger. He did a short spin to glance behind himself and saw that the ladies had stopped to look at him. He saluted and flashed a toothy smile, then continued with a long step and two short steps. It was fun to make people happy. He could definitely get used to this.

Across the street, Joseph noticed a man struggling with a heavy box across the sidewalk. Without missing a beat, Joseph ran over, grabbed the other end, and helped the man carry it to a waiting truck. Joseph pushed his end on the bed and kept walking. A diminishing "Thank you!" was called out and Joseph waved in the air, whistling his tune.

Up ahead, two grim men approached Joseph. They wore long slickers and watched Joseph intently as he approached. Joseph decided they needed a little joy so he cranked up his smile, advanced his stride, and spoke out:

"And a very good morning to you, gentlemen!"

The men remained downcast, bitter. Joseph thought he'd try again as he approached.

"Nice day, isn't it?"

Before Joseph knew it, the two men had scooped him up by the armpits and spun him 90 degrees into an alley. They looked around to make sure nobody was watching.

"Shut up and listen," the taller man growled. The men lifted Joseph over a pile of crates, and ducked behind them. One of the men quickly frisked Joseph, while Joseph's mind ran like a hooked tar pin.

Oh no. The taxes…

"I can explain. There weren't enough skins so I had to use the black market ones. I'll pay any taxes. I'm sorry."

The two men looked at each other, confused.

"What the hell are you talking about?"

"I uh—"

"I told you to shut up," the other man said. He pulled out a wallet and flipped open a badge.

"Yes, sir."

"Are you Joseph Mitsen?"

"Yes."

"We need to talk to you. It's very important, but we can't talk out here."

"My shop is just down the street."

"Is anyone there?"

"No, not until ten."

"Good. Let's go."

Joseph and one of the men walked ahead while the other hung back to see if anyone was following. They arrived at the store and Joseph unlocked the front door. As they entered, Joseph turned the lights on, but the man turned them back off.

"Better not to let anyone see us," he said. Joseph said a quick prayer and imagined Eva's horror-stricken face when she found his mutilated body lying on the floor of the shop, next to a display of brightly colored purses and shoes.

"I'm sorry to be so secretive, but we can't take any chances." Both men were looking out the window. So Joseph looked too. The men looked back.

"You were a gunnery sergeant in the Polish army?"

Joseph nodded. "Who are you?"

"I'm Agent Vorontsova, and this is Agent Rodkin."

Ah…Russians. Must be NKVD, the Russian's secret police force. They were known to make people disappear, but the curious way the agents were handling Joseph didn't exactly make him feel threatened. They could have taken him without a struggle much earlier. Joseph relaxed a little at this thought.

Agent Vorontsova pulled some photos out of his pocket showing man in different poses. One was a military ID photo, another was obviously shot with a telephoto lens, and one was of the man wearing Bermuda shorts and a silky shirt, seated on a rocky beach with a topless woman lying next to him. In the first picture the man was bald. In the last, the man had a brush full of short, blond hair. But the sullen cheeks, the deeply set eyes, and the crooked set of evil looking teeth could only be one person.

"Do you recognize this man?"

"I know this man. That's Muller. He was the commanding officer who led an attack on our border camp. He killed my family and many of my friends."

"Are you sure this is Muller?" The agent tapped the picture of the man on the beach and slid it toward Joseph.

"Positive. He has let his hair grow and his eyes are under a visor, but I'd recognize him anywhere."

Agent Vorontsova looked at his partner and when he made eye contact, the other nodded.

"Mr. Mitsen, we knew these first two pictures were of Muller, but this last one we weren't sure. Most people who have ever gotten close enough to see Muller are either dead or missing. We're sorry. We can feel your pain," Agent Rodkin said.

"Many good Russian soldiers were tortured and killed because of this man, but that's not why we want to talk to you," Vorontsova added.

Joseph sat on a stool and listened as Vorontsova continued. "Muller raided the people of each community he destroyed. When he got to Krakow, he took a stash of diamonds stored in a vault in Krakow."

"How much did he take?"

"Total about a hundred million US dollars' worth."

"And he's still alive?

Rodkin nodded. "He's been on the run ever since the Soviet army pushed the Germans out of Poland. One of our operatives took this picture a week ago in Athens." Joseph looked back at the picture again. Muller smiled at the woman lying next to him, obviously trying to get her attention. Joseph shuddered as he wondered what the woman's fate had been after the photo was taken. If she had refused him, who knew what he was capable of doing.

"Joseph?"

"Hmm?" Joseph stammered.

"We want you to help us find him."

"Me?"

"You're the only one we know who can quickly identify him."

"So?"

"We need your help."

"I'm kind of busy—my wife is pregnant, I've got a young son, and I've got a business to run."

Agent Vorontsova looked at Rodkin. "Agent Rodkin, would you mind if I spoke to our friend Joseph in private for a moment?"

"Not at all." Agent Rodkin wandered toward the back of the store and browsed at some belts. Agent Vorontsova took Joseph by the arm and led him near a corner.

"Do you know who Agent Rodkin is?"

"Eh, no."

"Alexander Rodkin is the chief investigator of fraud against the Soviet government. Last month alone he sent fifteen illegal importers, tax evaders, and money launderers to prison for a very long time." Joseph glanced at Rodkin who had picked up a small ceramic vase, took the top

off it, and sniffed inside. "Now, Joseph, my friend"—
Vorontsova turned him back to face him—"would you
like a cigarette?"

Joseph shook his head nervously.

"Then, do you mind if I smoke?" Vorontsova lit up and
let out a stream of smoke with a sigh. "I know about your
purchases of illegal skins for your business. I've known
for months, but I'm only involved in tracking Nazis."
Vorontsova took another puff. "Look, I know how much
of a struggle things are for you, especially being a Jew. I
know what you have been through and what was done
to you. I even know all about the homosexual camp
commander who tried to buy your son. I'm not here to tell
you what to do, only to give you options. We need Muller
to show us where he hid the diamonds. We can pick him
up, but we'll lose the goods. He's very adept at disguise."

Vorontsova waited for Joseph to digest the gravity of
the situation. "Let me ask you something, Joseph. Do you
hate Muller?"

"Yes, more than anything," Joseph said flatly.

"If Muller were brought to justice, could you imagine
telling him all the horrible things he's done to you and
your family? You would be sitting in the courtroom,
testifying against that monster before he is executed."

"I would like that."

"So would thousands of other Jews who lost their lives
at his hand. You were in the Polish army. What did they
teach you?"

"To take orders. To work hard. To fight."

"Right! Your country needs you again. It needs your
special abilities. You will be able to help us capture a

criminal and bring him to justice. Otherwise, I will be forced to give my folder to Agent Rodkin. If you help me, I will tear it up and make sure it is never mentioned."

Joseph leaned forward in the stool, staring at the floor. The agent put his cigarette out in a flower pot.

"Take your time. I'll be over here with Rodkin." The agent walked over to join his companion.

Joseph flashed several scenarios in his mind. None of them provided any favorable solutions. He walked to his office and got a drink of water from the ice box. He looked around the room, stopping at a picture of Eva, Pepi, and baby Haim. He smiled. The photo had been taken right after they had returned from Kazakhstan. It seemed like such a long time ago. His eyes traced a path up the wall, and he rested on a photo of him and Janek shortly after boot camp. He scanned more photos and stopped once more on a picture of him with his sister Miriam and his mom and dad.

"Go get him," his papa seemed to say. Joseph stepped back into the front of the shop.

"What do I have to do?"

———❧———

Joseph was given an address in a nearby city, just a few train stops away. He decided to keep this mission a secret from Eva—he hated lying, but he knew it was the only way to protect her. So the night before he left, he told Eva that he would be traveling for a few days to procure leather from a new supplier. He added that he would call her at the shop as it was her job to run things while he was gone.

While this was challenging for Eva, she enjoyed running the store. There was always something new going on and she always discovered new products that surprised her. She had been eyeing a certain pair of leather shoes that had been on the wall for a few weeks now. Maybe now was the time to let Joseph "buy" them for her.

—◦◦◦—

Rusted swings swayed in the breeze. Joseph looked over a concrete fence into an abandoned school's playground. The windows on the building were boarded up, but the latch was unlocked. He pushed the doors open and walked into the main atrium. The floor was freshly waxed and the lights in the hallway were all out. If he hadn't seen the outside of the school, he would have thought that it was still open.

Short footsteps echoed in the hall. At first he couldn't tell where the sound was coming from, but then he saw the source—a tall, blonde woman wearing a skirt that traced the contours of her long legs. She crossed the floor carrying a folder under one arm while her other was extended for a handshake.

"Mr. Mitsen, we've been expecting you. My name is Agent Banistov, but you can call me Mila." She shook his hand.

"You can call me Joseph"

"How was your trip?"

"It was fine."

"Good. Can I get you some refreshments?"

"No, thank you. I ate on the train."

"Very well, I'll show you around." Mila held her hand out to direct Joseph down the hall. "It looks like we'll be working together."

"Really?"

"You're to track down Friedrich Muller, right?" Joseph was surprised at her bluntness.

"Uh, yes. That's what they told me." Joseph eyed her suspiciously.

Mila detected Joseph's discomfort. "Don't worry, Joseph. We can talk openly. Outside we've got to be careful, but in here it's all business." Joseph caught a glimpse of the supine curve of Mila's long back, which ended in two firm protrudes. He held his glance a little longer than he planned and when he snapped his eyes back up, Mila was looking right at him with a big smile.

"Your report says you have blue eyes. I can see they didn't mention your inability to control them."

"Well, uh, I'm sorry. I uh…."

"That's okay. Just remember to stick to the business."

"Right, right."

They walked past several abandoned classroom desks, which were neatly stacked to the sides. Old posters and even student artwork still decorated the walls.

"The school was closed during the war and there weren't enough teachers to reopen it. There weren't enough students either." Mila looked at the floor. "We converted it to a training center a couple of years ago. Right now, we're on break for the winter. Usually there are agents wandering the halls, but right now we're just a skeleton crew." She stopped. "So it looks like we will be spending all of our time together." She smiled again and opened a door. Joseph could have sworn she was flirting with him, but then again maybe not. He forced himself to keep his eyes straight ahead when she turned around to open the door.

"This is where you'll sleep. I'm in the women's dorm across the hall." She turned on the light and rows of bunk beds ran down two sides of the room. "You'll have the place to yourself. The bathroom and showers are down the hall. I thought you might want to get yourself settled in before dinner. Afterward, you'll be debriefed and then we'll discuss your training."

"Where is the chow hall?"

"Oh, straight up the hall, you'll see the signs. Or you can just follow your nose. I hope you weren't expecting a five-star affair."

"Thank you. I'm sure I've eaten worse."

"Good. So I'll see you in an hour?"

"Great."

With that she turned with a quick smile and tapped away, her heels clicking with each stride. This time Joseph didn't look away, but watched with a carnal desire as this attractive woman, powerful and professional, strutted down the hall. He walked into his room and looked back out the door as Mila turned the corner. He closed the door, shaking his head.

"What's the matter with you?" he said softly. "Your wife is pregnant and you're ogling other women. Eva would kill you. This isn't biblical times where you can have a concubine. And you aren't a king." He sighed deeply. "But she sure can wiggle. Wow!"

Joseph threw his duffle bag on a bunk. Being in the army all those years, he felt out of place with luggage. He bounced on the hard mattress and kicked off his shoes. After a few moments, he let his mind wander. He made a mental note to ask Mila where the phone was to check in on Eva. Truth be told, he was having fun. He hadn't relaxed in a while and he was excited at the change of routine. Plus, there was something intriguing about Mila and he couldn't help but feel that the NKVD might recruit him. Sure, they used strong arm tactics, but it was better than being taken away in cuffs. Moreover, it gave him a chance to exact his personal revenge on Muller. With that thought, Joseph dipped into a deep sleep.

———∾∾∾———

"Sorry I'm late," Joseph said to Mila as he sat at the dinner table. "Where is everyone?"

"They went home."

"Oh."

"They got tired of waiting for you."

"Ah. I'm sorry. I fell asleep."

"Mr. Mitsen, we are here for a serious endeavor. I don't want to report that you are showing a lack of cooperation."

"I'm sorry. It won't happen again." Mila looked at Joseph and sighed. She pushed a covered tray across the table to him.

"It's probably cold. I'll have to debrief you while you eat. I hope you don't mind." Joseph opened the tray. The food was cold, but he was hungry. He ate it.

"So tell me about your first encounter with Muller."

Joseph told her everything he could remember. As he talked, she took notes. The only time she stopped was to adjust her glasses, and when she read a new question. She asked him about his family, about his fears, his relationships. She asked in detail about his imprisonment at the camps. She covered psychological questions, and even fantasy situations to gauge his response. The entire time she made notes and seldom looked up. Now and then she would unconsciously chew on the end of her pen, deep in thought. Joseph couldn't keep his mind from wandering toward Mila's soft features. He heard his name being called in the distance, but her perfect eyes, high cheekbones, and creamy skin had deafened him from the outside world.

"Mr. Mitsen?"

"Y–yes?" Joseph stammered.

"So you have shot an unarmed person?"

"No. I haven't."

Mila looked at him and then at her watch. She took off her glasses and rubbed her eyes.

"I think we've covered enough for tonight." She stood up and thanked Joseph for his help.

"Oh, can I ask where the phone is so I can call my wife?" asked Joseph.

Mila looked a little put off, but said, "Sure, I'll show you." She led Joseph to an office with a phone.

"I'll see you in the morning, Mr. Mitsen."

"Good night," Joseph said.

Once she left, he shook his head and focused intently on the turn dial. He called Eva, who was now cleaning up the shop.

"We made 1000 zloty today, Joseph!"

"That's great," Joseph said.

"Aren't you proud of me?"

"Y–yes! You are doing a great job."

"How are your negotiations coming along?"

The next morning, Joseph was called into the gym for training. Mila was wearing black fatigues, and Joseph entered wearing old shorts that had grown tight around his thighs. Mila chuckled.

"I didn't have time to buy any new clothes. These used to fit."

"I'm sure they did."

Several men trained in a corner of the large gymnasium. They wore gees and were throwing each other onto large mats using moves based on Judo.

"First we will determine your skills in hand to hand combat," said Mila. "Let's see how well you do against an opponent." Joseph looked at the two men. They looked like novices and in his estimate, they were not very fit. Sure he had put on a little paunch, but he was strong as an ox. He could take either of those guys. No problem.

"Okay, so which one is my opponent?" Mila looked over at them, then back to Joseph.

"Neither."

"Then who is—"

"You're looking at her."

"But—"

"Do you have a problem fighting a girl?" Mila smiled.

"I—"

"Don't say it. Just get ready."

Joseph followed Mila to a mat and settled into a ready stance. Joseph laughed.

"Are you sure? I really don't want to hurt you."

"I don't think you'll have to worry about that. I'd be more concerned with your own health." With that she spun and kicked Joseph squarely in the chest. He flew across the mat with both legs up and landed hard on his back. She walked up and stood over him while he gasped.

"You okay?" she asked sweetly.

"I–I…"

She extended a hand and lifted him to his feet. When he stood, he remained doubled over with his hands on his knees.

"You're good," he breathed.

"You don't know the half of it." She spun again with the same move, but this time Joseph side stepped it.

"I see your memory is working. Let's see about your speed." She initiated a brutal attack of martial arts punches and swift kicks. Joseph clumsily blocked and dodged at first, but soon matched her rhythm, blow for blow. When she backed off, she seemed impressed.

"Think of your family."

"I can do better."

She punched straight at Joseph's face. He grabbed her arm, twisted it around her back, and caught the other while locking her neck within his elbow. She stood straight up, her head pressed firmly against Joseph's shoulder, her hair running down his back. It smelled of sweat and lavender. It drove him crazy.

"So you're pretty proud of yourself?" she asked. Joseph pooched out his lip and nodded his head sideways with a slight grin. Mila stomped on the toe of his shoe with her high heel. Joseph yelped. Mila nimbly doubled over and reaching between her legs, grabbed Joseph's ankles and pulled. Joseph's feet were suddenly up in the air and he hit the mat with his back. Mila twisted her body and stepped, locking her legs around Joseph's. Joseph found himself flipped over and instantly in terrible pain as she leaned back, stretching his legs in an arch almost to his shoulders. Joseph slapped the mat and she let him go.

"That wasn't fair," Joseph said.

"Who said I fought fair?" Mila threw a series of jabs that backed Joseph up to the edge of the mat, step by step. He could see a strange fire in her eyes; something that, for the moment, made him uneasy. She seemed to want to kill him.

That's it. He was tiring of this silly game. Not that he was angry, but he was tired of her pompous attitude. He had been around the block; he knew he was a good fighter. It was Mila who needed to be taught a lesson. He blocked two more of her punches, then barreled a fist into her stomach. She doubled over, and he instantly grabbed her by the shoulders, then threw her over his knee and onto the mat. While she tried to catch her breath, he dropped an elbow on her back with all his weight. He could hear her vertebrae pop with the sudden impact. She let out a yelp and lay still as he got up. She slowly turned over and stared up at him, arms splayed out. Joseph cautiously leaned over her.

"Had enough?" he asked.

She tried to nod her head affirmatively. The fire was gone. She caught her breath and sat up on the mat with crossed legs. Her hair was matted with sweat and frizzed. *It looked incredibly sexy*, he thought. He held out his hand.

"You okay?"

"Yeah." She took his hand and stood on shaky legs. She tried to walk and fell into his arms.

"Take me to the chair." Joseph helped her sit down.

"Did you notice when you started taking this seriously?" she asked.

"When?"

She looked up at him like he was stupid. "When you quit thinking about how to get in my pants and started thinking like a soldier."

"Well, I guess that's true. It's been a while since I've been a soldier."

"We don't have time for you to relearn everything. I've got two days to get you ready for field work. You've got to take this seriously; your life or those working with you could be in jeopardy. And frankly, I don't want to have to protect myself and you too. We're done until after dinner. Don't forget to set your alarm clock."

With that, Mila walked out of the room. It was only then when Joseph realized the others who had been practicing had been watching the entire time. They gave Joseph a huge grin. Joseph looked at them and then made his way to the dorm as they all clapped.

"Glad to see one of us put her in her place," said one of the onlookers.

Joseph lay on his bunk for a moment, thinking about the fight. He decided he'd grab a shower. He pulled some clean clothes and a towel out of the duffle bag and headed to the communal shower. It was nice. Each stall had its own private screen, and the water was hot and felt good on his tired muscles. Maybe Mila was right—it had been a while since he was a soldier, and he was out of practice. Maybe he had lost his edge. He had to focus—to stop playing games. Yes, she was beautiful, but he was married. It was good that she was pretty as it had caught him off his guard and revealed a weakness.

He poured shampoo into his hands and worked it into his scalp. The hot water had started to loosen the tension. The steam was thick in the cool air of the bath and quickly filled the shower room. He was rinsing his hair when he felt something soft brush up against him. He jerked back and tried to open his eyes, but the soap burned them.

"It's only me."

"Mila?"

"Shh. Let me get that." Delicate fingers began massaging his scalp, rinsing the soap from his hair. When he could see clearly again, Mila looked up at him and smiled. Her hair hung straight on both sides of her face and twisted into casual curls on the end. Her breasts were as full and lovely as he had ever seen. She began to wash his body with a bar of soap.

"I'm sorry for the way I acted," she said.

"That's okay."

"It's not. I should have been more patient. This assignment was thrown on me when I had been planning to take some time off. I hope I can make it up to you."

"Well, you're doing a pretty good job right now."

"Good."

She was impressed with the numerous scars on Joseph's back. She ran her fingers over them, then rinsed his hair and saw the deeply grooved scar across the back of his head.

"Is that where Muller…"

"Yes."

She gently caressed the scar.

"That one nearly was the end for me."

She traced the scar from his elbow to his hand.

"Knife fight."

"You've got a story for each one?"

"Yeah. We collect them."

With that she turned around, showing a flawless rump. Across her back were several lash-like scars.

"What—"

"I'll tell you some other time." She turned to Joseph and looked up with deep brown eyes.

"You know I'm married and I love my wife."

"I know." She reached around his back and kissed him.

———≈≈≈———

The next day was filled with calisthenics and road work. Mila was slightly more affectionate. She didn't try to kill him this time.

"Come on! Catch up!" Mila shouted as she jogged in place on top of a steep hill, her ponytail bobbing. Joseph was out of breath.

"I told you—" she said

Joseph struggled to speak, wheezing between each word. "I…may…be…just…a little…out of shape."

Mila stopped jogging. "So how will you catch Muller when he runs? You know he was one of Germany's hopefuls for track and field at the '38 Olympics."

"Really?"

"Did he look out of shape?"

"No, not really, just very lean. Thin."

"Have you seen what a track star looks like?"

"Ah, I see your point. I wonder if he can outrun a bullet."

Mila frowned. "Let's go." She took off down the hill. Joseph stretched. Several bones in his back complained and he was off again.

———

The last day was spent mostly in meetings, but he did get some time in the indoor shooting range, with a new 9mm. Agent Vorontsova showed up and brought Muller's file. He, Joseph, and Mila all sat at a breakfast table together. Vorontsova slid several photos across the table, revealing a comfortable Muller lounging at an outdoor café, wearing the same dark glasses.

"We took these last week. He is staying at the hotel in Szczecin, Poland, on the sea. Your contact there is Agent Moniek Zilber. He will meet you at the train station."

"When am I supposed to leave?"

"As soon as possible. We don't want him moving."

"Any sign of the diamonds?" Joseph asked.

"None. We don't believe he has them on him."

"What about the hotel safe?"

"We've already checked."

"Couldn't you just catch him and torture him until he confessed?"

"He'd let us kill him. A man like that expects a violent death, and when you're not afraid of death you can withstand anything." Agent Vorontsova gave Joseph train tickets and then slid two others across—one for Eva and one for Haim.

"What are these for?" Joseph asked. He held up Eva and Haim's train tickets.

"Mila told me how close you and your family are and that you had mentioned how much your wife would like to go to the most beautiful seaside resort in Poland. This would be a perfect cover as a family vacation and she can see the sights while you work." Mila smiled at Joseph who sat astonished.

"But—"

"You can ask her tonight when you call," Agent Vorontsova said.

"Okay, thank you."

"Don't thank me. I could care less. Mila insisted on it. Her report was glowing. You really impressed her." Mila looked bashfully at the table. "You keep on impressing people, and you might want to consider this a new career. Find those diamonds and I can assure you that you'll have lots of friends in the Kremlin."

Joseph smiled, his pride swelling to greater heights.

"We know Muller is working with someone, or a group of someones," Vorontsova continued. "He has not made direct contact with them since we've been on his path. We're hoping that when you reveal yourself to him, he'll get nervous and try to move the diamonds."

"Wouldn't he just have someone move them for him?" Joseph asked.

"Muller is a very selfish man. He doesn't trust anyone. We don't believe he's told anyone where the diamonds are kept. Besides, can you blame him? He's a wanted man on the run. All they'd have to do is steal the diamonds and disappear, leaving him holding the bag." Vorontsova grinned. "No. He's got them at a safe place where only he has access."

21

Muller walked into a large retail store. Once inside, he spoke to an employee who promptly left to retrieve the manager.

A round man with a bib still around his neck was wiping his mouth as he approached Muller. Muller smiled a sinister grin, startling the manager, who immediately tried to breathe in a mouthful of chicken and started coughing. The manager had to stop at one of the saleswoman's desks, beg her for a glass of water, and wait until he could compose himself.

"Ah, sorry, Mr. Miller. Seems my food went down the wrong pipe. It's so good to see you again. Are you enjoying your stay?"

"Yes, yes. Very much. There is nothing quite as beautiful as the seaside resort."

"Quite right. So how can I be of assistance?"

"I came to get something from my storage box."

"Of course."

"Thank you." Muller followed the manager behind a metal gate and into a tiny room lined with metal storage doors. It looked more like a bank safe deposit room.

"Thank you, Mr. Miller. I'll see you out front," the manager said.

Muller pulled a long metal box from its cubbyhole. He carried it to a small privacy room and closed the curtain. Once he opened the top of the black box, he dumped its contents into the lid.

Crystal fire blazed in the room, sending a spectrum of fireworks across Muller's face. He snickered a congressed hiss behind wet teeth, as he ran his greedy fingers through the tiny ice crystals. A tear ran down his cheek. He held one gem up to the light and licked his lips. He turned it in his fingers, admiring the brilliant fire from a thousand tiny reflections.

"You are simply perfect, my dear." He brought the stone to his lips and kissed it, then placed it carefully in a glass vial and tucked it away in his pocket. He poured the rest back into the bag, closed it and returned it to the cubbyhole. His heart was light as he whistled a quirky tune and walked to the main hallway.

Muller removed a 100 zloty note from his pocket and tucked it in the manager's hand.

"Thank you, Mr. Miller!" The manager looked around and pushed the bill into his pocket. He watched Muller speak to one of the employees as he left. She wrote something on a piece of paper and handed it to him, and then he was out the door with a spring in his step. Once Muller had left, the manager returned his thoughts to the remaining chicken.

"You must be Joseph," Moniek said. He extended his hand and Joseph embraced it. "And this must be the lovely Eva and Haim. Joseph couldn't quit talking about you two," Moniek told Eva. "He's insisted that you join us in Sczecin, so how could we refuse?"

Joseph smiled. *It's getting deep*, he thought.

"It's nice to meet you, Mr. Zilber." Eva said.

"Call me Moniek, please."

Eva giggled. *Giggled?* thought Joseph. *She actually giggled like a school girl? We've only been here for two minutes and my wife giggled at him. Boy, he's smooth.*

"Let me take your things," Moniek offered. "The car is right around the corner. How was your trip? Have you traveled the beaches of Poland before?"

Oh come on, Joseph thought. *Enough.*

Moniek grabbed their bags from the station platform and carried them. Joseph tagged along with Haim.

"Really? I've lived all over the Middle East. In fact, I've had to move a lot with my business."

"You're in fashion, right?"

"Fashion? Is that what he told you?"

Joseph flashed a nervous eye at Moniek.

"I am not in fashion. Fashion is something that is here one day and gone the next. I am in apparel. I'm a prompter. I scour the world, looking for the most unique and highest quality apparel and accessories, and sell them in new markets. I'll have to send you some complimentary samples from our latest collection. I'll send them with Joseph."

"That would be very nice."

"We hope to be selling new items through your store in Wroclaw."

Eva smiled again.

She smiled again?

Moniek put the bags in the trunk and helped get Haim and Joseph situated in the back seat. Eva sat in the front with Moniek.

"There's more room up here and it will be easier to get in and out since you're expecting."

Eva blushed. "Do you have any children, Mr. Moniek?"

"No, unfortunately I am too mobile to put down any lasting roots."

"So there's no Mrs. Moniek?"

"No. Had a few close calls, but my job always took me away." They drove out of the station and headed down a busy street. "I guess you could say I was married to my work. Ah here, do you know much about this beautiful resort area? It is on the Baltic Sea with beautiful parks, resort-type shops, and restaurants. There is a about four hundred thousand people living here. A lot of German spoken here. This used to be part of Germany in the past."

"No, not really, I did not know that."

"Well, I know a personal tour guide who will take you and Haim around the city while I take your husband to boring business meetings. Tonight after you get settled in, I want to take all of you to my favorite restaurant, where you can sample some of the very best seafood cuisine. You will love it."

Eva smiled. "Thank you, that is very kind of you."

"It's the least I could do for the lovely wife of my favorite future business partner."

Joseph watched out the window as the blur of the street rushed by. He felt numb.

———∞∞∞———

Moniek was at the hotel early in the morning. Joseph kissed Eva and Haim good-bye and climbed into the passenger seat of Moniek's car.

"Good morning. How did you sleep?" asked Moniek.

"Terrible, I think I ate too much. It appears my stomach hasn't adjusted to seafood cuisine."

"Eva and Haim seemed to enjoy themselves."

"You are a smash hit with them. They are looking forward to touring the city. I'm sure they will see some amazing sights. I'd love to go with them."

"Ah, Joseph, you are quite the kidder. We've got a lot of work to do. Mila came in last night and was already put off that she didn't get to meet all of you. She's very dedicated to her work, eh?"

"Yeah, I guess so."

"Well, I've got some new pictures I want you to see. We're going to our safehouse where I can bring you up to speed."

Once they arrived, they were greeted with cold professionalism by Mila.

"Welcome to the Baltic Sea Coast. Are Eva and Haim enjoying themselves?" she asked.

"I think so. They were very excited. It's much better to take a train ride to a vacation than to a prison camp."

"I imagine so. Well, are we ready to get started?"

"Of course."

Mila led the men to a small room with photographs and maps spread out on the table. She stood with her arms stretched out.

"Muller is currently staying at a hotel down this road. He changes hotels every few days, which mean he's already very nervous," Mila said.

"Follow him, find his room, and search it. See if you can find the diamonds."

"What if he finds out?" Joseph asked.

"We must assume he'll notice someone's been in his room. He's too wary to let his guard down."

"But if you know he doesn't keep the diamonds in his room, why bother to look for them there?" Joseph asked.

"Because he'll make a move. We'll scare the fox out of its hole. He'll be forced to retrieve his diamonds and flee," Mila said.

"He'll run," Joseph said.

"With three of us waiting outside, he shouldn't be able to escape," she said.

"Where is the other picture?" Joseph asked.

"What other picture?" Moniek asked.

"The one where Muller was sitting on the beach with the topless woman."

All color faded from Mila's face. Moniek began looking around. He lifted a pile of pictures and sorted through them.

"That's funny. I could have sworn it was here yesterday."

"Well, I'm sure it will turn up," Mila said.

"We'll enter his room tomorrow when he goes out for dinner. Then we'll see what he does," Moniek said.

"Where are the retail stores in this area?" Joseph asked.

"Retail stores?" Mila asked.

"Muller has to have some place to keep his money. A man like him wouldn't risk carrying his treasures with him. If he's got diamonds he's probably pawning them off one at a time and keeping the cash in a storage box, rented at a local retail store. It would make sense that he's keeping the diamonds in a safe place. Local banks ask too many questions," Joseph said.

———

Joseph left. He looked around and walked around the block. Within minutes, he found Moniek.

"Have you seen Mila?" Joseph asked.

"No. I thought she was with you."

"I think I offended her."

"From what I know about her, that wouldn't be very hard to do. She probably went out to eat. I'm sure we'll see her later. You ready for tomorrow? I've got the key." Moniek held up a metal key on a ring. "He's in room 43."

"How did you get that?"

"It's my special skill. And you ask too many questions. We're staying a few doors down."

"Sounds easy."

"It is. Oh, by the way, I made some copies of the photos I misplaced." Moniek handed him a stack of three photos. The first photo showed Muller talking to a young woman wearing a large straw hat. Her back was to the camera. The second showed Muller touching the woman tenderly, and the third was a closer shot of the woman.

"Who do you think she is?" Joseph asked.

"Probably a prostitute, or a tourist."

"He seems rather comfortable with her if she is a prostitute."

"I've got dozens of pictures of him with prostitutes. One thing he definitely has is an active libido."

"That's true," Joseph said. He threw the photos back to Moniek, and resigned for the day.

———

That night, Joseph carried home some sample jewelry for Eva from Moniek.

"They're beautiful," she said.

"Did you have fun?" Joseph asked.

"We had a wonderful time. Haim got sunburned because he wouldn't leave his hat on. Tomorrow we're going to see more sights. You're coming with us, right?"

"I can't go with you. I've got a meeting and we're going to see a client," Joseph said flatly

Eva pouted. "Oh, pooh. What kind of vacation is this when we can't spend any time together?"

"I'm sorry, dear. Maybe we can go out to dinner tomorrow night."

"But, honey, I feel guilty getting to see all these amazing things without you. I want you with me so we can share these moments. You should see Haim. He won't stop asking questions."

"I'd love to go, but I've got work to do first. I'll tell you what—if I can wrap up my business tomorrow, I'll spend an extra day with you and Haim and we'll go off on our own."

"Okay, we'd like that."

"How's the baby?"

"*She's* doing well. I don't think she likes bouncing around in a bus, but otherwise she's fine."

"How do you know it's a girl?" Joseph smiled.

"She told me."

"She talks to you?"

"All the time—I can hear her in my sleep, and sometimes a thought will pop into my head and I'll know she wants something. Like today, I had a taste for something sour. I saw this man selling frozen juices so I got a green lemon. It was really tart. She loved it."

Eva kissed Joseph, and he smothered her in his arms. No matter how unfaithful he might have been, she was still a pillar of stability for him, someone he could rely on. He would have to be better at keeping away from other women.

—————

The next morning, Joseph headed for Muller's hotel, hoping he wouldn't see him. Not much chance of that, though. Muller exuded terror—in the way he crept about, in the way he contorted his thin lips into a hideous smile. Under the man's calm exterior, he emanated a sense of dread, a stench of death.

The hotel was a typical tourist trap. It looked very nice from the outside, but once he entered the hallway where the room was located, the smell of stale bedding and chipped paint revealed its worn-out soul. Joseph counted the doors, found 39, and knocked.

Immediately after knocking, someone exited their room four doors down.

Muller.

Joseph's heart beat quickly as he recalled the face behind the gun that had buried him underneath his comrades. The creature was wearing bright shorts and flip flops, and was casually carrying an empty ice bucket. It looked as if he had just woken up.

Joseph breathed deeply, trying not to draw attention. He knocked again at door 39 as Muller shuffled toward him. *Come on*, thought Joseph. *Open up!* Muller scratched his butt and coughed. He raised his peaked eyebrows at Joseph. Joseph locked eyes with him and froze.

"Hello," he squeaked.

Muller grunted and shuffled past. Moniek opened the door.

"About time," Joseph breathed. He pushed past Moniek and into the room, shutting the door behind him. Joseph looked out of the peephole and watched Muller stop for a brief moment and turn at door 39 with a curious glance. He shook his head, farted, and continued down the hall to the ice machine.

"That was Muller!" Joseph hissed.

"I know! Who did you think it would be?"

"I—I don't know! I didn't know what to do. Part of me wanted to kill him in the hallway, and another part wanted to run away with my tail between my legs. I couldn't believe he was so close to me."

"Did he say something to you?"

"No, not really."

"You all right?" Moniek put his hand on Joseph's shaking shoulder.

"Yeah, I'm okay."

"Make yourself a cup of coffee and get comfortable. We've got to wait until he leaves. Mila came by earlier. She said she had some things to do, but would meet us later."

"Oh, okay."

Moniek stayed near the door with it slightly ajar; just enough to see if door 43 ever opened. Joseph got bored and flipped through a tour magazine. He thought of Eva having fun without him. He sighed. He folded the magazine over and leaned back on the bed.

"There he goes!" Moniek whispered. Joseph sat up and a cold sweat broke out on his forehead. Moniek closed the door and listened. A door closed and footsteps approached the door. They stopped outside. Moniek looked at Joseph and they waited. The footsteps began again and faded down the hall.

Moniek waited a moment and finally opened the door. "Good luck."

"Thanks."

Joseph closed the short distance between the two rooms and looked down the hall. Nothing. He took a deep breath and reached for the doorknob to room 43. A Do not disturb sign hung loosely over the handle. Joseph reached into his pocket and produced a key, nearly dropping it when a noisy kid turned the corner of the hall and screamed back to his parents.

Joseph pushed the key in the lock and quickly turned the knob, entering the room and closing the door behind him. The room was a mess. Muller had a suitcase opened on a table and his toiletries in the bath. The closet was filled with several dress suits among other bright articles of clothing. Joseph was supposed to make it look like someone had been searching his room, so he began opening drawers and flinging out clothes. He pulled the bedding off the bed and turned the mattress over. He pulled the curtains back and even dumped the trash can over. Nothing. The man was traveling light. No diamonds here. They had to be in a safe deposit box.

Just as Joseph was about to leave, he decided to up the ante. He took a pad of hotel stationery and wrote:

We'll find them.

Joseph left the room and gently closed the door. Moniek was waiting with the door open.

"Nothing. Just some clothes. No diamonds."

"Well, he'll soon know we're onto him. Now we wait until he runs."

"If he leaves tonight, I'll follow him. I don't think he'll do anything until the morning. He's got a lot of thinking to do."

Joseph stayed up with Moniek until they heard Muller return. Joseph pressed his ear to the door and heard Muller enter his room. Moments later the man gasped, and Joseph quickly poked his eye through the peephole. He could barely make out Muller checking out the hallway to make sure no one had followed him. Then Joseph and Moniek heard Muller shut his door.

Joseph and Moniek spent the rest of the night planning how to nab Muller. The whole time, something tugged at Joseph's mind. Something he had missed. He casually flipped through the surveillance pictures of Muller. *We've got you now*, he thought. Once Moniek had the diamonds, Joseph planned to take some of his own vengeance out on Muller's hide. He laughed to himself as he thought of beating Muller senseless. He wouldn't want to kill him, he just wanted to make him suffer—for eternity. He found the picture of Muller and the woman on the beach and then it clicked.

"Moniek," Joseph said, excited. Moniek turned to Joseph with anger in his eyes.

"Shh!"

"Do you have a magnifying glass?"

"On the dresser. Be quiet!"

Joseph took the glass and the photo and sat at the table. He studied the picture, but this time he wasn't focused on Muller, but the back of the topless girl.

"Oh no," he said to himself. "OH, NO!" Directly above the woman's suit bottoms were several scars running diagonally along the woman's back.

"Mila," he exclaimed.

He rushed to the door, pulled Moniek back and closed the door.

"It's Mila," Joseph held out the photo. "It's Mila. The woman is Mila."

"How do you know?"

"Look here." Joseph held the magnifying glass up to Moniek. "There, on her lower back. See those scars?"

"Yeah, but how do you know that's Mila?"

"Because Mila's got scars on her lower back too."

"How do you know?" Moniek paused and a smile crawled up his cheeks. "You are a slick one, aren't you?"

"Never mind that! She's working for Muller. We can't stay here. Our cover is blown."

"I can't believe it's Mila. She was sent from HQ."

"There are many Nazi sympathizers in Russia," Joseph said.

"Right, because of their mutual hatred of the Jews," said Moniek.

"You're a Jew?"

Moniek nodded. "You're right, Joseph. We can't stay here. Muller will still run, but we're not safe. None of us are." Moniek's last few words struck a chord in Joseph.

"Eva," he gasped. He stood up and walked to the door.

"Where are you going?"

"I've got to get Eva. Mila arranged all her tours. She knows where she is."

"And she's been gone all day. I'll keep an eye on Muller. I'll switch rooms or wait across the street. Go find your wife."

"Be careful," Joseph replied.

Joseph got to his hotel and ran up to his room. Neither Eva nor Haim had been back. Joseph waited. The sun set and they still hadn't arrived. He passed a sleepless night, blaming himself for getting her involved. The next morning Joseph met Moniek at the café across the street. He hadn't slept either.

"Your face shows you did not find Eva," said Moniek.

"No. She didn't come back with my son."

"That's not good. I'll contact my up line and get some help to look for her. We'll find her, she couldn't have gone far."

"Did Muller leave last night?"

"No. I kept watch on the door from across the hall. He never opened it."

"Look!" Joseph exclaimed.

A man in an overcoat and hat pulled over his brow was walking their way. He looked around nervously every now and then.

"That's Muller," Joseph said.

"Wait until he goes closer, then we'll move into position."

Muller entered the building as Joseph and Moniek crossed the street and waited on either side. Several minutes later, as Muller emerged from the building, Moniek mouthed to Joseph, *Ready?* Joseph nodded in confirmation.

"Joseph! Joseph!" a voice called from behind him. A strained voice that he had heard before and it hurt him to his soul. He turned to see Eva holding Haim by his hand. He had been crying. Standing behind her, holding Eva's free arm in one hand and a pistol in the other, was Mila.

"So, Joseph, Eva and I have been talking," Mila spat. "We've had a nice long conversation. You know she loves you very much. And you, how could you? When she's done so much for you?"

Joseph turned around and Moniek was gone.

"Where's Moniek?" Mila asked, anxious.

"I don't know."

Mila shook Eva's arm. "Don't mess with me, Joseph. I'm not as easily fooled as naive little Eva."

Joseph took a step toward her. "No, you're not."

Muller walked out of the building door and looked straight at Joseph. He smiled with his wicked teeth and hissed a laugh as he walked by. He glanced at Mila and tipped his hat. He came to a stop and look at Haim, than quickly ran into the busy streets. Haim saw his face, his eyes, and saw the expression on his father's face. It was fear and hate. The boy never saw that in the past. The face of Muller was now registered in the boy's mind. He knew by his father's face that something was wrong.

"Moniek!" Joseph called out. There was no reply.

Mila pulled the gun from Eva's back and pointed it at Joseph.

"I thought I loved you, but I was wrong. You're just a dirty Jew. Good-bye, Joseph. It's your fault Eva is a widow and Haim has to grow up without a father."

Joseph's eyes fell on Eva's. They pleaded with him to do something. He looked back at Mila and a sudden, sharp crack rang out. Joseph looked down to see where he was shot, yet there was no entry wound. He looked back at Mila, and noticed a red splotch spreading on her white blouse, just above her abdomen. She looked down and then fell to her knees, toppling over on her face. Moniek came into view behind her, the barrel of his gun still smoking. Joseph rushed over to Eva and they embraced tightly.

"Moniek, get Muller!" Joseph shouted, pointing in Muller's direction.

But when Moniek turned his head, he saw nothing. The street was clear, except for a taxi rounding the corner at the end of the block. The cockroach had managed to escape yet again.

Joseph redirected his attention to Eva and Haim. She was crying uncontrollably, so Joseph held onto her, rocking her back and forth.

"I was so scared," Eva sniffed.

"I know. It's over."

The police arrived and an ambulance shortly thereafter. Mila's body was loaded on a gurney with a sheet over it.

Doctors examined Joseph and his family and soon released them. The police captain took them all to the station.

Joseph was first to be questioned, but Moniek interrupted.

"Captain, if I might have a word with you in private." The captain seemed put off by Moniek's candor. He looked at Moniek and then at Joseph.

"Don't go anywhere," he said to Joseph. The captain took Moniek into his office, where Joseph could see the two through the glass. The police captain held up Moniek's gun with a tag hanging from it and shook it at Moniek angrily. He pointed out his window, then emphatically slammed the gun on the table and yelled, constantly gesticulating for emphasis. Moniek listened patiently. When the captain calmed, Moniek opened his wallet and showed a badge. Then he took out a folded sheet of paper and gave it to the captain. The captain snatched at it and slowly looked up at Moniek.

After a few heated exchanges, a phone call, and a very disgruntled captain, Moniek left the office and winked at Joseph.

"Let's go."

"What did you tell him?"

"Oh, I showed him a letter of our assignment for capturing and bringing Nazi renegades to justice."

"We're free to go?"

"All free, let's go."

That night at the hotel room, Joseph was in the kitchen, contemplating his next move against Muller. Eva's hand caressed his shoulder as she approached him from behind.

"Haim won't sleep," she said softly.

Joseph turned to her, and smiled. "I'll go talk to the little guy."

He went into Haim's room. The boy was lying in his bed, his eyes wide open. He was staring at the ceiling.

"What's up, Haim?" Joseph asked with a grin.

"I'm scared."

"Of what?"

"Of that woman, and the ugly man that smiled at her."

Joseph sighed. "I know what you mean. She scared me too, but she's gone. She'll never come back."

"Why was she so mean?"

Joseph hesitated. "People…some people are filled with hatred for anyone who does not share their beliefs."

"But why?"

"I don't know…they just are that way."

"I think people should like each other."

"I think so too."

"Tata?"

"Yes?"

"Do you hate that man you saw today?"

Joseph paused for a moment. How do you tell your little boy an answer so simple yet if you told truth, you would feel like you were lying?

"Do I hate people?" Joseph was amazed at how his seven-year-old son had floored him with such a complicated question. "The truth is that I do. I hate what they have done to my friends and family."

"Okay, Tata. What about the scary man that walked by us, Tata."

"Can you go to sleep now?" Joseph asked.

"Yes. I hope I never have to hate anyone."

"Me too. Goodnight, my little guy." Joseph turned the light off.

"Goodnight, Tata. I cannot get that man out of my mind, I will remember that scary man for a long time. I love you, my Tata, good night again."

Eva was sitting on the couch, sipping a cup of tea, when Joseph came in and sat down beside her. She set her tea down gingerly and took Joseph's hand.

"I know why you lied to me. Mila told me everything." A worried look came over Joseph's face.

"What did she tell you?"

"She told me that she was a double agent, a Nazi sympathizer. She told me how Muller had met her through an underground network of...how did she call them...loyalists? She said she had sex with him and he paid her a lot of money. She bragged that she could seduce any man she wanted. She said she was planning to kill you in Poland, but that she fell in love with you." Joseph suddenly felt a cold sweat break out on his brow. "I can understand how she could. You're a special man." Joseph smiled a weak grin. "Anyway, she said she would kill you if it ever came to a decision between you and Muller. She had to be loyal to her employer."

"Of course."

"Thank God for Moniek."

"Yes," Joseph breathed.

"So why didn't you tell me about the NKVD?" Eva asked.

"They told me they would prosecute me for using black market skins for the shop."

Eva turned and held Joseph's hands. "I want to leave."

"We'll go home tomorrow."

"No. Actually, aside from being kidnapped and that scary bitch—"

"Eva!"

"Sorry. If I had a gun, I'd have shot her right in the face. Pow!" Eva held her finger out like a gun to Joseph's forehead and pulled the trigger. Joseph unintentionally blinked. "I want to leave Poland," Eva continued. "I want to go someplace where our children can grow up safely, without the fear of people trying to kill them because they're Jewish."

"Where should we go?"

"I spoke with Pepi, and she wants to go to Canada."

"Canada?" Joseph asked, shocked.

Eva smiled and nodded.

"They are very culturally diverse and it's a long way from here. Plus, I think you owe me." Joseph squirmed in his seat.

"Okay, but—"

"No buts. I want to get the papers in order when we get back, so we can leave as soon as the baby is born."

"Okay."

"And talk with your buddies at the NKVD. They owe me too—for lying to me and putting my family in danger."

"But—" Joseph started as Eva stared. "Okay, I'll ask."

"Good." Eva yawned. "I'm tired. I'm going to bed. Turn the lights off when you come to bed. Love you." She got up from the couch, kissed Joseph, and entered the bedroom.

Joseph sat and stared. He picked up her tea and started to drink, but it was cold and bitter.

22

There was a knock on the hotel door. It was Moniek, and he was holding a big box of chocolates.

"Can I come in?"

Joseph looked over his shoulder toward Eva, who was playing a board game with Haim. She looked up and saw who it was, but ignored him, looking back at the game. Joseph squeezed into the hallway and closed the door behind him.

"I don't think that would be such a good idea."

"I brought these for her—to say I'm sorry."

Joseph took the chocolates and opened his mouth to say something but changed his mind.

"Wait a second."

Joseph reentered the hotel room and Eva didn't even look up. He placed the chocolates on the table and turned around without saying a word. Joseph closed the door as he rejoined Moniek in the hallway.

"She's still pretty upset."

"I understand. I would be too."

"I don't think it's because she was scared, but more because I—" Joseph stopped short when the doorknob turned and Eva's face appeared.

"Please come in, both of you," she said.

Moniek looked at Joseph and Joseph smiled.

"Thank you for the chocolates," Eva sighed.

"You're welcome. I came to apologize."

Eva sent Haim to play in his room. "I wish I could just accept your apology, but I'm afraid you're going to have to do better than that." Joseph looked worried.

"Mrs. Mitsen, your husband had valuable knowledge of a Nazi fugitive, who was directly responsible for the deaths of thousands of innocent people."

"No one understands how evil that man was better than we do. He killed our parents and our brothers and sisters."

"Then you know why we needed Joseph's help."

Eva walked up nose to nose with Moniek and as she looked him straight in the eye she said, "That's the part that kills me the most! Joseph and our family have sacrificed more than enough. Why do you think that we owe you anything?" Eva poked his chest with her finger. "Not only did you put Joseph's life at risk, you put my whole family at risk, while you hunted down this criminal and I nearly got killed by a psychopath!" Eva poked Moniek so hard he rubbed his chest and backed up. Eva's eyes were smoldering hot. She had transformed into an intimidating feline warrior.

"Honey, it's probably—"

"*PLEASE!*" Eva snarled, cutting Joseph off midsentence, all the while never taking her eyes off of Moniek.

Moniek swallowed hard as Eva continued. "But it wasn't just the atrocities of the Germans, was it? The damn Russians had to add insult to injury. Why couldn't you have left us alone? Did you really have to murder Jews in the name of 'helping Mother Russia'?" Eva was now mocking the Russian accent. "You think we owe you anything? You think a little chocolate will make up for what was supposed to be a wonderful vacation?" Tears welled up in Eva's eyes. "We have tried so hard to rebuild our lives. We have worked against every kind of bigotry that's been flung at us and it keeps coming over and over and over again!"

By now Eva had backed Moniek up against the door.

"All I wanted to do was spend a little time away from the stress with my husband and little boy. You know I'm pregnant, right? Pregnant women shouldn't be put under this kind of stress." Eva beat on Moniek's chest with her fists, now stressing each word. "It's. Not. Right! She laid her head on Moniek's shoulder and cried.

Moniek looked at Joseph, who just shrugged his shoulders in an I-don't-know-what-to-do gesture. Moniek cautiously raised his hand and patted Eva's back.

"Why can't the Russians leave us alone?" Eva asked in a tight falsetto.

"I'm not Russian," Moniek said.

Eva looked up at him with a runny nose and red, watery eyes. "What did you say?"

"I'm not Russian, I'm Israeli."

Eva leaned back, wiped her eyes like a child, and sniffled loudly.

"I work for the Secret Israeli Intelligence Agency. We have been tracking Muller for months and needed someone who could recognize him. I had been working with the Russians as a double agent. When I found out that Joseph could identify him, I arranged it so we could have him sent to the Polish beach resort. It was supposed to be a vacation for you and Haim, but it was our cover. We knew that Muller had some local contacts and sympathizers, but we didn't know that someone within the NKVD would be working for Muller—that's the fault of the Russian Secret Service. That kind of carelessness would never happen with the Israeli Secret Service."

"But Israel just became a nation, what, two years ago? They already have a secret service?" Eva asked.

"Yes; they have a lot of people to choose from. We come from sixty-eight countries, and have a lot of talent, brain power, knowledge, loyalty, and worldwide connections. We have the largest network of secret service agents— they are the seven million Jews all over the world who were not killed, not only the two million Jews who are now in Israel. There are nine million of our soldiers that no one ever expected to fight back. Every Jew in the world will help us with almost anything we need, no matter what city or country we're in. All we need to do is ask," Moniek said. "I came here to apologize and to say good-bye. I'm going back to Israel."

"What about Muller?" Joseph asked.

"Muller will have to wait. We have to reassess our tactics. He's a dangerous man. That's the main reason I've been recalled. The situation is too dangerous if the NKVD has been compromised. It looks like we're going to have to rely on our own sources."

"But he's getting away!"

"He'll pop back up eventually. One thing I've learned about psychopaths like Muller is they have huge egos. They love to be the center of attention. They feed on it like a drug. It's their addiction. When they go into isolation, they literally go through withdrawal and have to satisfy their insatiable cravings by doing something that will gain recognition for themselves. That's when we'll catch him. Look at how comfortable he got here. He thought nobody would recognize him. We'll know better next time."

"Do you think he's still in Poland?"

"No. Muller's a smart man. It wouldn't surprise me if he's already left the country. He'll go into hiding for a while until he thinks the coast is clear, then he'll pop his head up and start moving around again. In one way, what happened was a good thing—he realized he's vulnerable to pursuit. He'll be living his life like so many other despots, hiding in holes and jumping at the sight of his shadow. It's good for him to be paranoid. I hope his nightmares are filled with images of the innocents he slaughtered."

"Will I ever see you again?" Joseph asked.

"The invitation to come to Israel is always open. We could use a man like you. I can't promise you a peaceful life, but I can promise that your job would never be boring."

Joseph looked at Eva. Eva took his arm and leaned against him.

"I–uh, I'm going to look for a place where I can raise my family without the worry. I want a normal life and a regular job, to settle down for a while." Eva laid her head on Joseph's shoulder.

"It sounds nice, but I'm a good reader of character and I bet in a short while you'll be traveling the globe, looking for adventure."

"You might be right. Joseph has always had lofty goals. That's why I love him. Most men were content to stay in their little box and do the little things men do. Joseph was never like that. He always had his eyes set on something bigger, on something exciting. And I love that about him. So if he does wander the world, I'll be with him."

Moniek extended his hand and Joseph shook it.

"Take care, my friend. You've got a good wife and wonderful family. I do hope our paths will cross again. Shalom."

"Shalom, Moniek."

Moniek tuned to Eva. "He's lucky to have you."

"I know," Eva said.

Moniek smiled, turned, and walked down the hall. Joseph closed the door to the hotel room.

Eva looked at Joseph. "Israel has a secret service? The country is only a few years old," she said. "They will grow to an awesome army of devoted agents around the world. Can you imagine how strong they will be in a few years? They will be a power to be feared. Muller and others like him can never hide from that power!"

⌒⌒⌒

Joseph, Eva, and Haim returned to Wroclaw, where life quickly settled into a routine. Soon Bella was born. She had Eva's brown eyes and locks. The synagogue gathered to celebrate the birth and everyone turned out to meet the newest addition to the Mitsen family.

Joseph and his family decided to visit Pepi, Motel, and their new baby, Abraham. Haim sat with his baby cousin on their apartment floor.

"Listen," Pepi said. Abraham cackled with laughter when Haim played peek-a-boo with him. "He's going to be a great father someday."

"Just like his Tata," Eva said.

Joseph and Motel lounged on the balcony and watched the city passing by on the street below.

"It's kind of sad—so many of the towns in Poland look so depressed. You go from one city to the next and you hope to see a flicker of life, but it just seems to stagnate," Joseph said.

"I know what you mean. I thought that after the war, things would get better." Motel turned to Joseph and paused. "There's another reason I invited you up."

"What's that?"

"We're leaving."

"You're moving to another city?"

"We're leaving Poland. We're moving to Canada. I just got the papers."

"But how? Poland won't grant permission."

"No, they won't, but they have to if you renounce your citizenship."

"But then…then you'll be a refugee—a family without a country."

"Australia, New Zealand, Canada, and Israel are all taking Jewish refugees. We just went to the Canadian embassy and got our papers."

Joseph stared at the floor as it all sunk in. He felt a little bit safe with Pepi only a train ride away, but this…this was something else. He'd be all by himself.

"What did Pepi say?"

"She wanted to, but she couldn't tell you. That's why she asked me to do it."

"When are you leaving?"

"Next month. I've already got the tickets and have scheduled packers to come in next week."

"Wow, that was fast."

"The time is right and that's why we want you to come with us."

"Me?"

"Look, Joseph. I know you've worked hard to settle your roots and to build a better life for your family, but no matter how successful you are, no matter how many friends you make, no matter where you live in Poland, eventually things will go bad and your family will be at risk again. You've experienced the anti-Semitism."

"Well…"

"Don't deny it. If I were to wear my yarmulke in the street, I'd be shunned. I don't see you wearing yours."

"Well, no. I guess you're right."

"Then come on. Let's go someplace where we can crank up your business and rebuild our lives."

"But I just rebuilt my life. I just went through all that. I don't want to do it again."

Motel sat quietly for a moment. He stood, put his hand on Joseph's shoulder, and said, "Think about it. Maybe not now, but someday when you decide you should, we'll be there to give you a head start—a leg up. Okay?"

"Okay, I guess."

"I'll be back in a bit. The ladies want to go to the store." Motel walked away. Joseph sat and watched the smoke rise from the chimneys, against a gray sky.

—◦◦◦—

Pepi and Eva returned from the store and made a fabulous dinner. Joseph found himself sticking close to Pepi. Wherever she went, he found himself beside her.

"I guess Motel told you the news," Pepi said as she washed the dishes.

"Yeah," replied Joseph.

"My little brother, you'll always be my little brother. You've been through enough trauma for five lifetimes, yet whenever you worry about me you still cling to me."

"I guess it's a natural reaction. I don't want to let you go, sis. We've lost everyone. I don't want to lose you too."

Pepi hugged him. "I'll be fine. Motel takes good care of us. We just feel that we'll be safer the farther we can get from Poland. There's nothing left for us." Pepi looked into his eyes. "Why don't you come with us? We'll rebuild our lives together."

"Motel has already asked me, but I'm not ready. I've finally got the business going and I was even thinking of expanding to other cities. Can you imagine how well we'd do in Warsaw?"

Pepi smiled. "I'm sure they'd love it."

"I'll keep that in mind. Motel is right. I just have to keep going."

"Well, if you decide, just be aware of how difficult it is to get your exit papers. The Polish government is extremely corrupt and we had to bribe several officials. It took some time but you can't give up."

"Thank you." Joseph smiled.

Pepi hugged her little brother and kissed his cheek. They hung the wet towels and joined the others in the front room.

That night the Mitsens slept in the guest bedroom. Joseph lay awake, watching the rain paint streaks of light down the windows. He listened to the soft breathing of Bella and Haim. He felt the rounded curve of Eva's backside pressed up against him. She was very warm. Joseph thanked HaShem (G-D) for his family. In these moments, when the world was still and his mind began to wander, he'd flip through the pages of his memories. The difficulties and frustrations would balance out with the love of his family. He didn't know if he could start over again. He didn't even speak English. How hard would it be to get a toehold in a strange land? Pepi seemed convinced, but Joseph had become more wary of rash decisions. He liked his routine: go to work, come home to a cooked meal, sleep in his own bed without fear. If he got a little bored, there were always supply trips to other cities. He loved to travel—more than that, he loved scheduling the trips to get the best value, or perks, or upgrades. Ritz had taught him well. He'd have to remember to pick up a bottle of vodka for him on the way home. Eva turned over and opened her heavy eyelids. The light from the window glistened on her eyes. She saw that Joseph was awake and stirred, so she laid her arm across his chest and squeezed him.

"You okay?" she asked.

"Just thinking."

Eva sighed and stretched her arms and legs out luxuriously. Her hair bunched up on Joseph's cheek, and he breathed it in deeply, taking in her scent. It was familiar, comforting. She nuzzled against his breast.

"So what are you thinking about?" she asked.

"About how much I love you."

"Keep talking like that and we'll have to get Pepi to watch the kids." Eva smiled. "So tell me, you don't stay awake unless something is bothering you."

Joseph turned toward her.

"Motel and Pepi invited us to go with them."

"I know."

"Would you go? To Canada?"

"I don't know. I haven't really thought about it. I'll go wherever you want to go."

"Really? So if I asked you to pack up and move to Iceland—"

"I'd go."

"Or Africa?"

"I'm there."

"Don't lie to me. I want your opinion."

Eva sat up, leaning on one arm. She rubbed Joseph's flannel nightshirt between her fingertips.

"I want what's best for the family. You've taken us through some hard times and we're still here. Many of our friends didn't make it, so I'm confident in your ability to do what's right. Where you go, I'll follow. You are my security."

"You're not being very helpful."

"I know. I guess I'm saying that if you think we should leave Poland, I'm fine with it."

"Thank you."

"You're welcome. Now get some sleep. We've got to be at the train station early in the morning." Eva kissed Joseph. "I love you."

"I love you too."

23

Two years had passed since Pepi left. She wrote frequently, sending postcards of all the wonderful places she had visited in North America. Joseph kept the postcards pinned to a wall in his office at the shop. Every now and then he would try to imagine what it would be like to explore the places in Pepi's photos. He imagined himself staring up at the huge Canadian Rocky Mountains or feeling the wet clouds of mist flow over him at Niagara Falls. The images seemed so colorful in contrast to the gray world of Wroclaw, Poland. He wondered why there weren't any postcards of places in Poland, and he realized that he had just answered his own question—who would buy them? The people in Pepi's postcards were always smiling, happy, and cheerful. He couldn't believe that such a place existed. *It must be made up, like the Hollywood movies*, he told himself. Yet still the images beckoned him. They spoke to his subconscious. His inner child cried and pleaded with him to go.

He was brought out of his haze by a ruckus from the front of the store. Joseph went to the door and looked out.

"They're a bunch of dirty Jews!" an elderly Polish woman shouted to the other store patrons. "I'd be dead before I brought a Jewish product into my house."

A scared cashier girl ran up to Joseph and said breathlessly, "I'm sorry. She saw my prayer book with the Star of David on the counter and went crazy. She started throwing things, so I tried to calm her down." The girl burst into tears.

Joseph walked past her, toward the elderly woman.

"Don't buy this garbage unless you're a Jew lover," ranted the irate woman. "They should have run them all out of the country, but no, we had to take all the bleeding heart refugees. They've got their own country—why can't they all go there? I'd pay to ship one there."

Joseph stepped up to her politely and said, "Madam, please—"

"Who are you?" the woman hissed with a sneer.

"I'm the proprietor of this store."

"You hire Jews? What's wrong with Poles? You're probably a Jew too."

"Madam, you should leave."

"You idiot, I *am* leaving. I just want to take my fellow countrymen with me. There are better places we can spend our hard-earned money instead of helping a bunch of thieving Jews!"

"Madam, you will leave now or I will have to escort you out of my store myself."

"You wouldn't dare."

Joseph grabbed the woman's arm roughly, knocking a package to the floor. He escorted her to the door while she kicked and screamed. Joseph opened the front door and shoved the lady into the street. She made an elegant, well-scripted pirouette and dramatically collapsed on the sidewalk.

"Did you see that?" she shouted to the passersby. "He assaulted me! You're all witnesses to it. That Jew attacked me. He nearly—"

Joseph closed the door, picked up the lady's package, opened the door again, and threw it at the lady as she continued her rant.

"Just wait. I'll have my boys take care of you! You'll see. They'll come and—"

Joseph slammed the door. The woman rolled to her knees and an elderly man helped her up. She gesticulated at the store with her arm, and then cursed at the sky. The man tried to get her to walk away as a crowd gathered. She smacked the old man on the back who promptly grabbed her and forcefully walked her down the street amid vehement protests.

The next day Joseph came to the store to find a red swastika painted on the front door. Human feces had been smeared on the walls. Joseph stood in front of the store for a few minutes, dumbfounded. Speechless.

Not again. It's starting all over again.

At first he was angry. He wanted to lash out at everyone who came anywhere near his store. But then he felt pity at how backward this society still remained. The world around Poland was changing. Israel had begun its life as a new nation, yet racism and anti-Semitism were alive and well. Joseph thought of the stories from the American Civil War, where hundreds of thousands had lost their lives over the plight of slaves, and here the Jewish population had been nearly obliterated yet the fanatics wanted more blood. Was there no end to their hatred? Were all his neighbors faking their smiles and speaking in platitudes, all the while cursing him and his family's very existence behind his back? He couldn't tell who was a friend and who was a foe. They all looked the same. They all looked just like him. He would bring it up with Rabbi Shlomo. He seemed to be able to navigate the gauntlet of hatred with a good sense of humor. Maybe he would have some answers.

Joseph went inside, filled a bucket with water, and began cleaning up the mess. Fortunately the thugs had come in the night to do their dirty work and it was still too early, so most shoppers wouldn't even notice what had happened. He prayed that it would remain an isolated incident.

—∿—

Alarming reports came in that made the entire Jewish community nervous. Rumors that an entire family had been found hanging from the rafters with swastikas painted on their bodies had bolstered the call for a plan of action. On Sunday night, Rabbi Shlomo held a meeting with his congregants. The synagogue was filled to capacity. The rabbi opened with a prayer and the crowd began murmuring. Rabbi Shlomo held up his hands.

"Please. Thank you. Let's begin. I wish we had such a group every Shabbat." The crowd chuckled. "But the reason for our meeting is as much political as it is spiritual. You have heard the rumors and the stories. Normally I would tell you that it is all a bunch of lies and gossip, but

I'm sorry to say—this time it's all true. In fact, it may be worse, much worse. Apparently the Russians are turning a blind eye to the brutality and racism perpetrated against the Jewish population remaining in Poland. This all bears echoes of Kristallnacht, when the Germans targeted Jewish families and businesses. We must be aware. Many of you are already very careful with the privacy of your religious beliefs and practices. This synagogue is evidence of your discretion. But I must ask you to be even more careful. If you go out in public, either hide your yarmulkes under a hat or better yet, leave them at home. When you wear tzi-tzis, make sure the tassels are tucked into your clothing. Be careful who sees you coming and going. Pay attention to who follows you. Don't go out in public by yourself. Stay in public areas and away from dark alleys. In fact, don't go out after dark, if possible, and don't open your door unless you confirm the identity of the visitor. While I don't condone violence, if you have a firearm, keep it ready, or at least have a hunting knife or solid club near the front door. If you are out and trouble starts, run. Protect yourself, protect your family, protect your home. Are there any questions?"

A burly man raised his hand. "Aren't you overreacting?" The man looked around the room. "I mean, it can't be that bad, right?"

Rabbi Shlomo nodded toward Joseph and Joseph stepped forward.

"Two days ago I might have thought the same thing. Some hoodlums vandalized my business with anti-Semitic graffiti. I have seen firsthand how the people you thought were your neighbors are in fact your enemies. Do not be naïve. Don't let your guard down. I'm not telling you to be paranoid, but you should listen to Rabbi Shlomo. There are people out there who only want to harm you."

Rabbi Shlomo finished the service with a prayer. Most people heeded the rabbi's warnings, but no one could expect how accurate his words would be.

—❦—

Joseph and Eva decided they were no longer safe in Poland. They called Pepi and told her what had happened. Her pleading convinced them. It was time to leave.

24

That week Joseph took some time from the shop. He, Eva, and the kids went to the Canadian embassy in Warsaw and were greeted by bright faces and a friendly staff. As soon as they saw the kids, two women brought out a tray of cookies and drinks. The children never even looked back at their parents as they walked away with a cookie in one hand and a drink in the other.

"I don't believe it," Eva said.

Haim reached up for another cookie with a mouthful of semi-moist mush. Bella toddled along and smiled as both the kids turned the corner into a colorful room.

"Our kids were just kidnapped," Joseph said.

"By women bearing cookies..."

A short man with a headful of silver hair approached. Eva was reminded of a smiling gnome.

"Hullo. Welcome to Canada!" he said. "Well, maybe not Canada, but technically the building belongs to Canada. My name is Jack Frink. I see your children have met our welcoming committee."

"I never would have expected my kids to walk off with total strangers," Eva said.

"Charlotte's cookies can be very persuasive, but I assure you, they're in safe hands. Happens every time. So how can I help you?"

"We want to go to Canada," Joseph said.

"You've come to the right place. We can get your visas right away. Please." Jack held out his arm toward an elegant wood desk in the corner of the main room. Behind it hung the flag of Canada and many beautiful photos of the country. Jack directed them to two large leather chairs as he sat behind the desk. He pulled out a folder and removed several forms.

"If you will let me see your passports."

Joseph looked at Eva, puzzled. "We don't have passports."

"Then what documents do you have?"

Joseph opened an envelope and pulled out two IDs and several folded papers. He gave them to Jack, who put on a pair of reading glasses. Jack read the cards and looked up at Joseph and Eva. He unfolded the papers and read them. After a strained moment, Jack took off his glasses and rubbed his eyes.

"Well, right now, the only one who can leave is Bella," he sighed. "You are refugees. She is Polish, she was born here. To get you to Canada, I need either a valid passport or I need exit papers. Most people have passports because, well, because few are willing to give up their citizenship."

Joseph took Eva's hand. They could hear a children's song playing on a record player and little Bella cackle with delight.

"Mr. Frink..."

"Jack, please."

"Jack, we have made up our minds. We are willing to do whatever it takes. My sister and her husband recently moved to Canada."

"Well, that will work for your sponsorship."

"So, can you help us?"

"Oh, no. I'm sorry, but we don't get involved in the internal affairs of Poland. You'll have to obtain the exit papers yourself, then we can help you the rest of the way."

"Do you know how we can begin?" Eva asked.

"That's a challenge." Jack looked toward the front door, then spoke in a quiet voice. "Many of the Polish officials are corrupt and it can be a…tedious process."

"Ah, I know what you mean," Eva said. She looked at Joseph with knowing eyes.

———⟊⟊⟊———

Joseph and Eva spoke quietly on the train ride home.

"The Naczelnik…I have to talk to the Naczelnik. He can help. He got us the permits for the business. He's been honest with me," Eva said.

"He's expensive."

"Maybe, but he's been reliable. We haven't had any problems with the government."

"That's true, but what if he can't help us?"

"He'll know who we need to talk to and where we need to go to get what we need."

"You do that and I'll speak with Rabbi. He might know someone who can help us."

"Have you told him yet?"

"No."

"That's going to be a long meeting."

—⁓—

Eva went the following week to speak to the Naczelnik. She explained how dangerous it had become for them to live in Poland, telling him about the store vandalism and their friends getting attacked on the street. They did not want to raise their kids in such an environment. They wanted to leave.

The Naczelnik sat with his fingers steepled and his lower lip puckered. He looked through Eva, drifting in thoughts of panic. He tried to show little emotion—a technique he always used in negotiations. Images of an angry wife yelling at him and an angry daughter telling him, "But you promised me, Daddy!" flashed through his mind. He was counting on Joseph's gratuity to pay for his daughter's wedding that summer, and during the winter, he was planning to take his wife to the Russian Riviera, to Rostov on the Black Sea, for their twentieth anniversary.

"Janusz?" Eva asked.

"Hmm? Oh…"

"What do you think? Can you help us get our exit papers?"

"Well, it used to be different," Janusz stammered. "It used to be whose palm you could grease and…well, one thing led to another. There still are some people like that— the ones who can make things happen, but it's difficult. So difficult that it makes things hard to do. It ends up not being worth the effort. Do you know what I mean?"

"Uh…I guess so," Eva replied but she didn't have a clue.

The Naczelnik's eyes lit up and he smiled as he escorted her to the door.

"Good! So just keep going and I'll talk to my guys and then when you come next month, I'll let you know. Okay?"

"But...it's going to take that long to find out?"

"You know government bureaucracy. Like I said, it's hard, so it takes time. Be patient and I'll see you next month."

"Okay, I'll...see you...then."

"Good-bye for now," he said curtly, shutting the door behind her.

—◦◦◦—

Joseph met with Rabbi Shlomo at the synagogue.

"I understand," Rabbi said. He adjusted in his seat to a more comfortable position. "Sorry, my shoulder is still sore. I don't blame you for wanting to leave. If anyone else had asked me, I'd have probably tried to talk them out of it. You've got to have a certain chutspa to make it out there and honestly, I don't think Poland is big enough for you." The rabbi opened a drawer in his desk and leafed through some files. He removed a folder and opened it with one arm, the other still in a cast. He tried unsuccessfully to pull his reading glasses from their leather case. Giving up, he turned to Joseph. "Would you please help me?"

"Sure."

Joseph pulled the glasses from the case and handed them to the rabbi.

"You're not the first person to ask for help." The rabbi flipped a couple of papers and found a mimeographed page. He pulled it out and slid it across the desk toward Joseph.

"You've got to fill out one copy of this form for you, Eva, and the kids. Then I need two, three-by-five centimeter black and white photos of each of you. I have a friend in Warsaw who has helped me get families out of Poland. But I must warn you, this process is very expensive."

"How expensive?"

"Five thousand US dollars for each of you—the kids, being minors, are free."

"Ten thousand?"

"Ten thousand and here's the details—he must have half up front and the other half when he gets the papers."

"That will be most of the money that we've saved!"

"It's worse. He won't accept Polish zloty; it has to be in dollars, German marks, or Russian rubles."

"But the banks won't authorize currency exchanges in that amount."

"I know. You'll have to buy them on the black market, and the exchange rate is never in your favor."

Joseph looked at the form, then back to the rabbi. "There's no other way?"

"Not unless you want to stay here."

Joseph sighed. "How long does it take?"

"Up to two years."

"What? Why so long?"

"It travels through many hands. And here's the part you don't want to hear—there is *no* guarantee."

"So I could lose the five thousand?" Joseph asked. The rabbi nodded. "Do you know how long it would take one of my employees making two hundred dollars a month to earn that much money?"

"A long time."

"A very long time!"

"A word of warning," the rabbi winced, shifting in his seat, "this is not a legal activity. If for some reason they believe that you will not pay the balance or if you make them angry, it would be easy to put those forms in the hands of the wrong government officials."

"I understand."

Joseph spoke with Eva that night. They phoned Pepi to discuss their situation and they prayed. They discussed it again over breakfast the next morning. The decision was made. They had to leave Poland, no matter the cost!

It took two weeks to buy the US dollars on the black market. Joseph was a little paranoid carrying that much cash with him. He thought every person he passed was watching him.

Joseph expected his contact's address to be located in a dingy apartment in a dark neighborhood. The address on his paper was at the Ministry of Public Affairs. Stephan Lapski was a supervisor! The rabbi had excellent contacts.

—⚬⚬⚬—

Joseph walked down a busy hallway. Families and workers waited impatiently, creating a noisy, blustery environment. In a strange way, Joseph found it comforting. He was used to loud environments and the noise was the music of activity, of progress, and it reassured him that he was doing the right thing. He hoped the rabbi was being a little overdramatic. He eventually arrived at Lapski's office door, and knocked.

"Joseph Mitsen! Please have a seat." Stephan Lapski had a round, pink face and a large smile. He wore a tailored suit. Joseph now understood where most of the money went. "The rabbi told me to expect you. Please sit down."

"Thank you."

Stephan turned in his chair and crossed his legs. "Now, he told me you wanted to leave our wonderful country?"

"Yes. I want to apply for exit visas for my family."

Stephan gave a hearty laugh. "You know we don't let citizens leave. This is a communist nation. Why would you think we would let anybody leave?"

Joseph took out the envelope stuffed with US dollars and set it on the desk. Stephan looked out of the large glass window to the hallway as people walked by.

"That would be a very good reason." Stephan reached across the desk to pick up the envelope. Joseph grabbed his hand when it was on top of the money. "Mr. Mitsen, it would be very wise if you would remove your hand. Did the rabbi not warn you of the sensitive nature of the service we provide?" Joseph held onto the money tightly.

"He did, but I want your guarantee that this money won't just disappear."

Stephan sat back, letting go of the envelope. He considered Joseph for a moment and looked into his steely blue eyes.

"I can tell that you are a man of resolve. If anyone else had touched me, I'd have called security and had you thrown out minus the contents of that envelope. But I tell you what, the rabbi told me of the good things you have done, and I promise that I will do everything I can to get your exit visas. You have my word."

Joseph relaxed a little.

"Do you have the forms?" Joseph pulled out a flat folder and slid it across to Stephan. He opened it and flipped through the pages.

"Lovely wife and beautiful children. I can see why you are so very protective. I would be also. Everything seems to be in order." Stephan held out his hand and Joseph plopped the envelope of money into it. "Good, I'll be in touch."

"When?"

"Soon."

Six months went by. Joseph spoke daily with Rabbi Shlomo, who encouraged him to be patient. Finally Joseph received an urgent letter from Lapski for him to come to Warsaw and "complete the transaction."

Joseph arrived to a grim-faced Stephan.

"Please be seated. There has been a problem. You understand how difficult these things can be…"

"What kind of problem?"

"It will cost you an additional seven thousand dollars to get your visas."

"Seven thousand more? On top of the five? That's"—Joseph counted but he was so flustered—"that's twelve thousand! But you said—you gave me your word—"

Stephan slid four visas across the desk with a big smile. "Got you."

Joseph caught on and punched Stephan on the arm. He snapped up the visas and looked at the photos with the embossed stamp and proper signatures. His heart floated.

"Thank you. Thank you so much."

Joseph gave Stephan the rest of the money and "floated" above the train all the way home.

Joseph contacted the Canadian embassy and spoke with Jack. The applications for Canadian visas were approved and were on their way. The excitement growing at the Mitsen household was palpable.

25

Joseph was able to condense the family's belongings to four sturdy travel trunks, by giving away the furniture to families at the synagogue.

Joseph phoned his contacts and booked passage on commercial ships and rail. He got a great deal on the short legs of the trip and was able to plan a little sightseeing along the way. This would be a memorable trip for the children. He saved on travel by leaving in the winter months. Their itinerary took them through France and Italy, and onward to Halifax. It was the largest port in Canada and even though it was thousands of miles away from their final destination of Calgary, where Pepi and her family lived, the train ride would give them a chance to survey their new home country.

The night before they were to start their journey, the synagogue gave a wonderful party.

"I'll stay in touch," Joseph told Rabbi Shlomo. "We'll write to you on the road and I'll send a telegram when we arrive in Canada to let you know we made it."

"I would like that. I'll keep you informed of our progress here too. It would be fun to come visit you," the rabbi said.

"When we get settled, I'll buy you both tickets."

The rabbi laughed. "I said it would be fun to go. I didn't say I could. These old bones aren't as adventurous as they used to be. What would I do with all the modern, hip people in Canada? No, I'm too traditional. It's built into me. I'm old fashioned, in an old fashioned home, in an old fashioned country." The rabbi took a sip from his glass. He grew serious as he stared into the deep crimson liquid.

"There is one place I've always wanted to go. I want to go to Israel—to our homeland. I want to go to Jerusalem before I die."

Joseph thought for a moment and smiled. "If there is any way I can ever help you get to Jerusalem, I will. You have my promise."

The rabbi put his hand on Joseph's and patted it. He wiped away a few sniffles, then all of a sudden his eyes lit up.

"This is not a somber time—it is a time for celebration!" The rabbi stood, and addressed the whole table. "If I could have your attention please. I want to propose a toast. Please refill your glasses and join me. Joseph, Eva, Haim, and Bella have been just like my own children and I love them the same way. When I first met him, I knew he was a good person and would become a great friend. Each of you I'm sure has a story or instance where Joseph or Eva has helped you in some way. I can truthfully say we've grown attached to them." He turned to face Joseph. "You will be deeply missed. I pray that HaShem blesses you and protects you in your travels and that someday we will all be able to share our friendship again." The rabbi raised his glass as did everyone else in the room. "To the Mitsen family: Success, blessing and health! La Haim."

Those gathered repeated, "Success, blessing and health! La Haim."

———∽∾∿———

The next day, the alarm clock sounded like hammers pounding on a gong. Joseph turned over in bed and looked—6:00 a.m. He pushed the alarm button and felt Eva stirring. He kissed her on the shoulder.

"Good morning," he said. His breath rolled out of him like a pungent fog. She pulled her pillow over her nose.

"Good morning," she said, her voice muffled.

They dressed and ate breakfast in silence, thinking of the big day ahead of them. Joseph took down his worn army coat and folded it on top of his luggage. It reminded him of the adventures he had been through. One of the men in the congregation borrowed a truck to take them and their belongings to the train station.

The last of the bags and trunks were taken downstairs and everyone climbed into the idle truck. Joseph went back to lock the door, and took one last look of his empty apartment. It was barren now, but he knew he was leaving a little piece of himself behind.

———∽∾∿———

He took down the mezuzah, the Hebrew home blessing, from his doorway and put it in his pocket. *For my next home,* he thought. He turned and walked down the quiet hallway.

Joseph had modified his family's shoes with special hidden pockets in the soles, to hide a few hundred dollar bills he had purchased on the black market. He knew traveling with a large amount of cash would invite robbery. He had also made a custom belt with a zipper in it, where he also placed a few of his bills.

The train station was empty of travelers. Joseph looked over the parking lot and could barely see traffic moving in the distance. Eva held Bella's hand and Joseph held Haim's. They were all wrapped up like snowmen, quiet, scared. Something cold touched Joseph's cheek lightly and he looked up. It had started to snow.

Joseph recognized this moment as another major transition in his life, that somehow his past life was now being tucked away in a filing cabinet. The next part was the beginning to another exciting chapter. He said a silent prayer and thanked HaShem for his generosity, for the opportunity to take his family to the new and safe world.

———

The train ride was uneventful for Joseph but he delighted in the excitement of the children. It was Bella's first train ride. For her, it was a fantasy trip to wonderland. "What's that? Look, a horse! Look at that! It's a lake. A cow, a duck, a bird." The wonders never ceased for her.

Haim played a game of I Spy out the window that went on for hours. The entire time, Eva sat and smiled and occasionally giggled at the children's fascinations. Joseph felt a darkness lift from the family the further they got away from Wroclaw and the closer they got to Gdynia on the coast, a port where they would at last leave Polish soil and cast out into the unknown.

The kids fell asleep immediately after supper. They were worn completely out after the excitement of the previous week. Joseph and Eva were in the berth below and for the first time in a month, they had time for a little hanky-panky as dessert.

"We're doing the right thing," Joseph said.

"I know."

"I want us to be happy."

"I want us to have the chance to be happy," Eva said. "I think we've had our share of repression. We've earned the right to a better life. I think it would be better if all the Jews left Poland. Let those bigots have their way."

"That's exactly why so many Jews are returning to Israel," Joseph said. He was surprised at the directness of Eva's comment, but agreed with her.

———❦———

The next morning, when they departed the train, Joseph could smell the sea air. It was wonderful. He inhaled deep breaths of the salty breeze. While Joseph picked up the tickets for a British passenger ship heading for Le Harve, France, Eva carried Bella on her shoulders and fed the seagulls. A cloud of birds circled the kids and Eva, swooping and diving. Haim threw bits of bread in the air, which the birds picked off midflight. Bella laughed with glee.

Even though their cabin was tiny, with barely enough room to stand, it had a porthole above a metal ledge—the perfect height for Bella to look out. Whenever they were in the room, Bella was glued to the window.

They toured the different levels of the ship. It was huge, at least in the mind of someone who had never been on an ocean vessel. They climbed to the bow of the ship and stood on the very tip of the nose, where the wind whipped their hair. The water rolled away to both sides as the ship cut through toward France.

They climbed to the pilothouse, where the captain guided the ship. As they walked along the narrow gangway under the tall glass windows, the captain opened the door.

"Would you like to come inside?" he asked.

The captain stepped back as Joseph and his family eagerly entered. Haim was awestruck. The captain took him by the hand and put a small crate beneath the ship's wheel.

"This is where we steer the ship. You slowly turn this wheel to make sure this indicator and this mark right here line up. That's how we know we're going in the right direction." The captain pointed to a floating compass with a gauge marked in segments. "Would you like to steer?"

"Really?" exclaimed Haim.

"Really. Hold on here and make very small movements like this." Haim held the wheel with two white-knuckled hands. Joseph thought his smile might flip back and swallow his whole head. Haim barely moved the wheel and the captain took his hands away. He put the captain's hat on Haim's head.

"You're steering the ship, my boy!"

—〰—

A few days out, the ship passed into a violent storm in the North Sea. There were waves rolling past that were higher than the bowsprits. The ship evenly cut through the waves but on deck it was like trying to stand on a roller coaster.

The captain ordered all passengers to their quarters. At first, Eva felt a little sick to her stomach. She was reminded of her morning sickness, yet the unfamiliar undulation of the watery horizon outside the porthole soon made her violently ill. Nothing would stay down. Once she got sick, the smell of vomit in the tight cabin tripped through the entire family like a set of seasick dominoes.

The next morning the sky had cleared and the captain gave the "all clear" over the PA system. Eva and Bella were happy to stay in bed but the boys wanted to breathe some fresh air.

The boat still rocked in the rough seas, which scared Haim. Joseph decided to make a game of it, trying to turn and walk up hill in the direction of the next wave. Joseph took off his belt and told Haim to grab the railing. He then wrapped the belt over Haim's hand and through the loop, tying him to the rail. Joseph took the other end of the belt and wrapped it around his own hand and tucked it in at the ends. They stayed like that for an hour in pure bliss.

Soon Eva ventured onto the deck on wobbly legs. She was tired of eating soup and was hungry for some "real food" in the mess hall. That evening they watched the flickering lights off the French coast.

Joseph carried a few cases of American cigarettes into the room. Eva was puzzled.

"When you take up smoking, you don't mess around, do you?" she said.

"I don't smoke. These are to negotiate our way around France."

"How do you figure that?"

"Ritz."

"Ritz?"

"Ritz told me that if I ever traveled through France, Italy, or Germany, I had to carry American cigarettes. They are an accepted form of currency and we don't have to lose money on the exchange rate."

"I don't believe it."

"Believe what?"

"That you were so dumb to fall for that!"

"It's true. He told me he did it all the time."

"But that was Ritz. He could pay for stuff with bottle caps and people would do it because it was Ritz. You are no Ritz."

"What are you saying?"

"I'm saying I can't believe you put our precious cash into cartons of cigarettes. And you don't even smoke. It'll take a week just to give them out to every smoker you meet."

"I bet you."

"You bet me what?"

"I bet you that I'm right and I can pay with cigarettes, or I'll eat a pack."

"No you won't. You'll sell every carton and make our money back."

"Okay, and if I'm right…"

"Yes?"

"If I'm right, I get it any time I want it. For a month," Joseph said with a smirk.

"You already get it any time you want."

"I do not. Not if you're tired or have a headache or maybe you just don't feel like it."

Eva thought about it. She loved Joseph in every way possible and even the thought of having to pay a debt with their favorite activity was appealing.

"Yes—I'll take that bet!" she answered, and they shook hands on it.

—◦◦◦—

They arrived in Le Harve, France, a week later. France was bright and colorful compared to Poland. Sophistication oozed from the cultural elite that plied the boardwalks near the pier. People seemed disgusted at the country pokes from Poland who wore rough wool coats and ancient clothing. It offended the French fashion sensibility.

Their cabdriver was a crazy driver who listened to a loud man yelling on a static-filled a.m. radio station. As they stopped outside their hotel, he hopped out of the cab and grabbed their suitcases and bags from the trunk. He stacked them in front of the hotel as a smartly dressed porter approached them. Eva watched intently as Joseph pulled out a carton of cigarettes from under his coat. Eva knew she had him and opened her purse to pull out a bill. Her mouth dropped open when the cab driver grew very excited and held up five fingers. Joseph dumped out five packs of Marlboros and handed them to the driver. The driver bowed and thanked Joseph continuously, all the way back to the driver's seat. When the porter saw the carton, he too grew excited. He practically drooled over them as he loaded their luggage and escorted them into the lobby. He said something to the check-in clerk and the Mitsens got a room upgrade. Joseph couldn't resist it anymore and shot a toothy grin toward Eva. Eva shook her head in disbelief, and patted Joseph on the back.

"Come on, Romeo," she said. Joseph giggled and rubbed his hands.

After breakfast and a lazy morning in the hotel, Joseph and the family headed for the train station. For a few more packs of cigarettes, the porter personally delivered all their bags to the station.

They boarded the train to Marseilles. Most of the passengers were locals. The businessmen crowded into the lounge to smoke and drink. Aside from the antipathy of their outdated fashions, hardly anyone said a word to Joseph and his family. It was like they had an invisible shield and the only ones who could see it were the passengers.

"These people dress so very nicely," Eva said. She looked at her own clothes and suddenly felt plain and unattractive.

"What's the matter, honey?" Joseph could tell something was bothering her.

"It's just…we finally get to France, ooh-la-la, the capital of fashion and culture. A girl's dream come true. It's just that I used to dream you would bring me to France for our honeymoon and here we are. And we're traveling on cigarettes."

"I know. It will get better. You'll see."

The train stopped at a station to refuel and the passengers disembarked for a short break. Joseph checked his watch.

"Apparently the French aren't as fastidious as the Poles on keeping schedules."

"Maybe you should learn to stop and smell the roses once in a while," Eva replied.

They clambered down the train steps and Haim was the first to spot the fruit vendor. Light-colored apples, bananas, oranges, grapes, pears, and cherries were overflowing in bushel baskets. They had never seen so much fruit at one time, nor such variety. In fact, they had never seen bananas before in their lives. They bought one of everything to try on their trip. Joseph paid with cigarettes.

When they climbed aboard and returned to their cabin, Haim sat with a full paper bag in his lap with fruit sticking out of the top. His eyes were big and he kept licking his lips.

"You hungry, son?" the American soldier asked as he as he sat with a group of GIs. Haim nodded his head enthusiastically. "Here, try a banana," said the soldier and handed one to Haim.

"Go ahead," Joseph said.

Haim gave a grape to his sister and he took and bit into the banana. Bella just looked puzzled as to why she got this tiny fruit and her brother got the big fruit.

Before anyone could say anything, Haim chomped down on the banana, peel and all. He sloshed the hard morsel around in his mouth, testing its flavor, and then sat back with a contented grin on his face. The soldiers, Eva, and Joseph laughed.

"No, son, not like that." Eva smiled.

"You've got to take the peel off like this," the GI said. The soldier peeled the banana. Haim took a huge bite, and his cheeks pooched out. Bella let out a small cry and pointed at the banana. The boy never had a banana before.

"Let your sister have a bite," Eva said.

Haim pouted, then broke off a piece and quickly ate the rest. Bella looked at the piece in her hand and tasted it. She popped it into her mouth and threw the grape at Haim.

"This is the best fruit I have ever had…even with the peel on!"

When they arrived in Marseilles, a new world opened up to them. A festival was in full swing, as revelers danced and drank in the streets. A band played under a decorative trellis and people sat at tiny tables, drinking tiny cups of coffee and talking. Vendors sold roast chickens and cookies. The smells were enchanting and after the family got their bags to the hotel, they immediately took to the town square to investigate the fun.

They wandered from booth to booth over cobblestone streets. A beautiful cathedral was the center of attention with its lofty spires and flying buttresses. Such beauty wrought in stone. Intricate gargoyles peeked over the eves, ever vigilant over the common folk below.

A crowd formed around a juggler. Haim was amazed at the feats of dexterity as the man threw batons, pins, balls, and fruit into the air in perfect timing. Bella was captivated by a mime who was now playing with her in a way only a child could appreciate.

As they wandered near the bandstand, Eva exclaimed, "Let's dance!"

Joseph hesitated. He still carried the trepidation that someone was following him. He was always on the lookout, always wary of people. Each movement was a military operation, moving the family from one position to another, then checking to make sure the coast was clear before continuing. Eva didn't know Joseph had brought a knife in his boot. She didn't know how nervous being in public made Joseph—until now.

"Joseph!"

"What?"

"I asked you to dance with me. What's going on? Why do you keep looking around?"

"There's a lot to see."

"That's not it. Come with me. Haim, watch your little sister. Mommy and Daddy are going right over there to dance."

Haim had a cookie in one hand and a slice of watermelon in the other. Bella had two hands wrapped around a slice the size of her head.

"Okay, Mommy."

Eva led Joseph by the hand. She turned and put her arms around him as the band played a waltz. She swayed back and forth while Joseph stood frozen. He looked around at the other couples spinning around them.

"Joseph?" Eva asked. "What's wrong?"

"I don't know."

"We're finally having a little fun and you're acting like you'd rather not be with us. I don't understand."

"I don't feel safe."

"Safe? What do you have to worry about? We're thousands of miles away from trouble. These people have hardly noticed us."

"I don't feel safe, okay?"

Eva stopped dancing. "Okay. Do you want to go back to the hotel?"

"Yes! Er, no. I don't know."

Eva then noticed Joseph's rapid breathing. Sweat dripped from his forehead and his palms were moist.

"Joseph, calm down. It's okay."

"We're not okay! We've never been okay! Don't you see?" Joseph shouted. Several dancers stopped their twirling to gawk. "We haven't been okay since the war. They've been after us ever since. Why can't they just leave us alone? What have we done to deserve this? What have we done?"

"Joseph, open your eyes. Look around. Look at your kids. Look at how happy they are. Look how safe we are. The demons are gone. It's over! We can live again. Like it was when we were kids. We can rely on each other. We can build together. You don't have to put all your energy into protecting us. You've done a great job, but that time is over. Now you can pay attention to me and the kids. Now we can continue with our lives the way we should have been able to do before. Things will be better. They have to be…"

Eva danced with Joseph there in the town square, until all the revelers were gone and their only audience was the pigeons. Eva bent down and picked up a sleeping Bella. Joseph picked up Haim and kissed him.

"I love you, Tata." Haim yawned. Joseph replied that he loved him too and walked him back to the hotel.

The next day they went sightseeing. They passed into the textile district and Eva was amazed at the colors and selection of clothes. This certainly wasn't like Poland. The latest fashions and the latest prices to go with it. The cigarettes served them well. They purchased beautiful clothing. The French clothes made them feel like they joined a new life.

—◇◇◇—

The next leg of their trip was to Naples, Italy. The ship passed up the coast of France. They saw the French Riviera, beautiful Monaco, and finally Italy. Tiny villages were nestled among the hills. The shoreline was sprinkled with yachts and fishing boats in their slips.

Eva put her head on Joseph's shoulder while the kids threw bread to the seagulls that followed the ship.

"I wonder if Canada is as beautiful as this."

Joseph smiled. "We'll find out together." He squeezed her arm.

—◇◇◇—

Naples, Italy, was a noisy city.

Their hotel was simple but clean. As they moved away from Poland, everyday technologies improved, making life more comfortable and leisurely. Eva was thrilled to have a bathroom in the hotel room. The landscaping improved and she spent an hour just looking over the balcony at the buildings and the city lights. She let go of her stress. She wondered about the phrase "being tightly wound up," because that's exactly what she felt like—something like a twisted rope was slowly being unwound, and with it, the core of her being became more pliable, like she could feel who she really was, instead of having to be on guard every moment. She saw it in the kids too. Where they used to cling to Eva's legs when they walked the streets of Wroclaw, now they wanted to explore on their own.

Joseph entered the room carrying big bags of fruits and vegetables.

"Tata!" Bella yelled. Eva took one of the bags and set it on the table.

"How did you buy all of this?"

Joseph looked at her and grinned.

"Cigarettes?"

Joseph nodded.

"Maybe you should list cigarettes as a new form of international currency."

"They already are," Joseph said. "Are we going to eat?"

"Yes, please," Haim said. "I'm hungry."

They stayed a week in Naples and Haim and Joseph even learned a little Italian. Later, they boarded a ship called *Saturnia*, bound for Halifax, Nova Scotia, on the east coast of Canada.

Their cabin was similar to the previous ship from Poland, except it was a little larger and had its own bathroom.

———

Bella didn't feel well. She had a fever. Eva did what she could but her condition worsened. The next day Bella was covered with small red splotches all over her body. They took her to the ship's doctor, and he didn't need much time to diagnose her. She had a classic case of the measles, which was contagious, so to keep the other passengers safe, Bella had to stay in an isolation room marked "QUARANTINED." Bella cried as a masked assistant showed her a bed in the corner of the nearly empty room. No one was allowed within twelve feet of her, at least until she was no longer contagious.

Haim, Joseph, and Eva all took turns watching over Bella. When she finally felt better, she would sit on top of the bed and pout, looking the most pathetic she could and it broke Joseph and Eva's hearts not to be able to hold her. Luckily, one of the nurses had a large collection of Italian fashion magazines. Bella spent her time looking at the clothing, fashions, and the many beautiful color photos of models. It was a big eye opener for her. She has never seen anything like it. "Wow," she whispered to herself. "Maybe in Canada I could be like one of these beautiful models." It gave her something to look forward to and gave her an exciting outlook.

Even while Bella slept, Eva remained by her side. Joseph entered with two cups of tea and handed one to her. It looked like she had been up for hours.

"Thank you. She just got to sleep."

"You ready to take a break?"

"Yes, my backside is sore."

"Good, go up on deck and get some fresh air."

"I'll stay and have my tea with you first."

"She's so cute when she's sleeping, isn't she?" Joseph said.

"She's still not feeling well."

"The doctor said it would be a few more days."

"She'll be all right. It's all part of growing up."

"I guess so."

"Oh, I forgot." Joseph pulled out a bar of chocolate.

"Where'd you get that?" Eva asked and Joseph just smiled. "Thank you. I love chocolate."

Two days before they were to arrive in port, the doctor looked Bella over.

"Okay, I think you're out of the woods. Go see your mother."

Bella walked across the room to hug her mother. "Mama, The doctor said I'm better. He said I won't ever get sick with that again!"

"Good, let's go tell your Tata. Thank you, Doctor," Eva said.

"Thank you, Doctor," Bella said.

"You're welcome."

———

Excitement was building on the ship as New Year's Eve approached. Decorations hung on the main deck with streamers and balloons draped around columns and tables covered with cloths and candles.

Haim and Bella went to be with other young people standing and dancing in a corner of the beautiful room.

"Do you think they'll be okay?" Eva asked.

"They'll be fine," Joseph said.

"We've never left them alone before."

"Don't worry, there is a large group of other teens and kids with them."

Joseph and Eva looked magnificent in the new clothes. A band played music as they entered the party. Couples danced on the dance floor under the twinkling lights of an open night sky.

The smell of the ocean and the fresh air seemed to rip away all of Joseph's cares. He took Eva to the middle of the dance floor and put his arms around her waist.

"You know, we've danced more on this trip than any other time I can remember," Eva said.

"I want to dance with you every night," Joseph said.

"I wonder if Pepi dances with Motel."

"I'm sure they do."

Joseph kissed Eva.

They drank wine and ate delicate cheese dishes. The captain stepped up to the microphone and held up a champagne glass in a toast.

"The New Year is almost upon us. I want to offer a toast and a prayer that your trip will be blessed and your lives successful. Don't forget the past, but learn from it and always try to do better than you did before. Okay, the time is closing in. Let's count it down!"

The entire party stopped what they were doing and counted down in unison. When they reached one, the captain shouted, "Happy New Year! Welcome 1960!" and the crowd erupted into a cacophony of cheers and glass clinking glass.

Eva and Joseph could still hear the band playing, even after they went to bed.

———

Early in the morning, Joseph woke the family. He took a chair and placed it in the center of the cabin. He addressed his children. When he spoke, he was overtaken by emotion. He told Haim and Bella about Rejowiec, his family, Rabbi Rosenfeld, Eva's family. He told them all he knew about the death camps and the slave labor camps. He told them about the murderer "Muller the Nazi," the man who killed most of their family. In front of his family, Joseph took a vow to spend the rest of his life dedicated to the capture of that murderer. He then asked Haim to take a vow to continue the search in the event Joseph was not successful. Haim stood silent and then took the vow.

Eva and Joseph both shed tears. Haim was shocked at what he learned. As he wiped away his tears, he felt both honor and fear as he understood the undertaking. He knew his family's burden had now become his. He was honored that his hero "Joseph" had entrusted him with such enormous responsibility.

An hour later, the ship pulled into Halifax, Canada. It was January 1, 1960. The deck was covered with snow, which excited Haim. He ran out onto the deck and immediately slipped and fell on the ice. He picked himself up and ran to the railing as they lowered the gangway. He felt a warm jacket being placed on his shoulders. It was Joseph's old army jacket.

"This will keep you from getting cold," Joseph said. "Welcome to Canada, son. Welcome to freedom, welcome to a new life with many opportunities. I know we'll be successful here. And I know you won't have the struggles that I had. That old army coat reminds me of the past struggles, May G-d Bless this family. The future is ours to build together!"

Eva carried Bella out wrapped in a coat and knit hat. They stood on the deck and took in the sight, thinking about the vast continent that lay ahead.

Along the coast ran a road with an unending row of single story houses opposite the sea. The snow covered the roofs and trees, giving everything a quaint fairy tale appearance.

"Tata, look, each house has a car in front of it," Haim said.

Joseph had to pause and take in what his son observed. He was right. Every house did have a car. In Poland practically no one had a car. Horses were still seen on city streets. There wasn't a horse in sight here, not even a barn. Haim looked up at Joseph and waited for an answer.

"Yeah, look at that. There sure is," Joseph said. He gathered his confidence and put his hand on Haim's shoulder. "We'll have a car in front of our house too."

"When?"

"Soon. You'll see. Soon."

THE END - Book Volume 1, look very soon for Book Volume 2, called: "West of Warsaw"